"I'm to become your mistress?"

"No. In exchange for physical protection, you'll become my lover."

"My lord. The end result is the same."

"Oh, no. It's not the same thing at all."

"No?" Her voice came out embarrassingly weak, almost breathy.

"No." Vaughn grinned. "A lover puts his partner's pleasure first. Or rather, her pleasure *is* his pleasure." He leaned forward, close enough for the scent of bay rum and warm skin to wash over her. Her mouth watered, forcing her to swallow. "When has your pleasure ever been the first and most important concern?" he asked.

Her eyes snapped up, riveted to him.

Never. Men paid for their pleasure to be the only concern.

"I propose to seduce you in stages, my dear. To make you beg for each and every intimacy."

"Beg?" A thrill coursed through her.

"Beg," he echoed with conviction.

Ripe for Pleasure

ISOBEL CARR

FOREVER

NEW YORK   BOSTON

This book is a work of fiction. Names, characters, places, and incidents are the product of the author's imagination or are used fictitiously. Any resemblance to actual events, locales, or persons, living or dead, is coincidental.

Copyright © 2011 by Isobel Carr
Excerpt from *Ripe for Scandal* copyright © 2011 by Isobel Carr
All rights reserved. Except as permitted under the U.S. Copyright Act of 1976, no part of this publication may be reproduced, distributed, or transmitted in any form or by any means, or stored in a database or retrieval system, without the prior written permission of the publisher.

Book design by Giorgetta Bell McRee

Forever
Hachette Book Group
237 Park Avenue
New York, NY 10017
Visit our website at www.HachetteBookGroup.com

Forever is an imprint of Grand Central Publishing.
The Forever name and logo is a trademark of Hachette Book Group, Inc.

The publisher is not responsible for websites (or their content) that are not owned by the publisher.

Printed in the United States of America

First Printing: May 2011

10 9 8 7 6 5 4 3 2

For Karin Tabke

ACKNOWLEDGMENTS

As implied in the dedication, I owe my friend Karin Tabke a huge debt of gratitude. Without Karin, this book wouldn't exist. She's the best non-agent a girl could have. I would also like to thank Jami Alden for being the best beta reader on the planet, and Jessica Cohen for brainstorming fantabulousness and always being available for cocktails and plotting. My San Francisco support network—Monica McCarty, Bella Andre, Carolyn Jewel, Poppy Reiffin, Veronica Wolff, Ann Mallory—as always, you ladies rock! Also, my fellow bloggers over at History Hoydens. For long-distance help and support, they're irreplaceable. My friends, whom I've largely deserted over the past year, know how much their support has meant. I owe more than I can say to my sister, Siobhan, for all the dog sitting it took to keep my mastiff Clancy happy and healthy while I worked. I'd also like to thank my team of "Alexes": my agent, Alexandra Machinist, and my editor, Alex Logan. Fantastic, insightful, supportive superheroines, both of them. A writer couldn't ask for a better team.

Ripe for Pleasure

❧ PROLOGUE ❧

T here are three private gentlemen's clubs on St. James's Street in London, each with its own rules and regulations governing membership. They are filled each day with peers who can't be bothered to attend to their duties in the House of Lords, let alone what they owe to their estates and family. Their ranks are frequently swelled by the addition of their firstborn sons, who gamble away their youth and fortunes while waiting for their fathers to die. What's less commonly known is that there is also one secret society, whose membership spans all three: The League of Second Sons.

Their charter reads:

We are MPs and Diplomats, Sailors and Curates, Barristers and Explorers, Adventurers and Soldiers. Our Fathers and Brothers may rule the World, but We run it. For this Service to God, Country, and Family, We will have Our Due.

Formed this day, 17 May 1755, All Members to Swear to Aid their Fellows in their Endeavors, Accompany them on their Quests, and Promote their Causes where they be Just.

Addendum, 14 April 1756. Any rotter who outlives his elder brother to become heir apparent ~~to a duke~~ is hereby expelled.

Addendum, 15 Sept 1768. All younger brothers to be admitted without prejudice in favor of the second.

❧ CHAPTER 1 ❧

London, May 1783

There was someone in her room.

The floorboards creaked, the wood protesting in its shrill way. Muffled footsteps sounded across the room, the tread far too heavy to be that of her maid. Viola Whedon froze beneath the covers, holding her breath. A faint line of candlelight licked through a crack in the bed curtains. Her heartbeat surged in time with the ticking of the mantel clock, a thready, sickeningly fast vibrato.

"It's got to be here." A man's voice, thick, angry, and entirely unknown to her.

"May'hap we missed it in the last room?" Another man, no more familiar than the first.

Viola carefully folded the covers back, the slight rustle of feathers and linen as loud as the clatter of iron-shod hooves on cobbles to her ears. She peered carefully out, not disturbing the curtains. Two men stood by the mantel, both squat and solid. The kind of men one passed near the docks or saw emerging from the slum of Seven Dials.

Just the sort of ruffians she'd have expected Sir Hugo to hire. They'd had such an enormous row when Sir Hugo discovered that he was to be included in the second volume of her memoir. It wouldn't surprise her at all if he were to attempt to steal. Or perhaps one of her other former lovers had hired them? Several who had refused to buy their way out of her memoir had made threats about taking more drastic actions to prevent publication. Despite the warm May night, Viola shivered. Did they know she was here? That this was her room?

One of the men held a candle while the other explored the mantel, clumsy fingers roughly caressing the wood. He made a disgusted sound in the back of his throat and spat. Viola clenched her jaw, revulsion pulsing through her. If only she were the heroine of a novel with a pistol under her pillow...If only she weren't alone in her bed.

Whoever had hired them, they weren't going to find her manuscript—not where she'd hidden it—and she wasn't going to simply wait for them to beat its location out of her. She needed the money that the manuscript would bring. Couldn't live without it, in fact, thanks in no small part to Sir Hugo. And she planned on living to spend that money as extravagantly as possible.

Viola took a deep breath, the familiar scent of her perfume and hair powder and crisp, clean linen not at all comforting, and steeled herself for a mad dash across the room. She was closer to the door than they were, and she had surprise on her side, because they'd left the door wide open.

She slid her feet over the side of the bed, eased the curtain back, and sprinted for the door. A startled oath burst from both men. Within seconds, they were pounding down the corridor after her, heels loud upon the uncarpeted floors, clearly not afraid to raise the whole house. One of them caught her hair and pulled, hard. She yanked her head free, vision blurring as she lost a chunk of hair.

Viola swung around the corner and half fell down the stairs, bouncing off the wall at the landing and skidding down the last flight, clutching at the banister to keep from falling. Her only footman lay facedown on the floor in the entry hall.

Viola vaulted over him. Her hands shook as she fought with the latch and wrenched the front door open. Please let there be someone on the street. Please.

One of her pursuers grabbed hold of her nightgown; threads popped and the gossamer nettle fabric tore. Viola screamed and struck him in the face with her elbow. He went staggering back, cursing. Warm air rushed over her as she ran down the front steps, searching the street for any sign of life, for any chance of rescue.

His cousin was a fool.

Leonidas Vaughn ran his fingers lightly over the cold hilt of his sword as two lumbering shapes slipped over the gate and into the small garden of number twelve Chapel Street. A horse blew its breath loudly through its nose in the stable behind him. A cat slunk by and disappeared into the dark recesses of the mews.

It was so like Charles to make a brash, frontal assault when the situation plainly called for subterfuge. For subtlety. For seduction. But nothing he'd said had changed his cousin's mind. Charles saw only what he wanted to see: a fortune waiting to be claimed.

It had been only a few months since they'd buried their grandfather. A bare week since they'd marveled at the cache of letters discovered among the mountains of papers at Leo's newly inherited estate. And in the days since Leo had followed his cousin back to town, Charles had already set the wheels of the hunt in motion…just as Leo had known he would. The fevered gleam in Charles's eyes had been all too clear as letter after letter revealed the details of the King of France's attempt to support Bonnie Prince Charlie's bid for the English throne.

They'd always dismissed their grandfather's tales of hidden treasure and tragedy as the stuff of legends, no different from the stories of Shellycoats and Kelpies Leo's mother had told them when they were boys. But the tragedy of Charles's family was real enough, and it seemed the treasure was, too. The small packet of treasonous letters left no other conclusion. Though the assumption that it was still waiting to be found—like a princess in a tower waiting for the first kiss of love—was questionable.

True or not, two villains from the stews weren't going to find it. But their intrusion would give him the opening that he needed, a chance to make the lady of the house beholden to him. And all he'd had to do to earn that opportunity was spend a few nights lurking outside her house waiting for his cousin to strike.

The night watchman had just turned the corner, his halloa of "all's well" echoing back faintly. Leo smiled into the dark. Any minute hell would break loose in number twelve. All he had to do was wait. Charles's men would deliver Mrs. Whedon directly into his hands.

A scream rent the humid darkness, bringing every detail sharply into focus as his pulse raced to meet it. A woman in nothing but her nightclothes erupted from the house. Her hair flamed in the lamplight as though it were afire, red-gold curls tumbling down to her hips. Mrs. Whedon. With that hair, it could be no other. Not a maid or a housekeeper but the lady herself. His luck was in.

Her eyes met his, and the night seemed to stretch. He could see terror there, a layer of anger below it, all the more intense for its impotence. Curses raced after her, low and guttural, intermixed with the sound of heavy, booted feet coming down a flight of stairs.

Leo shot out one hand and caught a flailing wrist, hauled her around, and held her fast. A scent that was pure summer—grass on a warm day, flowers drowsing in their beds—washed over him.

"Men. In my house." Her words were clipped, laced with fury. Her hand trembled, and she balled it into a fist, twisting in an attempt to free herself.

Leo thrust her behind him as a man in a dark coat came flying down the steps, a knife clutched in one hand. Leo drew his sword, using his left hand to hold Viola in place. It was only a dress sword, and though razor sharp, the rippled facets of the pastes covering the hilt were less than reassuring in the moment. Mrs. Whedon clutched the back of his coat, hampering him. A breath shuttered out of her, and her hand tightened, pulling him back.

"Where is it, bitch—" The man choked off as he hit the walk and his gaze locked on Leo's sword. He fell back a step, clearly assessing things, eyes darting about the empty street.

Leo shifted his stance, leveling his blade. "Wake the neighbors," he said over his shoulder.

His coat swung free. A flash of white and gold moved past the edge of his vision. Thank God. Mrs. Whedon wasn't famous for doing as she was told, but then what woman was? An unholy pounding resounded down the street as she beat against her neighbor's door, marking time as the seconds ticked by.

His cousin's gutter rat stared him down. The man's head sat upon his shoulders like a rock set on a stump. His jaw was heavy and his mouth hung open as though it were too small to contain his tongue. Not large enough to be a prizefighter, he had a menacing air all the same. A mad butcher's dog on the loose, capable of violence far in excess of his size. He hefted the blade, shifted his weight. Then with almost lazy disinterest, he thrust his knife into his boot and sauntered away, whistling. He turned into the entry of the mews down the block, nothing but the sharp notes of his ditty marking his presence, until that too dissipated into the gloom.

Leo glanced back over his shoulder. His quarry stood on her neighbor's porch, watching him. His hand shook as the rush of confrontation left him. He lowered his sword to hide it. He couldn't afford even the slightest sign of weakness. Not now. Not when Mrs. Whedon stood not four feet away.

"The knocker's off the door," she said matter-of-factly, one pale hand clutching the torn neckline of her gown. "No help there."

"Finally drive one of your protectors to murder, ma'am?"

A small smile curled the corner of her mouth as she descended the stairs, one slow, deliberate step at a time. Naked feet appeared and disappeared below her hem. Her toes gripped the ground. Her arches flexed, slim ankle-bones leading up to a flash of calf with every step. Her wisp of a gown slid from her grip, exposing one pale shoulder and a great deal of pale décolletage.

A deliberate maneuver. It could be nothing else. Like all women who rose to the top of their particular trade, Mrs. Whedon was a consummate performer. She had to be. Even under circumstances such as these. Gone was the fleeing victim, replaced by a feral Venus. Leo swallowed hard, wanting to touch, to reach out and grab. To possess that startling beauty, if only for a moment.

What man wouldn't?

"Possibly, my lord." Her reply jerked his attention away from her breasts. He'd been reduced to staring like a green boy by that damn wisp of a nightgown. "There were two of them, by the way." Her voice dropped, becoming an intimate, throaty entreaty of its own. "Intruders I mean, not protectors."

Leo smiled in appreciation. She'd certainly had more than two protectors. And based on that "my lord," she clearly knew exactly who he was, though their paths had never formally crossed. Paying for a bedmate was both repugnant and utterly unnecessary when the world was brimming with willing widows and unsatisfied wives. Besides, younger son that he was, he didn't command anywhere near the kind of fortune it took to secure a highflier like the one standing before him, even had he desired to do so.

A rivulet of sweat slid down his spine, like the ghostly touch of a past lover. He forced himself to ignore it, shifting his attention instead to the house. Armed intruders were far safer opponents than Mrs. Whedon. Especially when she was only a thin layer of cloth away from being naked. Even in the dim light, he could clearly make out the teasing circles of her nipples and the shadow at the apex of her thighs.

Lust grabbed disdain by the throat and shoved it down. Leo held his breath for a moment, searching for the control that seemed to have deserted him. Yes, he wanted her. And he meant to have her before all this was done. It was integral to the entire plan. But it would be on his terms, not because he allowed himself to be swept up in the drama and illusion of this not-so-chance rescue. And certainly not because he'd paid whatever price she might have in mind.

Leo turned away from her and strode into her house, making a vague gesture for her to follow. Inside, hysterical sobs greeted him. Two maids sat at the bottom of the stairs in a sea of flannel wrappers. A much older, harassed-looking housekeeper stood over them, nightcap askew, a large kitchen knife clutched in her hand.

One of the maids looked up and hiccupped, her face red in the candlelight. "He's dead. We came down when we heard you scream and found Ned like-like..."

Mrs. Whedon pushed past him, her hand perfectly steady as she shoved him aside. "Is there anyone else in the house, Nance? Did you see another man?" The sobbing girl shook her head from side to side, her hand covering her mouth.

"Back door was open though, ma'am," the housekeeper said.

"Then it's likely your other intruder has also left the premises." All four women turned to look at him as though he'd sprung from the ground like a fairy toadstool. The little maid sucked back another hiccup.

He picked up one of the candles and set his foot on the first tread of the staircase. "Stay here while I check the house. No, one of you had best wait out on the steps for the nightwatch."

The housekeeper nodded her grizzled head and turned toward the door. Leo put her, the sobbing maid, and the dazzling Mrs. Whedon firmly out of his mind as he crept up the stairs.

The house was utterly quiet. Soft, dark room after soft, dark room greeted him. The mantels had been swept clean, pictures ripped from the walls. A clumsy attempt to be sure. The treasure had to be better hidden than that. A porcelain figurine lay smashed on the floor of what appeared to be the only occupied room—Mrs. Whedon's, judging by the faint hint of *Eau de Cologne* that permeated the space.

Leo set the candle down and sheathed his sword. The men were gone, and his cousin had never been inside the house in the first place. A personal assault wasn't at all Charles's style. There was no point in roaming about armed like a buccaneer on the deck of a ship.

Her room was surprisingly simple. Plainer, in fact, than his own. It was hardly the lair of a woman famed for wanton indulgence.

No paintings or prints adorned the walls. The curtains surrounding the bed were a deep, solid blue. No embroidery to enliven them. No trim to soften them. The bedclothes spilling from between them were nothing but crisp, white linen. No silver brush sat atop the dressing table. No profusion of scent bottles lay scattered atop its surface. Just a few serviceable dishes and boxes, such as any woman might have for her powder and patches and pins. In fact, the only decoration appeared to be a mirror, a bit tarnished about the rim, and the smashed figurine.

Leo crouched down and scooped up a few of the larger, opalescent shards. Two legs ending in cloven hooves. A delicate head, ears pricked. A white deer. A symbol of good fortune in Scotland. A sign to the knights of old that it was time to begin a quest. A creature straight out of legend. Something not unlike Mrs. Whedon herself.

❦ CHAPTER 2 ❧

Viola yawned and poured herself another cup of tea. She fingered the hot, aching mark that ringed her wrist. In a few days, she'd be sporting a blue-black bracelet where her rescuer had manacled her wrist.

It had been a long night, hours spent waiting for the night watchman to summon the constable and for poor Ned to be taken away. Viola shuddered and swallowed a mouthful of lukewarm tea. Her stomach protested, and she set the cup aside.

She'd paced and drunk tea and watched with slightly horrified fascination as her rescuer stepped into the breach. He handled absolutely everything with the swift efficiency of a man who was used to giving orders, all the while giving every indication that he'd much rather be doing anything but helping her.

There were now a handful of hulking footmen guarding the house, and the hall had been cleaned by a swarm of women who'd arrived from his own home along with the footmen. He'd sent her own maids back to bed, an act of kindness that she couldn't easily dismiss.

It was fascinating. *He* was fascinating.

Lord Leonidas Vaughn. The Corinthian with the mismatched eyes. One blue, the other green, and both of them cold as the North Sea in February. Viola knew exactly who he was. One of the Mad Vaughns. The second son of the Duke of Lochmaben.

His grandfather was renowned for having intentionally burned down an entire wing of the family seat in a fit of rage, his father for kidnapping his bride from the steps of the church as she was arriving to wed someone else. And only last year, one of his cousins had been tried for the murder of his valet. He'd been acquitted, but all the same…There were rumors and stories of the Vaughn family's quirks and indiscretions going back to their knightly ancestor who had supported Queen Eleanor against her husband, Henry I.

Viola had been close enough on several occasions to judge those mismatched eyes for herself, but she'd failed to find them as arresting as the rest of London. Not until tonight, when she'd run headlong into him, while wearing just this side of nothing. Suddenly she'd been transfixed, for his famously frigid gaze had been anything but cold.

Viola stretched until her joints strained and her elbows popped. There was no point in dwelling on those eyes of his. He was notorious for never having kept a mistress, a fact much bemoaned among the ranks of the fallen, and she had neither time nor use for cicisbei. Only the money from her memoirs stood between her and debtor's prison, and the payment she'd received for the first volume was very nearly gone. But the offer she'd secured for the second volume would keep her in coal and lobster patties for years to come...

She wasn't an actress, couldn't sing or dance—at least not well enough for a career on the stage—and at seven-and-twenty, her days as one of the reigning belles of the fashionable impures were behind her. It was time to make do or suffer the lot of so many other fallen women: the slow slide down into common whoredom. A decline from which recovery was impossible.

Viola knew what she was, and she didn't regret the choices that she'd made, but she'd be damned if she'd let the sacrifices be for naught. She'd prepared so carefully, planned so thoroughly—and had been ruthless enough as she did so to earn the enmity of more than one man— only to see everything swept away by a few investments that had turned out badly and the actions of one petty baronet.

When Sir Hugo had discovered her working on the chapter about their time together, he'd stormed from her house and never returned. He'd even stopped the annuity that had been a part of their contract. Did he think she wouldn't find a way to avenge herself? That dropping her in such a way would somehow improve what she wrote about him? He was a very foolish man if he did.

She picked up the head of her smashed figurine and turned it over in her hands, watching the light play off the opalescent glaze. The last remnant of her girlhood. A gift from her father only days before she'd eloped... She set it in the saucer of her cup and rose to pace toward the window. It really wasn't worth mourning.

If she was going to indulge in that particular emotion, she had far more valuable losses she could contemplate: love, innocence, and reputation, all gone in one fell swoop. Viola swallowed a mouthful of air, pushing the faces that swam up from the recesses of her memory back where they belonged. Back where she kept them carefully partitioned and locked away.

Viola twitched back the curtain. A cloudless blue sky and a stream of sunshine greeted her. A small herd of sheep rambled down the street, their young shepherd marching beside them. A glossy coach pulled by four bays rattled past in the other direction, the livery of the footmen bright against the dark finish of the coach.

Just another May morning. Everything seemingly the same as the day before. Perfect. Beautiful. *Unbearable.*

A loud rap on her door made her jump. She turned to find Lord Leonidas framed in the doorway, his head nearly scraping the lintel. It was as though her house was simply unable to contain him. How had she never noticed that he was so tall?

His disordered hair was a deep auburn in the sunlight; strands escaped his queue and hung down at the temples. In candlelight, it was merely brown. It made her almost sick how badly she wanted to tuck those stray bits back into place, just to have an excuse to touch him.

His expression held both lust and revulsion, and not a little bit of self-loathing. An intriguing mix, as though he were aware of the contradiction. Men were usually so much clearer about their wants and needs, and they so rarely bothered to be squeamish or apologetic about them. To want, to lust, to need, that was enough for them. And

Viola liked it that way. It made them so much easier to manage.

Leo paused before entering Mrs. Whedon's boudoir, a sudden stab of lust burning away exhaustion. She'd pulled a flowery dressing gown over her wisp of a nightgown, but the sun blazing through the open window outlined her long limbs and trim waist perfectly through the thin cloth. Light filtered around the curve of her breasts and sparked her hair into a blaze around her head and shoulders. A Botticelli goddess without the half shell.

She dropped the curtain, and the room plunged into semi-lit darkness. She became merely an extremely beautiful woman, rather than something approaching the celestial.

Thank God for that.

"So what am I to do now?" Viola stepped toward him, and the whole room seemed to shrink.

"Go to bed, ma'am."

Her mouth quirked up, mocking him, as though she knew it was all that he could do not to beg to join her. As well she should, practiced coquette that she was. She could probably smell lust halfway across town. It was her stock in trade after all, no different from a tailor knowing the hand of his cloth.

"Practical advice, my lord. Will you be taking it yourself?"

Leo's mouth went dry. Was that an invitation or a taunt? His cock twitched, clear about what answer it wanted.

"Yes, ma'am," he ground out. "I was only stopping to take my leave. I'll return this afternoon to await the arrival of Mr. Addison's men."

One elegantly straight brow arched as she stared him down, blue eyes unblinking. There was a stillness about her that was fascinating, reminiscent of a doe as the baying of hounds washes over her and she takes stock of her options before erupting into flight. It made it hard to look away from her. Impossible really.

Leo caught himself and yanked his wandering mind away from her. He was tired. That was all. He was tired, and sleeplessness always bred fantasies and gave luster to otherwise mundane objects. She couldn't possibly be as beautiful as she looked at that moment. No woman could.

Annoyed with himself, Leo nodded, turned on his heel, and left. If he stayed a moment longer, he'd tumble into bed with her, and falling under Mrs. Whedon's spell was the last thing he could afford to do.

⚞ CHAPTER 3 ⚟

C harles burst into The Red Lion on a wave of gin. Leo allowed the upper edge of his newspaper to sag. The general din of conversation ended abruptly as his fellow League members watched Charles drop into a vacant seat.

A sprig of hope unfurled in Leo's chest at the sight of him, only to die just as quickly. Charles's hair was rumpled and hilly in its queue, as though he'd pulled it hastily back without the aid of a comb. His cravat hung loose and open about his throat, and his coat was nothing short of a disaster—a large water spot marred one whole side from shoulder to waist.

His disheveled state did not bode well. Charles had a mercurial temper: One moment he was amiable, jovial, the best of fellows; the next he was anything but. He could turn on you as quick as a mad dog, and today, they weren't even beginning with Charles in a good frame of mind.

"Long night?" Leo dropped the newspaper on the table and waved a hand. The owner's daughter appeared as though summoned by a spell. She had twisted her calico-coated hips through the crowd with practiced ease and set a steaming cup of coffee before Charles.

Charles didn't even reach for it. He just stared at Leo over the table. Hate scuttled through the recesses of his eyes, unmistakable even in so brief a flash. Where had that come from? How had he missed its inception?

Leo had been hoping that today, in light of his lack of success, Charles would listen to reason, would be open to joining forces. If what the letters hinted at was true, there was more than enough money there for both of them.

From across the room, Gareth Sandison caught Leo's gaze, his brows raised inquiringly. Leo gave him the slightest of head shakes. If Charles meant trouble, best not to antagonize him by bringing Sandison into their shared secret quite so publicly.

Leo pushed the steaming cup toward his cousin. Charles's gaze dropped, and his hand closed around it like that of an automaton. He raised the cup up and blew on it, holding it with unsteady hands.

"A long night…" He sounded pensive, but the anger laced beneath it was evident if you were listening closely. "You should know, Cousin. You were there, after all."

Leo sipped his own coffee and let the comment settle. The warm, earthy scent of the coffeehouse washed over him.

He and Charles hadn't been as close of late as they had been as boys. Leo had been hoping for something very different when he'd invited Charles to Dyrham Hall after their grandfather died. Some small part of him was still hoping…

"Charles—"

"No." His cousin slammed his cup down hard enough to send coffee sloshing over the rim. He yanked his hand away and shook off the steaming liquid. Leo held his breath.

All around the room, heads rose, attention shifting to Charles as though he were a fox scampering through a kennel of hounds. His cousin's mouth flattened, lips almost entirely disappearing.

"No, Leo." Charles's voice shook, and the vein in his forehead stood out in stark relief. "The money doesn't belong to your family. And it wasn't your family who suffered after the forty-five because of it. It was mine. Mine!" The final word erupted out of Charles. Spittle sprayed across the table, trailing behind like a comet's tail.

"We're both Vaughns." Leo kept his voice soft, low, as though he were speaking to a frightened horse. "And the fortune in grandfather's letters doesn't belong to either of us. It belongs to the King of France, or to the Cardinal Duke of York, if you prefer, but I for one have no intention of giving it to either of those bastards."

Charles wiped his mouth on his sleeve and chuckled, but the humor didn't reach his eyes. They stayed flat as those of a fish in a monger's basket. "I'm only a distaff Vaughn. We might share blood, but we're not the same family."

Leo opened his mouth to protest, but his cousin raised his hand to forestall him. A pale band on his ring finger marked a loss Leo had thought impossible. Things must be far worse than Leo had ever imagined if Charles had gambled away his father's ring.

His hand still held up like a shield, Charles said, "You'd say I was raised a Vaughn, but you'd be wrong. I spent every damn day of my childhood having my face rubbed in the fact that I was a poor relation. A duty. A burden."

Leo frowned. It was impossible that his cousin could say that, could feel that. Or it should have been. "You're my father's favorite sister's son. My father—"

"I'm a MacDonald." Each syllable was clipped, harsh, and emphatic. "The son of a disgraced and broken house, but I'm going to reclaim my birthright, my place in the world. And that money is the key to it all." Charles leaned forward, hands gripping the edge of the table, knuckles white. "You don't need it, Cousin. You've got an entire estate to entertain yourself with, thanks to Grandfather. Let it be."

"You know I can't do that, Charles. What I have is a house that at present isn't capable of—"

"Just stay out of it, damn you."

"And if I don't?"

"Don't cross me on this, Leo." Charles stood up and shook out his rumpled coat. The soft pile was smashed askew, making it dull and rough. He turned to go, but stopped before stepping away from the table. "That money is there for the taking, and I mean to have it. Neither you nor that whore is going to stop me."

Leo watched his cousin go with a sour taste in his mouth. He'd seen Charles work himself up about things in the past, but this cold fanaticism was something new. There was no hope of him seeing reason. Charles was beyond that now.

It wasn't just about the money. Leo turned his cup between his fingers, absently studying the blue transfer pattern of birds and teahouses, wishing he *could* simply let it go. Dyrham Hall was small, barely more than a house and a few acres of pasture, but it was also beloved, a love he and his grandfather had shared, along with their passion for horses and hunting.

The estate was simply too small to support itself, let alone support the care of the hunters who were its reason for existence. If Leo wanted to live there, to make a life there, he was going to need money. Quite a lot of money, actually. Far more than his younger son's portion.

Besides, whatever else Mrs. Whedon might deserve, she didn't deserve Charles. Especially in his present mood. No one did.

Leo was pulled from his introspection as his friends, Sandison in the fore, descended upon him. Most of them had been friends since they were boys, all except Dominic de Moulines. The Frenchman—bastard son of a French comte and his island mistress—had been inducted into the League when he'd come to London to give a fencing demonstration.

Roland Devere pulled a handkerchief from the pocket of his tobine coat and mopped up the table, fastidiously careful to keep his cuffs clean, before sitting down. Sandison simply sprawled at his leisure, prematurely silver hair swinging loose, looking very much as though he'd slept in his coat. Knowing Sandison, he probably had, if he'd slept at all. The others took the remaining empty seats and stared at Leo expectantly.

Devere wadded up the handkerchief and sent it sailing toward Anthony Thane, who caught it in midair and dropped it onto the folded newspaper. "Anything we can help you with?" Thane said, glaring at Devere.

"Not at the moment." Leo tossed back the last of his coffee and set the cup aside. "Just a family squabble."

De Moulines shook his head, just the way Leo's older brother did when he knew he was lying. "*Non.* No such thing with you damn Vaughns, this we all know. Mad, the lot of you."

"Besides," Sandison cut in, "MacDonald was quite loud: money, the forty-five, poor relation, birthrights."

"From across the room, it was all very intriguing," Devere said.

Leo held back a smile. Devere was always looking for an adventure, and Sandison, despite his sleepy appearance, was all too keen when it came to schemes and puzzles, while de Moulines was a fire-eater, ready to fight on the flimsiest of provocations. Only Thane could be counted upon to keep a cool head.

"No," Leo said, answering Thane and ignoring the others. "At the moment it's nothing but a family squabble. For now you'll have to excuse me. I'm off to call on Mrs. Whedon, and that most certainly isn't something I need any of your help with."

Devere's eyes narrowed, and Sandison went off in a peal of laughter, while the other two choked on their coffee. Leo shook his head at them and refused to be drawn in. He reclaimed his hat and swordstick from The Red Lion's porter and set off briskly toward St. James's Park.

His cousin's refusal to see reason still chafed, but it wasn't all that surprising. The cards had been dealt and the bets laid; there was no going back now. Leo stopped in the middle of the walk as a plan began to take shape.

A covey of giddy demi-reps out for an airing swirled around him. They sized him up as they went by, the stench of stale perfume and cheap cosmetics swirling in their wake. He could feel them weighing the cut of his coat, the expense of his boots, the value of his purse. They could probably guess his worth as well as any moneylender.

Leo adjusted his hat and flipped his swordstick up smartly under his arm as they drifted off slowly so if he wished to catch them he might. One of them smiled back over her shoulder, displaying her fine neck and an expanse of straight and surprisingly white teeth. Leo shook his head, causing her to whip back around. Her walk took on a decided flounce, skirts swishing, bouncing erratically over the false rump beneath them. He had a much more alluring conquest in mind. Beside Mrs. Whedon, the gauche girls before him in their rouge and patches didn't stand a chance. Just the thought of her set his mouth watering, made his pulse rise with expectation.

Leo plucked his watch from his pocket and thumbed the tortoiseshell case open: three-eighteen. He quickened his pace. He was going to be late to meet Addison's men, and he had a serious bit of seduction to get under way. A vision of flame-colored hair, slightly damp and tangled, hanging over him like a bedouin's tent made him inhale sharply. The loamy scent of the park washed over him, reminding him of her perfume.

He even knew exactly how to put his proposal to her...

"So, in exchange for your continued protection, I'm to become your mistress?" Viola smiled in spite of herself. Lord Leonidas had certainly found an original way of framing his proposal. He'd launched into it mere moments after the Bow Street runner had left them.

Her savior shook his head, mad eyes dancing beneath long lashes. "No. In exchange for both continued physical protection, and my letting it be known in certain quarters that you are under such, you'll become my lover."

"The term you choose makes no difference, my lord. The end result is the same."

"Oh, no, Mrs. Whedon. It's not the same thing at all."

Viola let out an unsteady breath. The hint of a growl in his voice set her nerves on edge and made her nipples tighten until they pressed uncomfortably against the stiff wall of her stays.

She wanted this man, much as she hated to admit it. Wanted him badly enough to consider breaking every rule she'd ever made for herself. And that was all the more reason to resist the impulse. The last time she'd felt this way, it had been disastrous, and getting what she wanted had only made things worse.

"No?" Her voice came out embarrassingly weak, almost breathy. She swallowed and balled up the hand he couldn't see until her nails bit into her palm.

Calm. Serene. Unflappable. That was what she was famous for being, what gave her the allure of being unobtainable. Calm, serene...

"No." Lord Leonidas smiled and abandoned his post by the cold grate to claim the chair across from her. His long legs stretched across the small space between them, boots nearly tangling in her skirts. Viola drew her feet back and tucked them under her chair. He grinned, clearly aware of her withdrawal.

"A lover, Mrs. Whedon, puts his partner's pleasure first. Or rather, her pleasure *is* his pleasure." He leaned forward, close enough for the scent of Bay Rum, warm skin, and sun-dried linen to wash over her. Her mouth watered, forcing her to swallow. One corner of his mouth kicked up as though he knew. "Just as his is hers."

Viola settled back into the embrace of her chair, moving away from the dizzying scent of him. She traced the bargello work with a nail, eyes on the intricate needlework that covered the chair rather than on Vaughn. "Her protector's pleasure is always a mistress's—"

"Exactly my point, ma'am. When has your pleasure ever been the first and most important concern of either person in your bed?"

Her eyes snapped up, riveted to him.

Never. At least not since Stephen died. Perhaps not even then. They'd both been so damn young... She pushed the memory away. Men paid for their pleasure to be the only concern. That was the whole point. Whether wife or mistress, a woman's pleasure was of little import.

A bubble of panic clawed its way up her chest and lodged beneath her heart, making it nearly impossible to breathe. To suggest that there was some mythical third option of *lover* made her want to slap him, but it also sparked a wild desire for him to prove what he said. Her lamentable curiosity was going to get her into trouble yet again. At least this time she had no reputation to lose. No family to embarrass or disappoint.

"So, in exchange for being allowed to put my pleasure first, you'll slay all my dragons." She did her best to be dismissive, to make his proposal sound as ridiculous as it was.

Lord Leonidas chuckled, a low, throaty sound that curled around her. "In exchange for being allowed to attempt to pleasure you, I'll slay any damn thing you like."

Viola sucked in a breath. His blue eye was steady, sincere, but the green one held a hint of mischief. That was the eye to watch, the one that gave away his secrets. It wasn't as simple as he made it out to be, but she'd be damned if she could fathom what his real motivation was. A bet perhaps? The challenge of climbing into bed with the most infamous whore in England without so much as tuppence changing hands?

"In fact, I propose to seduce you in stages, my dear. To make you beg for each and every intimacy."

"Beg?" A thrill coursed through her as her last shred of dignity evaporated. Her hands and feet began to tingle as heat pooled in her belly. The air between them crackled with tension, lust recognizing lust. What sort of man bothered to seduce a woman whose bed others had merely paid to enter? How badly did she really want to find out?

"Beg," he echoed with a conviction that unnerved her.

The muscles in his thighs bunched as he rose, straining the seams of his breeches. His large, square hands smoothed his coat into place, the subtle, striped silk sliding across his chest to mask the magnificent waistcoat beneath. Viola sucked in her bottom lip and caught it between her teeth. It was impossible not to imagine those hands touching her.

If she clung to that almost gaudy waistcoat, crushed the embroidered panels with both hands, would he carry her to the chaise? Or would he simply sink with her to the silk carpet beneath their feet?

How long had it been now since a man had touched her? Could it really be months? And how much longer than that had it been since she'd had a man with any real skill in her bed? Years? Forever? Never? The ones worth bedding were never the ones who could afford to keep her.

It simply didn't bear thinking about. A sudden wave of regret flooded through her. This wasn't the life she was supposed to be living...not the one she'd been raised to expect nor the one she'd dreamt of as a girl. Not even close.

Lord Leonidas circled around the back of her chair and leaned over her. "But for now, Mrs. Whedon"—his breath washed over her ear, and she shivered—"I'm afraid I'll have to leave you to your afternoon." He inched closer, until she could feel the slight abrasion of his cheek against hers, until the scent of Bay Rum flooded every pore. "You might indulge me and spend it imagining just what I might do, if allowed to touch you only below the knee, to induce you to beg me to touch your thigh."

And then he was gone, leaving her alone in her boudoir, flushed with anger and quaking with need. All she could think about were those long-fingered hands sliding up her calf...The bastard.

~ CHAPTER 4 ~

Viola handed her hat and gloves to Mrs. Pendergast's doorman and hurried to the parlor. It was evident, even through the closed door, that a lively discussion was already under way. As she pushed into the plush inner sanctum of London's most elite brothel, she heard Lady Grosvenor's laughter cut through the air like a soprano climbing to the top of her range.

Beside Lady Grosvenor were the other members of the New Female Coterie, demi-reps all. Lady Ligonier, Lady Worsley, Mrs. Newton, and the grandame of them all, the Countess of Harrington. Most of the members of their society were the fallen wives and daughters of nobility. Lady Harrington, on the other hand, was merely infamous, her husband having been more democratic in his views of wifely fidelity than most of his fellows. Of course, he was probably upstairs with one of Mrs. Pendergast's girls at this very moment...

Lady Grosvenor gathered her ever-present pug into her lap and patted the settee beside her, her eyes crinkling with mirth. "Mrs. Whedon, I hear such tales of you that I burn for corroboration. You were attacked? In your own home? And saved by Lord Leonidas Vaughn?"

"Yes," Lady Worsley said, leaning forward, anticipation writ plainly on her face. "Please do tell us that the rumors are true. That Lord Leonidas has fallen at last?"

"I'm afraid I'm the one who's meant to fall." Viola fingered the trailing ribbon of her sash. "And yes, I awoke to find housebreakers in my bedroom. They were after the manuscript for the next volume of my memoir." She shuddered at the memory. "Lord Leonidas was walking home from a late night of cards when I burst onto the walk."

"Thank heavens," Mrs. Newton said.

"Lucky girl, more belike," Lady Grosvenor replied with a hint of a smile. "What a savior to find at hand."

"Yes," Viola conceded, ignoring the flustered pulse beating its way through her veins. "He took care of everything, from searching the house to meeting with the runners." Her footman's lifeless body flashed behind her eyes. "The runner doesn't hold out much hope for catching them, though. He promised they'd do their best, but without more to go on, they can hardly accuse Sir Hugo publicly—though I know they must have been in the baronet's employ—and without Sir Hugo, the runners are unlikely to be able to trace my assailants."

"But Lord Leonidas has everything in hand?" Lady Harrington asked with a somewhat surprised expression.

Viola nodded. "He's taken the reins quite handily. I couldn't stop him if I wanted to. He's outrageous."

"But handsome."

"And rich."

Isobel Carr

"Not to mention, just think of the *size* of him." Lady Ligonier looked rapturous. "There must be only a handful of men among the *ton* who are anywhere near his height."

The first hint of a blush burned Viola's cheeks. She'd been thinking of very little else for days. "And entirely sure of himself," she added to their list. "You won't believe the proposal he's made me."

"Stingy, is he? I wouldn't have thought it of him. The Vaughns tend more toward grand gestures." Lady Harrington selected a small cake from the tray and ate it in one bite.

"I can still remember the wild, romantic tale of his parents' elopement," Lady Grosvenor said with a sigh. "I think it made far too large an impression on me as a girl."

Viola broke into a smile. "He's not offered to become my protector. Or rather, he has offered help with Sir Hugo, to quite literally protect me, but only if given the chance to seduce his way into my bed."

"Let him." Lady Ligonier fanned herself, batting her eyes playfully. "Lord knows I would."

Everyone broke out in laughter. Viola eyed her disarmingly frank friend. Lady Penelope Ligonier was well known for the fact that she thought infidelity the best thing she'd ever done, the freedom she found there beyond price. Yes, Penelope would have dragged Lord Leonidas down onto the carpet and had her way with him with nary a qualm or a thought.

"I haven't said no." Viola wasn't at all sure she could. "I haven't made any reply at all. And he's so confoundedly arrogant that I don't think he'd accept my refusal if I dared."

"Well, he is a Vaughn." Lady Grosvenor scratched her pug, sending the creature into a shivering state of delight.

"He sent a note yesterday inviting me to the theatre. I've half a mind to leave him kicking his heels on my doorstep—"

"And an entire body telling you not to," Mrs. Newton interjected. "Don't be a fool, Vi, really. Just think of it: *Lord Leonidas*. You'd be a legend. The only Cyprian to ever lay claim to a Vaughn, younger son or no. And think of the teeth gnashing among the widows of the *ton*? Their consternation alone would make it all worth it."

"And you'd have Vaughn in your bed in the interim," Lady Worsley said with a suggestive waggle of her brows. "I can't think of a more delightful way to spend the Season."

"Perhaps you're right…"

"If you let Vaughn slip through your fingers"—Lady Harrington eyed her indignantly—"I wash my hands of you."

Laughter bubbled out of Viola. The countess was every bit as decisive as Lord Leonidas. There was no questioning where you stood with her, and she never quibbled when it came to telling them all exactly how they should go on, almost as though they were her daughters.

"Yes, my lady. I shall do just as you say."

"Good girl. Now push that plate of macaroons closer to me, my dear. Thank you."

Leo leaned back against the squabs and studied Mrs. Whedon in the light thrown by the small lantern affixed to the carriage wall. With every bounce and jolt, brilliant

motes slid across her, drawing his attention from the
sweep of her clavicle to the swell of her breasts to the
hollow of her throat...each beautifully sculptured spot
calling out for a long, open-mouthed kiss. To be worshipped as it deserved.

Whore or not, she was magnificent. It was simply a fact.

Leo shifted in his seat, resisting the urge to climb
across the small space and pull her onto his lap. To
unhook her bodice and lift her breasts from their confinement behind layers of silk and whalebone. But that wasn't
the bargain they'd made, and he had every intention of
making her seduction a triumph. Tumbling her in the
coach, delightful as it might be in the moment, wouldn't
serve his purpose.

Mrs. Whedon sighed and sank a little farther into her
seat, long, fine hands quiet in her lap; restive, as she had
been that first morning in her boudoir. He moved one
foot, slipping it beneath her petticoats, careful not to so
much as brush her ankle. Her eyes widened, a pale blue
sea a man could drown in. The black silk beauty mark on
her cheek appeared to quiver. She was perfectly still, save
for the steady rise and fall of her breasts. One hand
clenched around her fan, the small sound of the ivory
sticks grating against one another was clearly audible in
the confined space.

Leo held back a grin and set his foot against the seat,
bracing himself, waiting for her to relax. The last thing he
wanted was for her to look like a frightened mare when
they arrived at the theatre. That wouldn't do at all. But
somehow he couldn't resist teasing her with small threats
of intimacy. Her shiver of anticipation was irresistible.

The hubbub of their fellow attendees washed over the carriage: shouts, laughter, the clang of steel-shod hooves and iron-rimmed coach wheels becoming a din of near epic proportions. Mrs. Whedon straightened, breasts swelling, threatening to spill from the absurdly low neckline of her gown. The tall feathers in her hair brushed the roof of the carriage, the longest curling down as if bowing.

Leo allowed himself a smile, picturing the looks on people's faces when they entered together. He was about to cause an unholy amount of gossip. But this very public display was necessary for Mrs. Whedon to continue in the belief that it was Sir Hugo she needed protection from, and that Leo had taken on the challenge. And when the lady did finally take him to her bed, that alone might make it worth the trouble. "Ready to face the lions?"

Mrs. Whedon smiled back, just a slight upswing of her lips, gone almost before it started, not even a crease in her powdered cheek to mark its passing. She ran her hands over her petticoats, smoothing them over her knees, then dipped her head and fiddled with one of the pins that secured her gown to its stomacher. "It's only the *ton*. I've faced worse."

Leo caught the tight expression on her face and was unsure whether to attribute it to the strain of their approaching debut or to give her words more weight than he normally would, considering her flippant tone. Before he could undertake any further interrogation, the carriage lurched to a halt and the door swung open, the steps falling with a soft *thunk* at the footman's instigation.

Mrs. Whedon met his gaze steadily, then rose and allowed the footman to hand her out. Leo jumped down after her and watched with amusement as she shook out her skirts, haughty as any of the grand dames of the *ton*. She had presence, and she clearly knew she drew the eye. She expected to do so.

Mrs. Whedon tipped her head and held out her hand. He took it, settled it on his arm, and led her toward the theatre's entrance, pushing past the gaping throng without so much as a nod. Let them wonder. Let them marvel. So long as they took note—so long as word got back to Sir Hugo, and whatever game he'd been playing with Mrs. Whedon ended before it interfered with Leo's own—he didn't care what they thought or said.

This was a grand performance. The protector claiming his mistress. The dog warning off the rest of the pack. This is mine. Don't touch. The point wouldn't be lost on Sir Hugo or Mrs. Whedon.

If it wouldn't have resulted in a screaming match with his mother—and one he was destined to lose—he'd have fastened the family rubies around Mrs. Whedon's throat as an unmistakable declaration of ownership. As it was, she was wearing a shocking collar of topazes, given to her by Lord only knew who.

The desire to rip them off nearly stole his breath. There was something deeply unsettling about having her parading about in another man's gift. The fact that it bothered him was more unsettling still. The performance was leaching into reality.

If she'd been truly his, an awe-inspiring parure would have been in order. Something to send those damn topazes to the bottom of her jewelry case for good. Peridots, or perhaps coral. Coral would be amazing with her hair.

But she wasn't. His. Not now, not ever. And even if she were, such a gift was well beyond his purse. Mrs. Whedon was a means to an end. A delightful means, but nothing more. Though it was all too easy to forget such quibbles when he looked at her, when he was plotting out how— where—to touch her.

Viola curled her hand more securely around Lord Leonidas's arm as they pushed through the crowd. His arm was hard under the silk, the veiled strength comforting in the crowd. For the first time in days, she felt utterly secure. Sir Hugo wouldn't dare bother her, under the circumstances.

After ascending several flights of crowded stairs, they arrived at the Vaughn family box. It was blissfully empty, a softly lit corner of the world where they were both entirely alone and dramatically on display, like a magnificent curio in a glass display case.

Viola took several deep, calming breaths and raised her chin a hair as Vaughn seated her on one of the dainty gilded chairs at the front. He sent his footman running for refreshments and claimed the seat beside her.

His shoulder crowded her, hip and thigh pressed against her, crushing her gown. He overwhelmed his seat as thoroughly as he overwhelmed her. It was unnerving.

Regardless of size, Viola simply wasn't used to being intimidated. Wasn't used to the anticipatory flush of excitement beating its way through her veins to lodge like a second heartbeat between her thighs.

Viola reached for the serenity at her core and found... nothing. Tears welled up in her eyes, and she let her breath out with a hiss to cover the surge of uncertainty.

He hadn't so much as touched her yet, nothing but gloved hand to gloved hand, an act so proper, so staid, it wouldn't inflame a virgin. But here she sat, the subject of a thousand prying eyes, nervous as a girl on her wedding night.

So much for Mrs. Whedon, famed courtesan. Right now, she might as well be Miss Perry, fifteen and green as grass, all over again. She certainly felt it at this exact moment, and the sensation wasn't at all welcome. It had been a decade since she'd been that girl, and she'd spent the intervening years in the arms of decadence and debauchery. And though she knew it was damning to admit it, she'd enjoyed nearly every minute of it. It had certainly been better than the alternatives.

She flicked her gaze over Lord Leonidas. He was magnificent. A dangerous creature masquerading as a gentleman, powdered hair and glossy black shoes a patent falsehood. The Duke of Richmond's tiger escaped to sun with the barn cats, tail flicking with lazy anticipation…

He'd planted the seed of her seduction so carefully, so perfectly, that she'd been undone before she'd known how to stop herself. The simple challenge of resistance inflamed her. The urge to beat him at his own game, to make him crawl and beg, was irresistible.

A week ago, Viola wouldn't have doubted her ability to bring a man to his knees. Tonight, she wasn't at all sure, especially when the subject of her experiment was Lord Leonidas.

The challenge was intoxicating.

He'd taken silence on her part for agreement. A sign of arrogance that had not been lost on her, and a trick of his nature that might prove useful at a later date. He simply couldn't imagine her saying no.

All around the theatre, quizzing glasses winked back at her. Fans fluttered and ladies shot her angry glances from the corners of their eyes as their male companions ogled her. Her friends were gathered together in the box of Lady Ligonier's current lover, all of them watching with avid interest. Sir Hugo was there, too, waves of anger emanating from his box like the heat of a blacksmith's forge.

Lord Leonidas sat beside her, languid and calm as a boat drifting in the doldrums. He caught her watching him, and his lips slid into a hint of a smile. His wicked green eye winked.

He was a devil, and it was all she could do not to melt onto the floor.

Humiliation and excitement warred within her, making her light-headed. Every nerve was alive with the idea that tonight Vaughn would fulfill his promise—his threat—to make her beg. Tonight those long-fingered hands would slide up her calf, strip off her garters . . . Viola caught her breath and forced it out in an audible huff. She was doing his work for him. Seducing herself. Damnation.

What had become of her famous self-control?

The footman returned with two glasses of wine. Vaughn accepted them with a nod, and the man slid back through the curtain into the corridor. Vaughn held one out to her, light flashing off the bubble trapped in the stem.

Viola took the glass, careful to avoid brushing her fingers against his, and raised it to her lips. The heavy flavor of oak and cherries and tobacco flooded her mouth and filled her nose. She took another sip, grateful for something to concentrate on other than Vaughn himself.

At last, the curtain rose and the babble of the pit rose with it. Viola took another draught and fastened her attention to the stage.

As the lead actress appeared to a riot of applause, Vaughn's hand slid into her lap, gripped her thigh, and his thumb began a slow, steady caress. A tiny thing really, just the barest hint of movement. It held her riveted.

The kidskin of his glove cloaked the strength of his hand. The cuff of his shirt likewise masked his wrist. But she was all too aware of the strength coiled beside her. All too appreciative.

Viola rapped his knuckles with her fan, and his hand jerked away. She kept her eyes firmly on the stage. "That part of my anatomy is considerably above my knee, my lord."

He'd be lucky if she didn't react like a combination of a
banshee and an avenging archangel when word of what he
was up to finally reached her in the hinterlands of Kinross-
shire. With any luck, she'd spend the summer mired in local
affairs and not give him, or London, a thought until Septem-
ber when it was time for his father's annual shooting party.

Leo settled back in his chair and let his eyes slowly
unfocus. The play was some trite affair by Sheridan, full
of characters with ridiculous names like Backbite, Ver-
juice, and Sneerwell. He hadn't come for the play. The
entire point of the outing was to be seen. To make enough
of a spectacle of themselves for polite society to sit up and
notice that Mrs. Whedon had passed into his keeping.
And by doing so, to take the first step down the path that
led to her eventual seduction and capitulation, and their
mutual pleasure. And it would be mutual, of that he was
sure. Anything else was unthinkable. Unacceptable.

The actors broke into a song about blushing maidens,
which meant he had at least another hour to go before the
play ended and the farce began. Sitting complacently beside
Mrs. Whedon for that length was insupportable.

What would she do if he knelt before her and took
what liberties he could in so confined, and public, a space
while the players cavorted below? Leo turned away from
the rather tepid fare being offered and caught her watching him. Their eyes met, and she held his gaze. As was her
wont, she simply waited. She didn't seem to be quizzing
him, nor challenging him, nor attempting to puzzle him
out. After a prolonged moment, when he was almost sure
she was going to lean in for a kiss, she blinked and twisted
her head back around to face the stage.

Leo tugged off his glove and dropped his hand to catch the silk of her petticoat. When she didn't protest, he slowly gathered the skirt upward, revealing first her ankle, then a good deal of her calf. Her breath hitched ever so slightly, but she kept her attention firmly fastened on the stage below.

He worked his hand under the hem, fingers sliding up her calf and over her knee, thumb sinking into the sensitive crease behind it. He traced the kneecap, skimmed up over the top of her knee, and slipped beneath her stocking, letting his thumb trace the edge where silk met skin.

Unable to stop himself, Leo leaned toward her, buried his nose in the small, alluring gap between her ear and her hair, and inhaled. As before, Mrs. Whedon smelled like sunshine and grass on a warm afternoon, underlain with the sweet scent of her own flesh. His hand left her knee, pushing up to the bare skin of her thigh.

Under the whorls of his fingers, the skin was soft, as supple as the glove he'd tossed to the floor. Suddenly her own hand locked about his wrist. She turned toward him, her cheek brushing his, her mouth perfectly poised for a kiss. Everything about her, save the steady grip on his wrist, spoke eloquently of capitulation.

Mrs. Whedon made a soft tsking sound, shaking her head no almost imperceptibly. "I was supposed to beg first, remember?" Her lips grazed his ear, and his whole body clenched.

Leo let his breath out with a laugh and rested his head more firmly against hers. "Ah, but 'bravery is a rampart of defense.'"

"Don't quote dead Romans at me. I'm not some village maid ready to be impressed by vague claims to education."

He pulled away to look at her, searching her face in the dim light for something he couldn't quite put a name to. "The claim isn't vague in the slightest. I've a very good memory for Tacitus." What was surprising was that she did as well. It certainly wasn't a common female accomplishment.

No getting around it. He was going to have to read the first volume of her memoir and see what it had to reveal about her past.

Her grip loosened, and he squeezed her thigh again before she shoved his hand away. "I don't suppose you'd care to leave now and let me resume my sortie in the carriage?"

She twisted about to face him, her expression triumphant. "Not a chance of that, my lord. We've the rest of *School for Scandal,* and then there's the farce. And during the break, you're going to fetch me another drink, and I'm going to enjoy a quarter of an hour's flirtation with all the gentlemen who even now are panting for a chance to be where you are."

"And then?"

"And then we'll see."

Mrs. Whedon turned her attention back to the stage and pushed her petticoats back into decorous order. Leo folded his arms and grinned. She could have her farce and her *we'll sees* if she wanted them. They changed nothing.

Onstage, the lead actress broke character to accept a rose from a man who'd climbed up from the pit. The crowd roared in disapproval, and the man slid back down, buffeted by a rain of rotting vegetables as he went. Leo sighed and blew out a desultory breath. It was going to be a long night.

When the intermission before the farce finally arrived, Leo stepped outside the box and sent his footman to fetch more wine. Now was his chance for a bit of public dalliance. It was now that he and Mrs. Whedon would perform upon a stage of their own for the eager masses.

He stepped back into the box, and Mrs. Whedon welcomed him with a cool smile and one slightly raised brow. She wasn't going to make this easy. Good. The seduction was half the fun. More than half, if he was to be truly honest.

All around them, faces were turned eagerly toward their box. Leo nodded to a few of his friends across the open expanse of the pit. From his own box, Sandison raised his glass in a toast, before returning his attention to his own guests.

Leo reclaimed his seat and took possession of one of Mrs. Whedon's long-fingered hands. He unclasped the bracelet she wore over her glove and tucked it into his pocket. One side of Mrs. Whedon's mouth slid up into a grudging smile. Leo tugged at the tip of each finger, loosening the glove, then he pulled it off and stowed it with the bracelet. "You have lovely hands." He kissed her palm, then slid his mouth down to the pulse point at her wrist.

Her charming intake of breath became a hiss of displeasure as a male voice interrupted them. The man's sputtering, inchoate curse erupted into an uproar. "You've no right, my lord! No right at all." Leo pushed his thumb in lazy circles across Mrs. Whedon's palm. He ran an eye over Sir Hugo. The baronet was a big man, not overly tall, but with a pugilist's formidable build.

"I've a contract signed and sealed." Sir Hugo's face flushed from pink to puce, and his glare locked on Mrs. Whedon. "She's mine through the end of the year. Bought and paid for."

Mrs. Whedon was also flushed. Anger seemed to be choking her. Leo raised her hand and brushed his lips across her knuckles. "Was he always this crass? It must have been a chore to put up with him, let alone bed him. You have my sympathy, madam."

Mrs. Whedon's eyes widened, and after a pregnant pause, she burst into laughter. Sir Hugo lurched toward them, hands balled into fists. Leo shot to his feet, grabbed hold of the other man's coat, and wrestled him out of the box.

The crowded corridor parted around them, ringing them in quite effectively. Sir Hugo looked close to apoplexy. He straightened his wig as though he were donning a helm and squared his shoulders.

"Fair warning, my lord," Sir Hugo spat out. "You're trespassing."

Leo nodded. It was entirely likely that he was. "You have my apologies, sir. You can be very sure that I will have my solicitor review your contract with Mrs. Whedon. If she's found in breach, I'll be sure you're made whole."

The crowd tittered and jeered. Sir Hugo ground his teeth, his hands flexing as though he were imagining them around Leo's neck. "I should like to teach you a lesson, whelp. But this is neither the time nor the place."

Leo raised a brow by way of response. The baronet must know such contracts were nearly unenforceable. And the theatre was the perfect place for such interactions. Public exhibitions of personal lives were practically the only reason anyone came.

Mrs. Whedon approached from behind, her skirts fluttering against his legs. She placed one hand just between his shoulder blades and leaned forward so that she could see around him. "I'm not some scrubby schoolboy," Leo said, not taking his eyes off the seething baronet. "Whelp or not, I'm still the son of a duke, and Mrs. Whedon is no longer your concern."

Sir Hugo's breath huffed out of him as though he were the bellows in a smithy. "I hope she bleeds you dry, Lord Leonidas. Lord knows it's what you deserve."

Charles frowned as the crowd exiting the Haymarket swelled, pushing past him in a torrent of silk and lace and the heavy stench of violet hair powder. He raised his handkerchief to his nose, trying to block out the stink.

His cousin Leo was a few yards ahead of him, his height making him conspicuous, easy to follow. Beside Leo, Charles could just make out the Whedon woman's mass of curls and the bob of her very expensive feathers.

He'd watched them from the pit all evening. Leo might as well have bent her over the railing and fucked her in full view of the entire audience.

What was the point of bringing such a woman to see a play? Of treating her like a lady? Of wooing her? Everyone knew she could be had for a price, and it hardly added to a man's reputation to be seen groveling and pandering in such a manner. His cousin was making a fool of himself, and for what? Because he wasn't man enough to simply take what he wanted.

It was ridiculous.

Charles gritted his teeth as the corridor swelled with people, and he was relentlessly borne along with the tide of humanity. A man jostled him, elbowing him smartly in the ribs. Charles glared and shoved back. The man threw him a frightened glance before stumbling away and disappearing into the throng.

Damn Leo. This was too important a matter for him to simply let Leo win, as he always had. Leonidas: the golden boy of the Vaughn clan, for all that he was the younger brother. Always the best at everything, or at least always the one praised for being best, singled out for reward simply for being born who he was. The pampered spare who had to neither live up to an heir's responsibilities nor scramble to support himself. He was like a pug, pampered and sheltered. Useless.

It was to him that their grandfather had left an estate. What had Charles got? A yearly annuity of a few hundred pounds. Leo could insist they were both Vaughns, but their grandfather's will had made it perfectly clear that they weren't equals. Leo was to become a landed gentleman, to have a life worthy of a duke's son, while he was left to scrape by as best he could on his wits and a pittance. The duke had even gone so far as to recommend the Church.

Charles's stomach clenched. A pinch-penny vicar, that's what the mighty Vaughns thought appropriate for him. Damn them.

But Leo wasn't going to prevail this time around. Charles couldn't allow it. Wouldn't allow it. His great-uncle's involvement with the Jacobites had been all it took to bring the entire family to its knees. Heads had rolled, titles had died out, and fortunes had been lost. Children like him, the final fruit of those pruned vines, had been left to fend for themselves as best they could.

Most people supposed him lucky to have been taken in by his maternal family, but they were wrong. Every moment of every day simply heaped further insult upon injury. Every triumph of his usurper-supporting family was another blow. The prince had been their rightful king. Charles's family's reward for doing what was just, what was required by God and honor, had been destruction, desecration, and ruin.

But the money hidden in number twelve would change all of that.

❦ CHAPTER 6 ❦

Before Mrs. Whedon had time to fully settle onto the velvet seat of the carriage, Leo clambered aboard and crammed his way onto the seat beside her. She twisted, putting her back to the corner, hoops and skirts riding up. Her wary eyes gleamed in the dim light cast by the linkboys' flambeaux as they ran past, shouting for custom.

The coach rocked hard as it set off, the muffled voice of the coachman cursing at those blocking his way. "How long do you think it will take to clear all this?" Leo said, drawing her feet up into his lap. "We might not get home till dawn." He eased off one shoe and flung it carelessly across the coach, diamond buckle and all. "If we're lucky."

Anticipation curled in his belly, crawling up and down his limbs with the same tingle as a lightning storm. Outside, there was chaos as sedan chairs vied with carriages and footmen fought over the placement of their masters' coaches. Inside, it was the eye of the storm, just quiet enough for him to hear her small gasp as he pressed one thumb into the soft arch of her silk-clad foot. Beneath his fingers, the delicate bones shifted. Kidskin slid over silk, promising something entirely wanton.

Mrs. Whedon bit her lip and flexed her toes like a cat responding to a hand down its back. Leo turned his head to hide his grin and bent all his concentration on Mrs. Whedon's foot. Nothing else existed, save the fact that it led—irresistibly—to a finely turned ankle and shapely calf.

She made a small contented noise in the back of her throat as he slid his hands up her calf and slipped a finger beneath her garter. Leo thumbed the hook loose and tugged the garter free, then bent and kissed the bend of her knee. The intoxicating scent of warm flesh filled his nostrils; the knowledge that her naked thigh lay just out of bounds was torturous.

He gripped her stocking with his teeth and pulled.

"Those are twelve shillings a pair."

"And worth every penny." He stripped it from her leg and flung it after her shoe. "But you really should have much more engrossing things to think about just now than the exorbitant price you've paid for stockings."

She chuckled and pushed against him with her bare foot, her leg lolling outward in what he dearly hoped was a blatant invitation. Leo put his open mouth against the soft flesh on the inside of her knee and sucked, and then blew across the wet mark he left behind.

"My lord—" Her protest cut off as he bit softly above the mark left by her garter.

"My lady?"

"My lord." Her breath hitched, her tone pleaded, and her hands were locked on his coat.

He licked a short trail up and over her knee to the inside of her thigh.

"I wasn't—"

"Of course you weren't," he agreed, not moving from the spot. He knew begging when he heard it, and this was just the beginning of their evening...

The sound of gunshots brought Leo upright and out of the haze of seduction as thoroughly as a cold bucket of water. The coach shuddered to a stop, and he pushed Mrs. Whedon behind him. A second shot burst the small window in the door, sending a thousand minute projectiles raining down upon them. Outside, there was shouting and the unmistakable sound of a horse in pain. Leo flipped up the opposite seat and grabbed one of the pistols kept there before he flung open the door and waded into the fray.

He emerged into darkness that was only vaguely pierced by the greasy glow of the streetlamps. Leo cocked the gun and took the scene in with a clarity that seemed to come only in times of crisis. One of the horses was down, thrashing in its traces. Its mate was sideling, tossing its head in terror.

His father's coachman, Tompkins, was struggling to cut the wounded horse free, while the footmen were locked in combat with multiple ruffians armed with cudgels and knives. Leo shot one of them, then turned the gun about and hit a second man with its heavy butt. He went down silently, but with a sickening lurch. Leo stepped over his body and pulled a man in a rough frieze coat off one of the footmen.

A shot rang out from behind him, and the man in the frieze coat fell back, screaming. Leo spun about to find Mrs. Whedon, the second pistol drooping in her hand. Their eyes met, and he thought she smiled, and then she was falling back into the coach, screaming.

For the first time in his life, Leo actually understood what it meant to see red.

He got halfway to the coach before someone grabbed his arm. Nothing existed except his fists, the fools who had undoubtedly been sent by his cousin, and the need to get to Mrs. Whedon. To Viola.

Leo didn't realize that it was over, his cousin's men either dead or fled into the night, until Tompkins—wig missing and livery coated in blood—caught his wrist. "My lord, have done."

"Mrs. Whedon?"

"Here." Her voice was high, clearly frightened. Rage flushed through him anew. This wasn't how a man did things. Wasn't how he or Charles had been raised to treat a woman. But Charles had turned his back on everything he'd been raised to believe, been raised to be. And tonight Leo was ashamed to call him cousin.

Leo pushed away from the body on the cobbles and stumbled toward the coach. Mrs. Whedon was sitting in the doorway of the coach, her gown in ruins, hair tumbling down her back, and blood trickling down one side of her face, dripping onto her chest.

Leo swallowed hard as his heart missed a beat and attempted to crawl up his throat. He pulled her up— perhaps a bit roughly, judging by her hiss of pain—to examine her head. A bloody scrape marred her temple, but that was all. Thank God. "Well, aren't we rather rough and ready with a pistol?"

Viola flashed a wan smile, shrugging almost imperceptibly. Blood trickled over her brow. Her eyes fluttered, lashes batting against the dark stream. One feather bent ridiculously over her forehead while the other stuck straight out.

She was more than she presented herself to be. More than he—or the world—gave her credit for. And it was his fault she was hurt. He should never have shown those damn letters to Charles.

Leo wiped his thumb over her brow, clearing it for the moment. "We need to get this seen to immediately."

"It's just a head wound. They *do* bleed. I'll be fine once it stops."

"Perhaps…" Arm still locked about her waist, Leo glanced over his shoulder. All of his servants were still standing, but they were clearly the worse for wear. One of the footmen had found his wig and was beating it against his leg, sending up a cloud of powder. The other was clutching his arm, a grimace turning his face into a mask.

A crowd had begun to form; coaches and sedan chairs built up behind them as their owners disembarked to goggle at the scene. A sudden disturbance ran through the gathering horde, and a familiar silver-headed man sauntered forth like a champion come to save the day.

"Sandison," Leo said with relief. "Please do me the favor of seeing Mrs. Whedon home. Mrs. Whedon"—he swung her up into his arms and nodded to Sandison to lead the way—"you can trust Mr. Sandison as you would myself."

"So not an inch further than I could push him," she said with a brave attempt at a chuckle.

"As you would myself," Leo repeated, giving her an extra squeeze for reassurance. "I'll be with you as quickly as I can. Have Sandison send for a surgeon. No arguments."

She blinked, eyes huge, as though she were still trying to make sense out of the evening's events. Leo placed her in Sandison's coach and stooped to rest his head against hers, nose to her ear, lips briefly brushing the corner of her jaw. That simple promise was all he could give her in haste.

Knowing she was as safe as he could make her, Leo clapped his friend on the shoulder and waded back through the crowd to the scene of misery his cousin had created.

"Aren't you a fright." Anthony Thane stood like the mountain he was in the center of the street. He took a pinch of snuff and surveyed the wreckage rather like a traveler viewing some impressive foreign vista.

Leo yanked his cravat loose and passed it roughly over his face. No amount of laundering would save the frill of ruinously expensive lace, so he might as well make use of it.

"It's a certainty that blood and hair powder don't mix."

"Very helpful, Thane." Leo scrubbed at his face one last time and thrust his cravat into the pocket of his coat. "Am I reduced to a minor horror? Yes? Excellent. I see the night watchman has arrived, for all the use he'll be. Can you handle him while I see what can be done to clear the road? I don't think I'm prepared to be polite at the moment."

Thane spun on his heel and marched off in the direction of the watchman, who stood with his club dangling from his hand, a look of pure shock upon his face.

~≈ CHAPTER 7 ≈~

Viola accepted Mr. Sandison's proffered handkerchief and held it to her temple. The edge drooped, obscuring her vision. The blood was already drying, the tightness on her skin distracting with each and every breath. Her hand shook as she pressed the linen more firmly in place.

She'd shot a man. She'd never shot at anything but the pips on playing cards, and tonight she'd shot a man, maybe even killed him. It had been absurdly easy. Seemingly unreal. Lord Leonidas had leapt from the coach, gun in hand, leaving the pistol's mate glinting in its secret box.

It had been in her hand before she'd even realized she'd reached for it...

As the coach rumbled into motion, Vaughn's friend opened a panel behind him and withdrew a large, double-barreled pistol. The panel closed with an almost silent *snick,* and he sat, leg braced against the door, gun resting loosely in his hand: a guardian at the portal.

"Do you all go about armed? Does every coach in London have a secret panel?"

Mr. Sandison chuckled, his whole demeanor seemingly relaxed as he swayed with the coach's motion. "Life in London does seem to call for a weapon far more often than one might assume." He pushed the curtain aside with the barrel of the gun and stared out into the dark street. After a moment, he let the curtain fall closed again. "Or at least my life certainly does."

"Lord Leonidas's as well."

"Yes." Mr. Sandison nodded in agreement. "Vaughn does seem to lead a most exciting life."

He was looking directly at her, and Viola felt a blush rise in response. Ridiculous. She never blushed. Never. Though that seemed to have changed of late... She pursed her lips, refusing to be baited. She pulled the handkerchief away from her head and was relieved to see the flow had greatly lessened.

Mr. Sandison glanced at her. "Best keep it there a while longer." He pushed the curtain aside again and returned his attention to the streets. The occasional flash of light as they passed a streetlamp illuminated the coach for brief moments before plunging it back into darkness.

The plush seat embraced Viola as she sagged backward, only her stays keeping her from crumpling into a ball. The invasion of her house had been terrifying, but this, to be attacked on the streets, to see men wounded defending her... It was too much. She simply couldn't make sense of it. This clearly hadn't been about seizing her manuscript. It had been about her. She'd never imagined Sir Hugo would go to these lengths.

Did he think killing her would stop publication, or was he merely that angry over his humiliating encounter that evening? And he was in breach of their contract. Had been for months, ever since he'd failed to make the quarterly payment that was due. Ever since the first volume of her memoir had thrown him into an inexplicable rage.

Her hands began to shake, her stomach churning violently against the pressure of her stays. Her mouth watered as though she were going to be sick. Viola shut her eyes and concentrated on the simple act of breathing.

The sooner she finished her manuscript and handed it over to her publisher the better. Once it was gone, she would be safe. There would no longer be any reason—logically—to harass her. Though Sir Hugo might burn for revenge when he read his chapter.

Killing her after the book was in production would only ensure it was the biggest hit of not just the Season but possibly the century. The murder of the Earl of Sandwich's mistress—also committed as she left the theatre, now that Viola thought of it—was still being talked of in lurid whispers four years later. If poor Martha had written a memoir, it would have been a sensation. Viola shivered and thrust the memory of her dead friend away.

The carriage rolled to a clattering stop, and Viola opened her eyes as Mr. Sandison leapt down, the magnificent silver braid that edged his coat sparkling in the welcoming light of her home.

"Stay inside while we check that the street is clear," he said before shutting her up again. The distinct sound of knuckles on wood was followed by muffled conversation.

The coach rocked gently as one of his footmen swung down. Minutes passed in tense silence. The door opened, and Mr. Sandison's gloved hand appeared.

"All clear, Mrs. Whedon. Let's get you inside before that changes."

Mrs. Draper stood in the doorway, crowding aside Sandison's bulky footmen like a broody hen making room for her chicks. As Viola's foot touched the cold metal of the coach step, she remembered her shoes were missing and that she was wearing only one stocking.

Mr. Sandison swept her up into his arms. "Pretend I'm Vaughn. Better yet, pretend I'm someone far more handsome and desirable than my deplorable friend." He smiled, flirtatious, but harmlessly so, as they ascended the stairs.

In moments, she was in her own boudoir with her maid and housekeeper fussing over her. Mr. Sandison made her a profound leg and excused himself. "I'll be downstairs until made superfluous," he said, before whisking himself out of the room, the skirts of his coat swinging with an almost jaunty air.

Viola stared at the door. Sandison was enjoying himself. It was appalling, and yet she found herself smiling. What sort of man enjoyed such an evening?

Dismissing him from her thoughts, Viola crossed the room and collapsed on the seat before her dressing table. Tentatively, she leaned forward to examine the damage. Blood streaked her hair, covered one side of her face and neck, and crimson and burgundy rivulets traced a path down her chest to bloom onto her gown like some exotic Chinese flower. Against her powdered skin and hair, the effect was garish. She turned her back to her reflection and began to strip off her gloves.

"Mrs. Draper, can you please get me some hot water?"

Her housekeeper nodded her head decisively, enormous nightcap flapping about her ears. She rushed out the door, bellowing for the maid of all work at the top of her lungs.

Her ladies maid gave her a wan smile as she stood. Viola tossed her gloves on the floor with a shudder. Nance tsked over the state of her gown as she stripped it off her. "At least your stays haven't been touched, and I think it's likely I can get the few spots on your shift clean if I wash it immediately."

"Never mind about that." Viola flicked the pile of expensive silk away from her with her foot. "Burn it all, throw it in the midden. I don't care. Just get rid of it."

Viola pulled on her oldest and most comfortable dressing gown, its frayed velvet cuffs oddly comforting. Mrs. Draper reappeared with a pitcher of steaming water and an armful of towels. Behind her, little Sally bustled in with a tray of small lemon cheesecakes and a glass half full of amber liquid.

"Brandy, ma'am. Mr. Sandison's orders." She said it as though that made it law.

Viola felt a bubble of laughter swelling within her chest, pushing the cold horror of the evening to the fringes. While her servants fussed about the room, Viola returned to her dressing table and forced herself to eat. The filling was sweet on her tongue, the crust simply melted, a thousand layers of buttery flakes. She washed it down with a healthy amount of brandy, letting the warmth seep through her, from lips to throat to stomach and out to her frigid limbs.

Nance lit the candles that flanked her mirror, smoke curling up from the twisted length of paper in her hand. Viola turned her head to the right, and a pristine, if tired, woman gazed out at her. Only the deep circles under her eyes spoke to her true state. Turning her head to the left revealed the ghostly apparition of a murdered queen. Something right out of Shakespeare.

She picked up a towel, soaked it and rung it out, and began cleaning the blood from her face. The hot water stung, but she held the cloth firmly to her wound, loosening the clot that matted her hair.

Nance finished disposing of her clothing and returned to brush out her hair, carefully stripping out the powder along with the tangles. She was making the small clicking sound with her tongue that she always made when distressed. Pin after pin clinked into the black, japanned box on the table as Nance plucked them from the wreck of her coiffure.

A second towel joined the first in a damp pile draped over the empty ewer before a peremptory knock on the door set Viola's heart racing, and Vaughn appeared behind her in the glass. Even in reflection, his eyes burned, and the set of his jaw was impossible to miss. He hadn't calmed down one iota since she'd seen him last.

She'd watched him beat a man with his fists, possibly to death. There'd been rage behind his actions, but there had also been cold calculation, precision, and no hint of indecision.

Viola twisted about to face him. He was dirty, rumpled, and nearly as blood-streaked as she'd been. But even under all that blood and grime, the hard, masculine planes of his face were distinct, like an ancient marble statue just reclaimed from the earth. And her impulse was the same as anyone discovering such a treasure: to revel in its glory.

He was hers, at least for the moment.

"Nance, that will be all." Viola wet the edge of a clean towel and stood, her robe swirling around her feet in heavy folds. The click of the door shutting signaled her maid's swift departure. "Sit."

She took his arm and pushed him into the small chair she'd just vacated. He tensed, then sank obediently.

Viola passed the towel across his forehead, trying to be gentle. "Are your servants all right?" The splinters of window glass had sliced his cheek in multiple places.

As with her own wound, the blood made it look far worse than it was. The only real damage was one nasty slice that ran along his cheekbone like the scratch of some great cat, though it was clear he'd have a black eye come morning.

"Yes." He winced slightly as the towel passed over the largest cut, his wicked green eye closing tight, tiny rays of smile lines running down his cheek. "A broken arm and a knife wound that needs stitching are the worst of it. Lucky for us, most of my family's footmen are veterans of the King's Royal Ethiopian Regiment. They're a bit more useful in a fight than their London-bred counterparts."

"Really?" Viola stood back to admire her handiwork. She cocked her head and wiped off one last smudge near his ear, allowing her fingers to linger on the hard edge of his jaw. The faint burr of whiskers pulled at the fabric of the towel. "I had wondered why most of your footmen and grooms were Africans."

"My uncle was one of the officers in charge. Promises were made for their support. Promises that haven't been kept for the most part. When he returned after the war, he retired, and now he spends his days finding employment for as many of his men as he can."

She ran her thumb over his cheek, holding her breath to prevent herself from leaning forward to kiss his wound as though he were a child . . . or a lover. He was in need of a shave; the dark whiskers gave his jaw a faint velvet sheen in the candlelight. It must be later than she thought, for he'd been immaculate at the theatre.

Lord Leonidas plucked the towel from her grasp and rose. One hand caught her chin and tipped her head for his inspection. His eyes narrowed, and he dabbed at her neck. Clearly dissatisfied, he tugged the collar of her robe open, exposing her shoulder and very nearly her breast.

Viola bit the inside of her cheek to keep from smiling. "Once again, my lord, you're considerably above my knee."

"What—"

His look of bewilderment set off a peal of laughter.

"Very funny, my lady." He thrust her down into the chair and began scrubbing the dried blood from her shoulder with much the same air as an annoyed governess with a recalcitrant and muddy charge.

"Is your uncle an abolitionist?"

"Of the strictest order." He soaked a new towel and continued his almost rough ministrations. "No sugar. No rum. No cotton. Rides about distributing pamphlets. Even paid for his secretary's memoir to be published last year."

"He sounds like an admirable man."

"He is." Lord Leonidas tossed the towel into the basin and dropped a casual kiss on her still-damp shoulder. Her lungs seized, shriveling away to nothing inside her chest. "He's also an incredible bore."

She shuddered as the ability to breathe returned. "Most reformers are."

"We're a wicked, ungrateful pair, you and I."

"Bound for hell. I've known it for years. Makes me all the more determined to enjoy this world." Viola locked her hand in his lapel and pulled him toward her, raising her face for a kiss. She needed it. The warmth of it, the reassurance of it, the celebration of it. Needed it more than she needed to maintain control.

He stiffened, resisting, finally raising one hand to engulf hers. She winced as he removed her hand. Lord Leonidas simply stood staring at her wrist, cradling it as though it were a captured butterfly.

"You didn't get that tonight." His brow furrowed as his thumb made a small circle over the bruise that stood out livid and ugly just above the bones of her wrist.

"N-n-n-no. It's from the night those men—"

"But they didn't leave this." His voice was flat, a thread of pure anger laced through it. "I did." His thumb continued running back and forth over the bruise as though he could wipe it away.

Tears burnt behind her eyes. She willed them away with a shuddering breath. If she started crying now, she didn't think she'd be able to stop.

"I'm sorry." His apology rumbled through her, shocking and warm as the brandy she'd drunk earlier.

"For saving me? Nonsense."

Something other than tears burned behind his eyes. For a moment, both the blue and the green looked equally sad. Equally defeated. Viola caught her lip between her teeth, mind racing to understand the fleeting grief. It seemed too intense for something so small as a bruise.

~ CHAPTER 8 ~

Leo swallowed down the anger that had been building all evening. She hadn't needed saving tonight. This attack had been meant for him. He wasn't yet sure if it was a warning, or if his cousin really had meant him harm, but either way, he was ultimately responsible for Viola's wounds. All of them. The fact that he'd left his own mark on her simply added an undercurrent of self-loathing to his rage.

Doubt rattled through his brain, coursed through his blood, pushed farther with every beat of his heart. He squashed it down, let it mix with embers of anger and subside into a cold, dark lump in the center of his chest.

Now wasn't the time for repentance. He'd set the wheels in motion, and either his cousin or he would come out the winner in the end. It would certainly be better for Viola if it were him.

A race to the treasure, that had been easily foreseen. How far his cousin would take things, what he would do to win, Leo hadn't been prepared for. A mistake he wouldn't make a second time.

Leo ran his thumb lightly over her wrist again.

"Come to bed, my lord." Viola rose and tugged him toward her.

He planted his feet, rooting himself to the floor. The assortment of ointment bottles and small china dishes on her dressing table rattled softly.

He couldn't. Not tonight. Not like this. Capitulation was one thing, but his was something else. And it left him feeling unclean. Unworthy. Which he supposed he was. He'd never meant for her to be hurt.

A short indulgence—which she'd enjoy every bit as much as he—and then he'd be a rich man. She'd be none the wiser, having lost something she'd never known she'd had. Something that was hers only by a random act of fate.

When the idea had come to him, it had been simple. Easy. Suddenly it was something else. Something sordid and cheap and unworthy of a Vaughn. And that nasty realization was all his damn cousin's fault. Telling her wouldn't help a thing. She'd banish him from her presence, leaving herself prey to Charles.

Her hands were on his chest, her face upturned. Damp eyelashes framed those magnificent eyes of hers. Eyes the color of the Aegean. Eyes that pleaded. Her lips were parted, a sweet entreaty all their own. But there were shadows of exhaustion beneath her eyes, and the beauty mark she'd worn so saucily as they'd set out for the theatre had been replaced by a raw, angry-looking cut.

Leo cupped her face, caressing the high arch of her cheekbone, savoring the warm velvet of her skin, like the skin of a peach fresh from the tree. "I think that would be breaking our bargain."

Her face crumpled, the shadow under her eyes becoming hollows that reminded him far too much of the mark on her wrist. "Please? Isn't *please* begging enough?"

Leo shut his eyes as her plea dragged a smile out of him. "Yes, my dear, but of entirely the wrong order. What you want tonight is sleep. But if you want me to stay, I can dispose myself on the chaise with perfect comfort."

Viola eyed the chaise in question, then flicked her gaze up and down his length. "Doubtful as I find that, my lord, it won't do." She shivered, pressed closer, and laid her head upon his chest, hands still clutching at his coat. "I don't think I can stand to go to bed alone tonight. To *be* alone tonight."

Leo clenched his jaw, fighting the impulse to simply acquiesce. It would be so damn easy. "I can't pretend that fright is a suitable substitute for desire." He swept her up into his arms and marched into her bedchamber. "What you want is comfort. What you need is sleep. The first I'm more than willing to provide. The second—I think—will come to us both readily enough."

He deposited her beside the bed, shaking his head at her rueful expression, wanting to laugh or to cry. The cold spot that had taken up residence just behind his breastbone burned, seeming to expand with every falsehood and deception. With swift efficiency, he stripped her of her dressing gown and bundled her, naked and fuming, into bed.

He'd thought this would be easy.

The alluring flash of skin—pale as the moonlight that limned it with a faint celestial glow—was almost more than he could bear. The heavy sway of breasts, the flare of hips below a trim waist, the rounded perfection of thighs, all of it beauty personified.

Had he really just sworn to sleep chastely beside her?

Leo undressed quickly, dropping his clothing unceremoniously onto the floor. Most of it was ruined anyway, fit only for the rag-and-bone man. Wearing his drawers as a masculine chastity belt, he climbed into bed beside her.

As he slid beneath the covers, Viola fit herself to his side: head on his chest, breasts pressed close, thighs embracing one of his own. Leo wrapped his arm around her and kissed the top of her head, letting the faint, lingering scent of lavender hair powder invade his senses and lull him into a merely lustful stupor.

Viola made a sleepy, unintelligible sound and burrowed into him like a kitten, her breathing changing almost instantaneously into the soft, steady rhythm of sleep. Leo stared up into the dark recesses of the canopy and cursed himself for a fool.

Viola woke to screams.

She sat bolt upright, hands flying to her mouth, terrified the sound was coming from her own throat. Her head swam, pounding painfully as her heartbeat surged.

The sound went on: men and horses and the terrible roar of fire behind it all. An unholy red light flooded through the window.

Lord Leonidas was gone, the indentation he'd left in the mattress, stone cold. His coat and stockings lay abandoned, a milky pool against the dark wood of the floor.

Viola staggered from bed, shrugging into her dressing gown as she rushed to the window. The mews were afire.

Half-dressed men struggled with fear-maddened horses. Smoke poured up to meet heavy clouds, the promise of rain a cruel taunt in the face of such disaster.

Her gate burst open. A tall figure, hair flowing around his shoulders and mirroring the flames behind him, led a plunging horse into her garden. He yanked the halter from its head, and the animal caroled away from him, a fierce display of muscle and bone that sent Viola's heart straight into her throat. Two more horses joined it before the gate snapped shut, and Vaughn disappeared back into the smoking mews.

Viola ran into the street barefoot and in her bedclothes for the second time in as many weeks. A horse burst past her, dragging a groom with it. Its hooves hit the cobbles with a sound like a smithy.

Viola pressed herself to the wall, aghast as the groom swung himself onto the back of the moving horse and held tightly as the animal broke into a gallop. A second horse flew after them, leaving only the impression of terrifying strength and the rolling flash of the whites of its eyes.

As Viola rounded the corner, the sky opened with a thunderclap that made the ground shake. The deluge soaked through her dressing gown instantaneously. She shoved wet hair back, twisting it into a knot, impatiently searching the crowd for Vaughn. Gads, tall as he was, he should be easy enough to spot, but he wasn't.

They all paid a small fortune for the fire crew that was furiously battling the flames, water flying through a giant hand pump on wheels, aided now by the sheets of rain pounding down upon them all. Men swirled around her, calling out warnings, fighting to pull carriages from the building, and struggling to control maddened horses. The spotted carriage dog that belonged to her neighbor wove through the crowd, its white coat dulled by ash so it was almost unrecognizable.

A great cracking rent the air, and a shower of sparks erupted out the stable door, hitting the rain with an insidious hiss. Viola's hand again crept to her mouth, holding back a cry that seemed to deafen her from the inside out.

He wasn't there. He simply wasn't anywhere in the crowd. Another shower of sparks erupted as the stable fell in upon itself, the first story crashing down into the stalls.

A man stumbled out and was caught up by the crowd, their hands slapping out flames as quickly as the rain. Her heart turned over, but it wasn't Vaughn.

Viola stepped back as a coach was dragged past her, paint bubbling up on the door, obscuring the crest. She spun about, lost in the crowd, and bumped into a horse. She shrank away as it lashed out. Teeth caught her sleeve, yanked her off balance, and sent her sliding across wet cobbles and down into a crumpled heap.

Her cry as she hit the cobbles was drowned out by a deafening boom of thunder. Someone caught her from behind, lifting her up and away from the animal's nervously mincing hooves. Viola wrang her hand over her mouth, stifling a sob.

"Hush bunting, you'll frighten the horses."

Wet, bedraggled, and holding firmly to the halter of a trembling horse, Vaughn wrapped one arm about her and held her tight. His hair was half black with soot. Rain ran from it in great, gray runnels, streaming down his ruined shirt.

Lord Leonidas. Leo. He kept up a soft, singsong patter, though she couldn't for the life of her tell if it was for
her or the horse. The horse dropped its head, exhaling
loudly enough that she could feel it ripple through her.

"That's a pretty girl." He dropped his death grip on the
halter and ran his hand caressingly over the horse's neck.
"Let's put her in with the others, shall we?"

Viola nodded, not trusting herself to speak. She blinked
water out of her eyes, letting Vaughn lead her toward the
gate to her own yard, along with the mare.

He pushed the horse in, the wet slap of his hand on her
rump sending her tail flicking. She nickered, and the others rambled toward her, ears pricked with interest.

Viola bit her lip and looked helplessly at the ruin of her
garden. The neat beds had been trampled into a soggy
morass. One bench had been tumbled over, the seat knocked
from its base. The garden had been about the only thing
that hadn't been invaded and turned upside down during
the invasion of her home.

She sighed and then pressed her lips together disap-
provingly as Leo chuckled softly in response. His arm
snaked around her waist, and he propelled her up along
what was left of the gravel path.

The gravel bit into the tender flesh of her feet, causing
her to walk slowly and take each step with deliberate care.
The rain continued unabated. Her wrapper seemed to have
tripled in weight, its heavy folds making every step a struggle.

Once inside, they hurried up the servants' stairs and
into her room. Water dripping from his hair and pooling
beneath him, Leo heaped coal into the grate. Viola left to
rummage through the linen press. She returned with her

arms loaded with towels to find Leo stripping off his wet shirt before a crackling fire.

Her mouth went dry even as her hands shook. Firelight washed one side of him with ruddy warmth. The creeping dawn eased through the window, limning the other side with a soft, radiant glow.

He caught her watching, and his eyes crinkled with merriment. One large hand snatched a towel from her grasp. He disappeared behind a curtain of white Turkish cotton, emerging with his dark hair in dramatic disarray.

Heat flushed through her, driving back the cold of the wet cloth that still clung to her. If she shrugged it off and reached for him, would he resist? How much humiliation was she willing to accept in a single night?

He toed off his shoes and turned to drape his shirt over the fire screen. A powerful ripple of muscle moved beneath his skin with every gesture. Viola clutched the towels to her chest.

It wasn't fair that one man could be that perfect. That she could desire him as much as she did. It was frightening and exhilarating all at the same time, like being driven too fast in a high-perch phaeton. The thrill made it hard to breathe, hard to think, and it made her long for more.

Leo glanced over his shoulder. Viola was still rooted to the same spot, towels clutched to her chest as though they were some kind of shield. He stepped toward her. Her eyes widened, pupils spiraling out, obscuring the vivid blue. With an unmistakably wanton sigh, her lips parted. The soft lining of her lower lip called out for a kiss, for his mouth to meet hers, damp heat to damp heat.

His hand closed over her upper arm just as the door burst open and her housekeeper erupted into the room. "Water's heating for a bath, ma'am." She completely ignored him, gaze avoiding him with practiced perfection. "The fire in the mews is out, and I've sent one of his lordship's men off to fetch him dry things. In the meantime, I've got one of poor Ned's nightshirts for him so he doesn't catch his death."

Quick, efficient hands deposited the promised night-shirt on the bed and plucked up wet clothing and the other detritus of their evening's adventures. Viola's eyes met his, bewilderment evident in the slight pucker of her brows.

"Tha-uh-thank you, Mrs. Draper. Can you fetch my green banyan? And then, yes, I think a bath is more than called for, for both of us."

A sharp stab of lust shot from groin to throat at visions of Viola smiling up from a tub, rosy and wet, her hair swirl-ing out in the water like a mermaid's. But the tub in question wasn't some small wooden affair or a dainty tin slipper tub.

No, he wanted to see her naked in the bathhouse at Dyrham. Surrounded by a Roman-inspired sea of stone and a deep tub of hot water most commonly found only in London's bagnios.

"I'll not put your staff to the trouble, my dear. I can easily take myself home for my own ablutions."

Viola turned to leave, throwing him one last rueful smile, bedraggled hair falling from its knot as she did so. Her housekeeper swept out after her, tutting and fussing like a hen.

Leo shucked off the last of his wet clothing, pulled on the deceased footman's too-small nightshirt, and settled in to wait for his own clothes to arrive. From soup to nuts, his evening had not gone as planned. His seduction had been interrupted, and so had his subsequent explorations.

Unable to sleep, he'd been quietly searching for a loose floorboard or a trigger lock for a secret door when the commotion in the mews had intruded. He'd yanked on breeches and shirt, thrust his feet into his evening pumps, and gone to see what was happening. After the past week of deadly maneuvers, something that raised the entire neighborhood boded ill.

He couldn't be sure his cousin had set the fire—a groom coming home from a late night might have just as easily overturned a lamp—but he wasn't fool enough to believe it a mere coincidence. Leo walked across the room, checking boards for telltale squeaks and looseness as he did so. He couldn't possibly allow Viola to stay in London. Not with his cousin clearly willing to do whatever it took to best him. And that meant that it truly was time to bring the League into things.

"So you've finally decided to include us in your adventure." Devere yawned behind his hand and slouched lower in his chair, balancing his booted feet on the fender as though preparing for a nap.

Sandison rolled his eyes and ignored him. "Shall we invite the entire membership, or just Thane and de Moulines?"

Leo pulled the packets of letters from his coat pocket and handed them over. "When you've read these, I think you'll agree that this is one adventure best kept within our smaller circle."

Without comment, Sandison untied the bundle, unfolded

the first letter, read it over—turning it about and squinting to make out the crossed lines—and then, with a low whistle, passed it on to Devere. When he reached the third letter, he began to shake his head and click his tongue. When he finished the last one, he sighed and downed his untouched glass of brandy in a single gulp.

"You've got yourself into some very dangerous territory there, Vaughn." His incongruously dark brows were pinched over his nose. Leo could practically see the clockwork of his brain whirling behind his eyes.

Leo nodded. You could always count on Sandison to understand just where all the pieces stood in any important game. Thane kept the coolest head, and Devere was often first to act, but it was Sandison who saw things clearly. "There's nothing to link my family to the plot—"

"Thank all that's holy for that," Devere said, *sotto voce*.

"But," Leo said loudly, cutting off his friend's mumbled comment, "it's always risky to cross paths with treason, even a generation later."

"Especially when you're not the only one who knows about it and the other party is—how shall I put this?—not entirely friendly."

"Not entirely sane," Devere said, folding the final letter and dropping it onto the table as though it were scalding his fingertips.

"Charles isn't mad. He's just decided he's entitled to take what he wants, whatever the cost, and he's not willing to share."

"And just how determined are you?" Sandison cut straight to the heart of the matter, his query as sharp as a knife.

For the barest moment, Leo felt a flicker of greed and shame burn within his chest. Things had already gone further than they should have. He'd already failed Viola and his own sense of honor. "I won't kill for it."

"And your cousin already has." Devere looked unusually somber, his dark hair and dark eyes sliding from deepest brown to black—a mere trick of the light, as a cloud passed over the sun, but chilling all the same.

Leo nodded. "Not Charles himself, but his men, yes. They killed Mrs. Whedon's footman, and you both saw what they did to the lady and myself." He waved a hand over his face, past the mottled bruise around his eye and the split and swollen lip.

Sandison tied the letters back up and handed them over with a hard look. "Burn these. There's nothing in them we'll need to revisit, and they're dangerous."

∼ CHAPTER 9 ∼

Viola fumed inside the velvet cocoon of Lord Leonidas's well-sprung coach. Her maid dozed on the opposite seat, the ruffles of her cap swaying. Leo himself had chosen to ride, thundering along beside them on a glossy blood bay that made the team look like ponies.

Unlike his family's now-damaged town coach, this one had no coat of arms upon the door. The grooms were dressed in simple, serviceable clothes rather than distinctive livery. They had slipped from the city in the predawn hours, slipping past those of the late-night revelers with anonymous ease.

The sun had risen as they'd sped past Luton. The roads had quickly dried after last night's storm, making the journey far easier than she'd thought it would be. The lone window was a blur of blue and green, with occasional flashes of her protector's oatmeal coat, dark queue, and glossy mount.

Viola shifted position, sliding across the plush upholstery to sit closer to the door so she could keep Leo in sight. What was it about a man on a horse? Watching them parade up and down Rotten Row had been a favorite pastime for years. But this was far more satisfactory. An intimidatingly handsome man with an equally splendid mount, the two of them racing, hair and mane flying, and powerful muscles straining.

The attraction was magnetic, as enchanting today as it had ever been. She couldn't bear to take her eyes off him. Couldn't help but know, bone deep, that he would touch a woman with every bit as much skill and control.

God, how she wanted to find out.

Any other man would have joined her in the coach. Would have made love to her to while away the drive. Leo had handed her a novel and a loaded pistol and shut her up like a jewel in a box.

Eventually he slid out of her view and she let herself sink back into the corner. The novel Leo had given her still lay open on the seat. Viola picked it up and resumed reading.

Her stomach growled as they clattered into the yard of a coaching inn. The door opened, and Leo practically yanked her from the coach.

"You've got as long as it takes to change the horses, to eat, stretch your limbs, and use the necessary. Bing," he said, calling to the publican by name. The grinning man thrust out his chin by way of acknowledgment. "Get the lady whatever she requires. My men and I will have ale and meat pies. Mrs. Whedon"—he bowed and brushed his lips over her hand—"I'll return to fetch you in just a few minutes."

Leo strode off, claiming a tankard of ale as he went,

shouting for the ostlers to hurry. The innkeep looked her up and down, the knowledge that she was no lady writ plain upon his face.

"My maid and I shall have tea, and if there's somewhere I could tidy up…" She let the question hang. Lady or not, welcome or not, Mr. Bing wasn't likely to risk the future custom of the Vaughns just to put her in her place.

True to his word, Leo reappeared before she'd even had time to finish the small cup of weak tea that had been grudgingly provided. "Wrap the pie in your handkerchief, love; we're off."

He hustled her back to the coach, Nance trailing behind them, as if they were in the midst of an elopement and a mob of angry brothers was closing in. The door was already open, the steps let down, awaiting her. The coachman and one of the footmen stood to one side, heads together, a hushed argument raging between them.

"—not a chance. You get it out."

"It's your job, Sampson, to see that things like this don't happen. *You* get it out."

"Get what out?" Lord Leonidas's curt question cut them both off. The footman, Sampson, glanced into the coach and then back at him. Viola craned her neck, trying to catch a glimpse of whatever it was that had caused such consternation.

"It's-it's a dog, my lord," the coachman said. The animal in question jumped from one seat to the other, causing the entire coach to bounce. It flopped down, tongue lolling out as it panted.

"A huge black one, like some sort of monster."

"Must'ave jumped up when we was changing the

horses. And now it's sitting there like it was the king himself and won't come out no how."

"Queen," Viola said, trying not to laugh.

"What?" All three men looked at her.

"Like she was the queen herself. That's a bitch."

"Bitch or dog, it won't come out of the coach, my lord. When we—"

"I!" the footman insisted testily.

The coachman glared at him. "When Sampson here tried to grab it, it growled and bared its teeth."

Leo grumbled under his breath and took two steps toward the coach. "Out." He snapped his fingers and pointed. The dog cocked her head and obligingly leapt down, then trotted over and flopped down at Viola's feet, catching her skirts beneath it and pinning her to the ground. Nance squealed as though she'd been bitten and hid behind the footman.

Viola tugged at her skirts, but they remained firmly trapped beneath the enormous dog. Her eyes welled as she took in its state. It was dreadfully skinny, mottled with patches of dirt and dried blood. Large patches of fur were missing, and what were clearly bite marks stood out in several places. One ear was caked with scabs. Its stump of a tail was broken in several places, kinking to one side like a pig's.

A fighter, now groveling at her feet. A creature who did what it had to do to survive. Recognition burned.

The dog rolled over, exposing its belly. Viola knelt and ran her hand over the expanse of soft, pink skin. The dog whined and licked. Viola looked up to find Leo glaring at her, every inch a duke's son, impatience writ large on every bit of him.

• • •

Leo prayed for patience as he saw Viola's hand splay protectively over the mangy cur at her feet. She was damn lucky the thing hadn't bitten her. God only knew what the mongrel's parentage was, but, at a glance, he'd guess someone's mastiff had got at the local butcher's dog and the resulting pups had ended up being used for some sort of blood sport. Bull baiting? Bear baiting? It was impossible to say. Whatever its past, it was no lady's lapdog.

"My lord?" Her voice was tentative, but the plea in her eyes was easy enough to interpret. Viola was going to keep the damn thing. And nothing he could say was going to dissuade her. The mulish set of her jaw was incontrovertible.

He let his breath out, tasting resignation and defeat. Viola's hand absently stroked the dog. Its mangled tail churned the dust beneath it.

Leo knocked a bit of mud off the skirt of his coat with his crop and gave in to the inevitable. "I believe my proscribed role is that of *he who indulges every whim and fancy*. If you want to brave the ride with that beast locked up beside you, who am I to deny you?"

Viola smiled brilliantly, joy leaking out her pores. It hit him like a wave, like something physically manifest rather than an emotion. It infused her whole being and left his chest with a hollow ache behind the sternum. He'd never seen her smile before. Not like this.

This wasn't the polite smile of a practiced seductress; it was simply her. Pure, true, original, and heartrending. The taint of betrayal was like acid on his tongue.

She stood and, in clear imitation, snapped her fingers and pointed at the coach. "Up, sweetheart. Up!"

The dog heaved itself to its feet and scrambled back into the coach. Viola caught him by the arm, lips brushing his cheek, there and gone before the kiss had even registered.

"Thank you, my lord."

He simply handed her into the coach, head swimming with the rush of something so simple. She plumped her skirts, spreading them out onto the seat. The dog pushed closer, its enormous head burrowing into her lap.

Leo stepped back to allow Viola's maid to enter, but found that she was instead being boosted onto the seat beside the coachman. "What, Nance, not going to share your seat with the beast of Avon?"

Flustered, back stiff with annoyance, the little maid glared down at him. "I'm not getting anywhere near that animal, my lord. Not if it means my job. You can leave me right here in the yard if it comes to it."

"It won't," he assured her.

Sampson grinned at him as Nance wedged herself in beside the coachman. Leo nodded back at his footman. Sampson always did like them dainty and willful. With a shake of his head, Leo knocked his hat against his thigh and turned back to the open coach.

"My lord?" Viola's voice trapped him, hand still on the door. "Could you fetch another pie? I'm afraid she's eaten mine."

Leo gave in to the moment, laughter impossible to resist. It filled the hollow in his chest and flooded his limbs with warmth. "Handkerchief and all?"

She held up the soggy, chewed scrap of linen and lace that had so recently held a pie.

"I'll bring you several. I doubt one has satisfied that beast in the slightest, and I'd hate to arrive at Dyrham to discover she'd eaten you, too."

∾ CHAPTER 10 ∾

Washed in moonlight, Dyrham slid into view as Leo broke from the avenue of lime trees that curved from the road to the house. He was home. A nightingale's call wove through the sound of iron-shod hooves on gravel and the dull grind of the wheels of the coach.

The stone façade of the house, half-mantled in creeping ivy and wisteria, looked almost blue in the night. The large lamps on either side of the door were overshadowed by greenery, but welcoming all the same. Before the coach had even stopped, the front door opened, spilling forth his small staff of servants.

Leo swung down from Meteor's back, transferring his pistol from holster to pocket as he did so. He tossed the reins to the groom who came running from the stable block and gave the bay a final affectionate slap as the boy led the gelding away.

Tension leaked out of his shoulders. They'd arrived without a single mishap, if one didn't count Viola's new pet. Footmen were already disappearing into the house with their trunks as he opened the door to the coach. Viola yawned behind her gloved hand and pushed the sleeping dog off her lap.

"Come along, my dear. I'm sure my staff will have supper ready for us, and arranging for a plate of scraps for your dog should be easy enough."

"Boudicea."

"Queen of the Iceni?" Leo's eye twitched.

"The first warrior queen of England. It seemed appropriate."

"Beau won't thank you for that."

Viola put her hand in his and stepped down. The dog bounded out behind her, and he could have sworn he heard his steward mumble, "Sweet Savior, deliver us."

"Beau?"

"My sister, Lady Boudicea Vaughn. If she discovers that I have a bitch at Dyrham who shares her name, I assure you there won't be a safe place in all of Britain for me to hide."

"We can't have that, can we?" Viola ducked her head, a grin curling up the edge of her lips.

Leo ushered her into the house, waving back his servants as they stepped forward as if to block the dog from following. He heard Sampson laugh, the groom's deep basso profondo drowning out Viola's maid's indignant protest. His grandfather had always had a dog or three about the place, and though there'd been none here of late, he had no doubt his household would make the necessary adjustments. And so would Viola's maid.

"Perhaps you'd like to wash the dust, and dog, off," he added with a laugh, "before we dine?"

•   •   •

Lord Leonidas's butler led her to a room that was large and plush. A silk-upholstered settee sat before the fireplace. Matching silk hangings curtained the bed. Everything in pale shades of pink and primrose.

Nance bustled about the room, muttering under her breath.

"Oh, do stop fussing."

The maid's head snapped around, and she flushed. "I'm sorry, ma'am. It's just that between that beast of a dog and that monstrous footman . . ." She let her voice trail away.

Viola eyed the blush. She'd bet her favorite earbobs that Nance was very well pleased with Sampson's attentions. She'd seen the smile that had accompanied his pinch and her hand slapping.

Viola pulled down her hair and shook out her curls. Nance was in the process of pinning it back up when Sampson arrived with a pitcher of hot water. He bobbed his head, set it down, and left, while Nance blushed red as a boiled lobster.

"Monstrous, is he?"

"Yes, ma'am. A cheeky devil, too, not above pinching."

"Quelle horror."

Nance schooled her temper, her expression shuttered. Viola shooed her away. "Shake out my calico."

Viola took her time dressing. Lord Leonidas was waiting downstairs, and he was every bit as monstrously cocky as his footman. He'd taken control the moment they'd met and not let the reins slip once.

It couldn't be allowed to continue.

~⚹ CHAPTER 11 ⚹~

I was thinking about Hippolyta, or perhaps Penthesilea."
Leo chewed thoughtfully, nodding. Amazon queens
seemed a likely enough namesake for the beast currently
sleeping on the rug at her mistress's feet, a joint bone
gnawed to a naked stub beside her.

"Something of a mouthful." And names that only someone as well versed as his father in the writings of Homer
and Smyrnaeus was likely to have dredged up. Who *were*
her people? Most women had quite memorable scandals
attached to their debut among the ranks of the fallen, but
he could remember nothing of Viola's story. "Not to mention a name only a scholar could love or pronounce. Was
your father a vicar with a penchant for history? A Latin
tutor? Can you read Latin and ancient Greek, or do you just
know the stories?"

Her face went blank for a moment, panic and something like pain shooting through her eyes. "Yes, my father
was a man of the cloth, and yes, I can actually read both
Latin and ancient Greek, a good bit of Hebrew as well—

but I put myself beyond Christian forgiveness and they cast me off, and there's an end to it."

Leo frowned. That wasn't an ending. That was a beginning, or at least a very muddled middle. Viola dropped her eyes to her plate and pushed the remnants of her meal about with her fork. After a moment, she said with forced brightness, "She could be Polly or Pen for everyday use. Of course this is assuming you don't have another sister already so christened?"

"No, just the one sister."

"And one brother, if memory and Debritt's serve."

Leo studied her for a moment. The shadows were back beneath her eyes. She looked almost crushed, almost weak. She shook her head slightly and reached for her glass, resolution in the set of her jaw.

"Yes, one brother as well: Alexander William," Leo said. "Damn lucky to have been born first and got the more unobjectionable names. And he isn't forced to use them, having been the Marquis of Glennalmond since the moment of his birth, so it seems doubly unfair that he shouldn't have been burdened with Charlemagne or Battus."

"Or both." Viola smiled, the edge of anger and despair seemingly gone, glossed over quite adroitly. The dog scrabbled in its sleep, chasing imaginary rabbits, nails loud upon the floor. "Is it too rude to ask whatever possessed your father?"

Leo sighed and refilled both their wineglasses. He swirled his about, watching the heavy, dark liquid color the glass. Should he give her the full history? "My father was born a younger son. Did you know that?"

She raised her brows inquiringly and sipped her wine

by way of answer. The deep burgundy stained the seam of her lips until she licked it away.

Leo blew out his breath in a soft huff, desire flooding out from his groin. "He spent his youth in a classical fog. My mother—God love her—has an equal passion for the histories of England and Scotland. Hence our names: one for father, one for mother, and nearly all of them ridiculous."

"Except for Lord Glennalmond's." The corners of her mouth mocked him with a hidden smile. "What outrage did your mother perpetrate upon you?"

Leo gave her a smile with an edge of teeth. It was inevitable that she would ask. "Roibert, after the Bruce." He drained his glass and reached for the bowl of nuts and sweetmeats. He plucked a walnut from the pile and cracked its shell between his palms.

He extended the broken nut across the table. Viola took a large piece of the meat, lifting it from his hand with long, pale fingers that ended in polished nails.

"Crushed with your bare hands? Impressive." She placed his small offering in her mouth, pink tongue darting out to tease him again.

"Just a boy's trick. I could teach you as easily as my father taught me."

"Don't." She selected another and held it out to him, her grin returning as he broke it neatly in two. "So much more interesting to allow me to go on thinking you as strong as your legendary namesake."

"If you like." Leo shrugged. She was flirting. Teasing. Offering...but something didn't feel quite right. There was a brittle edge to her smile.

She rose, skirts rustling almost imperceptively over

the snoring of the dog. She'd changed out of her dusty traveling gown, reappearing for supper in a simple gown of printed cotton. A fichu obscured her décolletage, its two ends primly tucked into her bodice. She tugged them free as she stepped toward him, letting the delicate wisp of embroidered gauze float away as she moved.

"I believe you'd reached my knee when we were interrupted." Viola swallowed convulsively as she faced Leo down. It was time to act. Time to regain control. She had to return to a scenario she knew how to manage. Allowing Lord Leonidas to continue his game of seduction was too unnerving. Letting him talk, letting him ask questions, was even worse.

And she could manage it... and him. She just had to make the effort, and everything would fall into place. He was just a man, after all.

Leo tipped his head and leaned back into his chair. A smile cocked up one side of his mouth, causing the cut that marred his cheek to tighten and pull. His wicked green eye glinted, as if it could laugh all on its own, even past the bruise that shadowed it.

One large hand shot out to grip her skirts, pulling her toward him. His fingers grazed her hip as he tightened his hold. "Search your memory. I think you'll find I'd reached your thigh and was well on my way heavenward."

"Really?" Viola raised one brow, gazing down at him, trying to look arch and mocking. It had always been so easy, controlling men. And when you controlled them, controlling yourself, your world, was easily accomplished. But she was clearly not in control with Lord Leonidas

Vaughn, and tonight she could barely keep her hands steady. She had to concentrate just to place one foot in front of the other, her nerves jangling with anticipation.

"Really." Leo stood suddenly, chest scraping the length of her, the buttons of his waistcoat stuttering across the hook and eyes that held her gown closed, popping the uppermost free. She fell back a step, his firm grip on her skirts preventing her from retreating farther. Her breath caught in her throat as her lungs seized.

He yanked her closer, head dipping to her ear. "But perhaps I'll start over from the top." He caught her lobe between his teeth and kissed the pulse point behind her ear, mouth hot, breath moist.

"And work your way down to hell instead?"

He laughed, hands sliding around to grip her bottom. Her feet left the floor, one shoe falling to the carpet with a muffled thud. He sank back into the chair, dragging her with him, her thighs splayed wide, embracing his ribs. A flurry of panic beat its way up her spine.

Leo hadn't pulled her into his lap because he'd lost control. He'd put her there because, in such a position, she had almost none. Physically she was trapped, restrained . . . lost.

His mouth was at her throat. His teeth slid roughly along her clavicle. His hands slid up her thighs, gripped her hips, and tugged her forward in his lap. Her skirts rose in a froth between them. Leo shoved them back, leaving her naked nearly to the waist.

Warm as the night was, the air felt cold as it washed over her exposed skin. Excitement mounted, desire threaded through her.

"If this is hell, I'll be happy to forgo Christ's promise of forgiveness."

Viola gasped, as much from his easy blasphemy as from the shock of his knuckles running lightly over the straining peak at the base of her mons. She arched, body seeking more, spine fighting against the embrace of her stays. One nipple slid free of her bodice, and Leo captured it with his mouth.

His cock was hard against her thigh. The promise of earthly delight blatant and tantalizingly close. He bit lightly down on the bud of her nipple, opened his mouth, and sucked hard, teeth sharp on the tender flesh of her breast.

Her hands locked in his hair. Her hips rolled as his hand possessed her, long fingers filling her, thumb circling, teasing, torturing.

Her thighs shook as she leveraged herself up so she could open his breeches. She yanked his shirt loose, fought her way past his drawers. His hand left her, slid around to manacle her wrist.

She caught a sob at the sense of bereavement that followed. She was hollow, aching, her whole being wound down tightly to the throbbing between her thighs that had replaced her heartbeat as the measure of life. As the only thing of import in the world.

"Have we reached the begging stage already?"

The chuckle that followed caused her spine to stiffen. Lust and need died away as though she'd been slapped. Her breath left her in a huff, and she found herself staring into eyes filled with cool assessment. He was as rampant as a statue of Priapus, but he hadn't lost one jot of his self-control.

"Not quite, my lord." Viola forced every bit of frustration into her voice, and prayed that it sounded more like annoyance.

Leo grinned back at her, clearly not at all fooled. He let go of her wrist. His fingers trailed lightly up the inside of her thigh. His teeth slid along her neck.

"Shall I resume where I left off?"

His thumb pressed against the tendon where her thigh joined her body. Fingers circled the secret folds, blazing a path that left her with an aching need for more.

"Or shall I retrace my steps?"

One finger slid tantalizingly across the very peak of her clitoris, then slid down to circle the entrance to her body. Her thighs quivered, and her womb pulsed. His fingers circled again, flittering over her, leaving a teasing promise of delight in their wake.

"Let me make this easy. Do you want me to touch you here?" He pushed against her clitoris.

"Yes." The word shuddered out of her.

"Here?"

His hand slid downward, and one long finger pushed inside her. Viola's throat tightened. Her hands gripped his coat hard enough that they shook. "There."

A second finger joined the first inside her. His thumb returned to its rightful place at the center of her being. Leo nipped at her neck and bit her shoulder. His fingers moved within her, curling, pressing.

Tension coiled in her belly, her core turning to liquid, pleasure sliding into pain and back again as she came. "Not enough." Her own plea shocked her. Humiliation and need spun together, coalescing sharply between her thighs. His fingers pushed deeper, and her body throbbed in response.

Viola yanked the fall of his breeches open. "I need—I want—"

Leo pushed her hands away a second time. "If that was you begging, Love, you'll have to do better. Much, much better."

An annoyed huff was all she was able to manage. She wanted him inside her so much that her body ached. Her hands were cold. Her fingers and toes tingling.

Viola clutched his shirt and buried her head in the crook of his neck. She took a deep breath. Linen and leather, warm skin and Bay Rum. God, but he smelled good. She swallowed hard and took a shuddering breath.

This was supposed to be a contest of wills. Why had hers utterly deserted her? She'd desired other men. Enjoyed their touch, but this was different. Her friend Lady Ligonier would smirk and put it down to her prolonged bout of abstinence. But she'd be wrong.

It was desire—raw, hot, and irresistible—spiraling between them. Hers fed on his; his fanned hers to greater heights. One-sided, it was merely lust. Her coin of trade. Shared, it was another thing entirely. A passion that almost frightened her.

Leo nudged Viola's head up from his shoulder. Her eyelids fluttered, finally settling half-open over irises that had darkened to azure in the candlelight. Curls tumbled about her face, transforming her once more into the Italian goddess of their first encounter.

He dipped his head, capturing her mouth with his. Her

tongue met his, dipped and stroked. Their kiss intensified, becoming a battle all its own. Her hand twisted in his hair, ripping his queue free of its ribbon.

Leo surged out of the chair, sweeping Viola off his lap and into his arms. He strode toward the door. Carrying his acknowledged mistress through the house would hardly shock his all-male staff, and Viola's maid must be inured to such experiences.

Once in his room, Leo kicked the door shut behind him. Viola slid out of his arms, regaining her feet. He yanked the hook and eyes that fastened her bodice with enough force to bend the last few. The tapes that held her skirts were quickly dispensed with, as were her stays and shift. He left her standing in nothing but her stockings and garters.

Blood pounded in his ears in deafening waves. Viola raised her chin, gaze holding his, skin flushed and damp and radiant. He wanted to push her beneath him and thrust into her, to lose himself in her, to ride her to sweet incoherence. But he wasn't going to do so, at least not tonight.

Leo pulled her toward the bed, tipped her onto it, and sank to his knees. He wrapped his arms about her, slid her forward to the edge, and leaned in to take one taut nipple between his teeth.

Viola hissed. Her knees gripped his ribs, squeezing, tugging him closer, trapping him against her. The damp heat of her cleft burned through the fabric of his shirt. His cock pushed against the layers of linen and leather between it and its goal.

Leo opened his mouth wider, took more of the flesh of

her breast between his teeth, and sucked hard enough that Viola whimpered. His cock was going to have to wait. Tonight was about her. Tonight, he was dedicated to her complete seduction, her pleasure, and her surrender. Simply fucking her wouldn't achieve any of his goals, though the tight ache in his balls and his painfully hard erection argued against his plan.

Viola clutched at his shoulders, hands pulling at his shirt. "Please, Leo. Please."

"Please, Leo, what? Please, Leo, touch you?" He flicked his tongue over her ruched nipple. "Please, Leo, taste you?" He blew across the wet peak. "Please, Leo, take you?"

Leo cupped her breast, caught the tight bud of her nipple between his thumb and forefinger, and squeezed. Her eyelids fluttered, her spine arched, and her lips parted. Sweet Jesus, he wanted to fuck her.

He rolled her nipple between his fingers, and Viola's nostrils flared as she breathed in sharply. Her legs gripped him, pulling him in. She leaned forward and brushed her cheek against his like a cat greeting its mate.

"Please, Leo." Her words slid across his skin, scalding hot. "Taste me."

Her lips found his, her tongue invading his mouth. Leo slid away from the kiss, mouth trailing down her neck, over her breasts and stomach. He pushed her back onto the bed and held her there, arm across her hips while he shouldered apart her thighs.

Her secret folds were slick and swollen from the last time he'd brought her to climax. Leo dipped his tongue into her and she bucked, thighs locking about his shoulders.

Sweet and salty at the same time. Peaches and balsamic vinegar. Dessert in Rome on a hot summer day. Leo licked and sucked, fixing his mouth over her pulsing clitoris.

Viola's hands slid into his hair, pulling him closer, trying to pull him away. He couldn't tell which, and didn't care. She was panting, twisting, legs trembling as they gripped him. Her hands suddenly clenched, nearly ripping his hair from his head, and she gave a high, keening cry that ended in his name.

Leo ran his tongue up her cleft, flicked it over her clitoris, and let his teeth slide lightly over the tender peak. Viola shook and pushed at his shoulder with her foot.

Hands resting on her thighs, Leo sat back and simply allowed himself to enjoy the trembling aftershocks of her climax and the knowledge that the next time she came, his cock would be buried inside her.

❧ CHAPTER 12 ❧

A fat, lazy bee droned among the hollyhock and pinks, the spring's bounty too much for even its greedy forging. Viola twitched her skirts aside to avoid its pollen-drunk flight.

She hadn't been stung since she was a girl, but she remembered it clearly enough not to want to repeat the experience. No more than she wanted to repeat the dizzying thrill of infatuation...but her own feelings, her own memories, were harder to avoid than the bee.

Penthesilea grumbled behind her, breaking into a full-throated bark as a butterfly had the temerity to flutter across her path. Viola shook her head and quickened her pace. She'd caught a glimpse of water from her window that morning as she'd dressed. A pond? A stream? She hadn't been able to tell, but the promise of shade, cool water, and a peaceful spot to think was irresistible.

She'd woken in her own bed, the memory of Lord Leonidas carrying her there hazy, mixed up as it was with that of climax after climax. It had been a night filled with teasing, with sweet, erotic torture. And when she'd complained that hands and mouths were not enough, he'd simply smiled and brought her to orgasm again.

The path of crushed oyster shell turned to dirt as it meandered into an artful copse of trees. Nuthatch and robins darted through the dappled light. A squirrel dashed up a tree, scolding as it went. Pen sneezed derisively, ignoring it in favor of crashing through the foliage beside the path.

Birds erupted in all directions. Pen woofled, chasing after them, far too slow to catch one but happy to try all the same. She had been pronounced to be, in general, healthy and likely to recover in full.

The local hunt master clearly hadn't been delighted to minister to Viola's mongrel, but he'd done so all the same. Undeniably only as a favor to Leo. He'd left with promises of dire consequences if Pen were to interfere with his hounds and general predictions of doom attached to her adoption of such a beast. That Leo had gone with him had been a relief.

The ground rose slowly until the path became a rough set of stairs. Stone steps emerged as she rounded the hill. A stone wall, damp with moss and lichen, rose along one side. A few more steps and then an outer wall began, and then she was climbing into the ruins of a small, square tower.

It was enchanting. A garden folly of epic proportions. She hurried upward, winding past several narrow windows before reaching the top.

A vista of rolling hills, green with grass and dappled with trees, greeted her over the uneven, broken balustrade.

The small rise where the tower was built was littered with broken stones. They tumbled down until they met a wide stream that wound through the open field and lapped at the tower's base. Pen was circling and sniffing among them, rooting in the tall grass.

Viola sat down upon the uppermost edge of stone and stared out toward the ha-ha. Her head ached. Likewise her wrist, but it was the weakness in her thighs that stood out, that reminded her that last night she'd sailed off the edge of the map. The waters here were deep, filled with hidden shoals . . . teeming with dragons.

The previous evening's misadventure left her with no illusions. She had attempted to claim the reins and failed. Lord Leonidas had emerged the victor in that particular struggle for power—utterly, completely, delightfully. All that was required now was her complete surrender. But allowing herself to succumb to pleasure, to simply receive, to take was inadvisable and dangerous. Not to mention utterly infuriating, just like the man himself.

"Rapunzel, let down your golden hair!"

Viola nearly fell from her perch as Leo's voice startled her. He was mounted on his blood bay, the horse's front hooves firmly in the water. Pen gamboled about them, splashing, whining with excitement.

"Alas, my lord, my hair is red. Not at all the proper color for a princess."

"Nay." He smiled up at her, the shadow of his hat hiding the bruise she knew ringed one eye. " 'Tis gold, with flame running beneath it, just as a princess's hair should be."

A smile tugged at her lips. She caught her lower lip

between her teeth to hide her grin. Her hair was red, no denying it, though she'd escaped the plague of freckles that so often accompanied such coloring.

He urged his mount forward and abandoned it to crop grass at the base of the tower. Her pulse surged. Lust, ripe and heady, washed through her. Try as she might, she was no more composed today than she had been last night.

Mere moments after he'd disappeared from view, he was pushing in beside her, crowding her, hip balanced against the top of the wall. Did he do it on purpose? Was he even aware that he always dominated a space in such a manner?

"I see you've found my Tintagel," he said, one hand reaching into her hair. He gently pulled a leaf free and stood turning it in his fingers.

"Your what?"

Leo chuckled, the sound rumbling through her. "My Tintagel. My Tower of London. Occasionally even my Nottingham Castle." He turned and sat beside her, gazing out over the field and stream. "No, to be truthful, it was my brother's Nottingham."

"Did your father build it here for you?"

"No, my grandfather built it for my grandmother, but she shared it with us, along with stories of King Arthur, Robin Hood, Cú Chulainn—all the myths and legends that Father and Mother eschewed in favor of truth and history."

"But the stories are so much more satisfying, aren't they?"

Leo nodded, still playing with the leaf. "More happy endings anyway. Good wins over evil. Right triumphs in the end..." His voice trailed off, and he tossed the leaf over the edge.

Viola watched the leaf spiral down until it disappeared into the climbing roses that girded the tower's base. "It's a beautiful folly. It must have taken quite an effort to create it."

He ground a weed under the toe of his boot. "It's a miniature version of the ruins of Kirby Muxloe. Grandmother loved the place. It's only a few miles off. I should take you to see it. We could ride over tomorrow if the weather stays fine."

"I don't ride."

Leo shook his head, a smile growing on his face. "Honestly?"

Viola shook her head and shrugged one shoulder, wishing madly that she did ride. "This is the first time I've ever been to a country estate. Not much call to ride in town."

"You can't always have lived in London?" He looked shocked. As though he couldn't fathom the idea of being born and bred in a city.

"No, but I've never lived in the country. A sedan chair is a simpler, and cheaper, option regardless of what city one is in."

"Not ride." He turned the concept over, his brows drawn up in disbelief. His eyes took on a familiar spark of devilment. "Well, that will have to be fixed, and what better time and place than this?"

"Oh, nooooo..." She let the word drag out as uncertainty washed over her. "Thank you very much, but—"

"You aren't afraid, are you?" His eyes were still dancing. "The divine Mrs. Whedon, not ride? It's an outrage. For heaven's sake, think of my reputation if you've no concern for your own! Lord Leonidas Vaughn, Corinthian, owner of Dyrham, breeder of some of the most sought-after hunters in all of England, to have a mistress who *doesn't ride*? I'll be a laughingstock."

His feigned outrage set her laughing until she had to place one hand across her stomach, afraid she'd burst her stays like the subject of some rude cartoon.

"You see, even *you* find it ridiculous." His blue eye had taken on the teasing nature of his green one.

Viola gasped for air and blew out a long breath. He was going to wheedle and tease until he got his way. She was done for. "Have you ever taught a woman to ride? Do you even have a lady's saddle here? And what am I to wear for this adventure? I've no habit, and I'm certainly not going to attempt to learn in this." She waved one hand to encompass her simple *Chemise a la Rein*.

"No, I've never taught a woman to ride, but I was present when my sister learned." He ticked off one finger. "Yes, we have several ladies' saddles here, as all the women in my family ride." Another finger bent to his accounting. "Also in consequence of which, I'd be willing to wager that at least one of them has left behind a habit or two you can make use of—and no, you certainly shouldn't make the attempt to learn in that wisp of a gown." He made a sweeping flourish with the hand upon which he'd just counted off his points.

Viola wrinkled her nose. "But I'm not your mistress. You said so yourself. So my lack of equestrian skill shouldn't matter in the least."

Leo gave a shout of laughter. "Minx. You're not getting off that easily. Are you afraid of horses?"

She shook her head. "I'm not afraid of the horse itself; it's the fall."

"Then don't fall." He looked perfectly serious. As though it were really that simple.

"*You* perch five feet off the ground, clinging to a scrap of leather with your knees while the animal it's attached to moves of its own accord, and *then* we'll talk about not falling."

"Is that a wager?"

Viola narrowed her eyes. "Is what a wager?"

"If I can ride sidesaddle, you'll learn?" His slow grin set off a burning sense of indignation deep in her chest. If he didn't already know for a fact he could do it—and she was almost certain he did!—he wasn't the least bit worried about attempting it.

"If you can do it *just as I'll have to,* I'll attempt it," she agreed. He wasn't the only one who could turn a situation to his favor.

A sudden crease appeared between his brows. She saw comprehension flare, followed by amusement and something indefinable that must be whatever it was that prompted men to wager on everything from raindrops racing down a windowpane to who could seduce the latest ballet dancer.

"You mean to put me in skirts, do you, vixen?"

"I do, my lord. I should have to wear them after all."

"What if I put you in breeches instead? You wouldn't be the first. Doesn't Mrs. Bing make a spectacle of herself in them regularly?"

Viola shrugged. "Either way, my lord. Me in breeches or you in skirts."

Leo grinned evilly. "I think I rather like the idea of you running around in breeches. Such a lovely view of your otherwise hidden charms...but for now, let me show you something you'll like far more than the folly."

"It's hard to imagine that the estate has anything more beautiful than this view to offer." She pushed herself off the wall and turned her full attention to the vista that spread out from the tower. Rolling hills, speckled with sheep. A group of thatched cottages in the distance. Dense woods beyond them and the gleam of flowing water twisting through it all.

"You're correct. The view couldn't possibly be more beautiful." His voice brought her back to the fact that he was staring at her, not the landscape, as he spoke. "But you'll like my surprise all the same."

She eyed him warily. He looked too pleased with himself to trust him entirely.

"Come." Leo held out his hand. She hesitated for a moment, then allowed him to lead her down the stairs. The warm leather of his gloves slid against her naked hands with a seductive softness. She forced herself to ignore the sensation and the thrill that coursed down her spine. When they reached the bottom, he caught her about the waist and pressed in for a kiss.

His mouth met hers with an urgency that belied how lightly he held her. Viola sagged back against the stone wall for support and Leo followed, hands splayed out beside her, caging her in.

He moved to her jaw, traced a searing path to her ear,

sucked hard on the sensitive spot where neck and jaw met. Her hands crept inside his coat, slid around to his back, sliding between the layers of silk with ease.

She—they!—were going to ruin her dress, and she couldn't find it in herself to give a damn. A gown was a small price to pay. The knowledge that he was every bit as susceptible, every bit as powerless, was priceless.

CHAPTER 13

Leo broke off the kiss as Viola's dog nudged into them with her head, knocking him off balance. Pen sneezed, blowing petals off the roses, and grinned up at him. Her tongue lolled out the side of her mouth, spilling from beneath an impressive display of teeth.

Leo steadied his hand, flexing it against Viola's tightly corseted waist. "You're a damn inconvenient beast," he said to the dog. Her grin widened, and she rocked back and forth on her front paws. He reluctantly stepped back from Viola, taking her hand and pulling her along toward his horse.

"Tell me again why you insisted on keeping her?"

Viola shook her head, tossing her loose curls away from her face. One curl slid back, and she tucked it behind her ear. "Because she needed rescuing, and you can't tell me, in this of all settings, that you don't know a damsel in distress when you see one."

A frown pulled at Leo's mouth. He forced a smile instead. This entire trip to Dyrham was nothing but a ruse. A fantasy. The fact that she thought him a hero ate at him like a canker. At least his conscience was clear where the dog was concerned. "Take your shoes off and dip your toes in the water."

"What? Why?" She didn't look as though she trusted him in the slightest. Somewhere deep down, her instincts were correct, but not in this instance.

Leo shook his head. "It's a surprise." She narrowed her eyes and shot him a quizzical glance. Her hair, gloriously loose, swung around her shoulders, tips bouncing about her hips. "Trust me. It's one of the best parts of Dyrham."

She rolled her eyes, but stripped off her shoes and stockings all the same. Naked, familiar feet padded through the grass. She gathered up her skirts, exposing limbs like those of a statue, long, beautifully molded, and pale, save for the love bite he'd left just above the inside of her knee.

She stepped carefully off the bank, toes disappearing into the water. "It's warm." She twirled about, eyes wide enough for him to drown in, lips parted in surprise. The hem of her skirts trailed in the water as she waded in.

"There's a hot spring on the estate. If you look upstream, you'll see the real surprise. It's a bathhouse. You'll never be satisfied with a tub in your room again."

Water spilled from a stone pool into an enormous soaking tub before swirling away down a sluice and out of the building. Steam rose off the pool's surface. Light poured in from the glass roof. Viola sat on the pool's edge, skirts damp and filmy, clinging to her thighs, feet dangling in the water.

"If I owned this, I'd never leave." She splashed her feet in the water, sending waves sloshing over the edge and into the tub. "I'd put a bed in one corner and a table in the other and I'd live right here."

"Like a sultana in a harem?"

"Why not." Viola sighed and stretched her neck, face going soft and dreamy. "I don't think I can imagine anything more wonderful than endless, everlasting hot water." She pulled her feet from the water and stood. The wet linen of her skirts plastered itself to her legs. Leo swallowed hard. Why was something almost visible infinitely more alluring than something fully exposed? He'd seen her naked, but somehow this was far more exciting.

"Stay and enjoy it then. I'll send your maid."

Her brow furrowed, and her lips compressed into what he was coming to recognize as her secret smile. "Only if you'd rather *not* join me, my lord." She tilted her head, chin raised just enough to emphasize the challenge in her declaration.

Leo grinned. She did so like to have the upper hand. Almost as much as he did. "Not today, my dear. Today—though it breaks my heart to say so—I have a meeting about a horse. But we'll have plenty of time to play the sultan and the concubine while we're at Dyrham. In fact, while I'm gone, you can pick out a spot for that divan. But for now"—he pulled his watch from his pocket and thumbed it open—"yes, for now, I really must leave you to your own devices."

Leo sketched a small bow and strode out of the bathhouse. Viola was clearly not pleased. For a woman who had made her living pleasing men, she apparently had little skill masking her anger. It was possible that none of her former protectors had ever provoked her, but— knowing his own kind as he did—that seemed unlikely. Perhaps it had been the other way around, and they'd been the ones who made every effort to please? Having one of her select set in keeping was considered something to brag about. Losing such a woman was certainly an embarrassment.

Viola's dog raised her head as Leo emerged from the bathhouse. She gave him a long, penetrating look before laying her head back down upon her paws with a protracted and almost artfully woeful sigh. Whatever inconveniences might arise from her adoption, at least he need never worry that his cousin could slip in unnoticed. Pen had clearly set herself the task of guarding her mistress, so Charles would never get past her.

Leo took Meteor by the reins and led him toward the stable. Squire Watt should be arriving at any moment. The man had cast a covetous eye toward several of Leo's hunters last season, and Leo could think of nothing better than having the legendary man spend the upcoming season mounted upon an animal from his stable. It would be good for his reputation, and that in turn would be good for business, crass as it was to admit.

And Dyrham was going to have to be a business. It didn't have the vast acreage necessary to support itself. There was no coal or iron or other valuable resource. What it had was location and reputation. It was in Melton territory, prime hunting all around it, and at the moment, he had one of the best strings of hunters anywhere in England eating their very expensive heads off in his stables.

It had been one thing for his grandfather, the duke, to support such an establishment. It was something else for him to try to do it without the resources of Lochmaben to draw upon.

If he could maintain the estate for a few years, he could set himself up as a breeder and trainer. Most of his hunters were worth more than a pair of perfectly matched carriage horses, more than your average vicar, barrister, or doctor made in a year, more than the grooms who cared for them made in a lifetime.

But in order to make such a dream a reality, he had to have money, far more than his younger son's portion. Without the prince's treasure, he'd have to sell off all those magnificent horses, might have to sell off Dyrham itself in a few short years.

His first attempt to search Viola's house had been interrupted by the fire in the mews, and though he'd tasked the League to make a more thorough attempt, he'd received no letter announcing success.

He'd have to invent an excuse to return to town sometime in the very near future, an excuse that would allow him to leave Viola safely—and ignorantly—tucked away at Dyrham.

❧ CHAPTER 14 ❧

A loud, repetitive, and most determined thumping echoed through the house. Charles smiled to himself and continued to explore Mrs. Whedon's bedchamber.

The footman must have regained consciousness. His men had overpowered him with a blow to the head and locked him in the kitchen's small cellar. They'd reinforced the door with the large chopping block after shutting it. There was very little chance of Boaz getting loose anytime soon.

There was nothing here in her room. No secret panel in the wall. No hidden passageway behind the clothespress. There wasn't even anything worth stealing. No silver brush set. No jewelry. The house had been quite carefully packed and closed before she'd left.

The sound of a large piece of furniture being shifted caught his attention, and Charles wandered down the corridor to find his men dragging a large bookcase away from the wall. Books were scattered in piles across the room, open, closed, pages bent and torn. His uncle, the duke, would have apoplexy on the spot.

"Nothing, sir," Cooper said.

Charles turned slowly about, looking the room over. She obviously used it as a study. A small writing desk sat under the window, framed by curtains. The walls were lined with bookshelves. A watercolor of some ancient Mediterranean ruin hung above the fireplace.

"You've checked behind them all?"

"All the ones as ain't built in, sir." Cooper's partner, a shambling ex-pugilist whose name escaped Charles, pointed at the chaos they'd created.

Charles raised one brow. "And which of them are built in?"

"Them two." The pugilist pointed to the small shelves flanking the fireplace.

Charles crossed the room and ran his hands lightly over the seams where both cases met the wall. There was a slight gap around the left one. It could be nothing but poor craftsmanship, or it could be something more. No, there it was, an almost imperceptible draft.

He tossed all the books over his shoulder and ran his fingers slowly over each shelf, looking for anything that could be a trigger. Nothing.

Charles set his shoulder and shoved. A groan, but no movement. There was something there.

"We could rip it out of the wall, sir," Cooper said.

Charles brushed off his hands and stepped back. "It may well come to that, but let's not be hasty. If the trigger's not in or on the case itself, it must be close by... No, not one of the floorboards. Not the baseboard either. Nothing behind the painting. No bell pull in the room. That would be too damn easy, wouldn't it? No, but it really has got to be close."

He cocked his head and studied the fireplace. No fanciful carvings. No roses or roundels to make a button out of. He ran his fingers under the mantel, behind the small lip. Yes, there it was. A knob. He fiddled with it until it moved, sliding to one side. There was a distinct *snick,* and the bookcase wobbled slightly.

Charles pushed it with his foot, and it slid back into the wall. Cold, musty air flooded out. He slipped in, shoulders scraping the sides of the narrow passage. A few steps and he was in a small room. A dark oubliette.

"Fetch a candle," he yelled back over his shoulder.

A few minutes later, a wavering light licked past him, shivering over the dusty room and its scant contents. It was nothing but a priest's hole. Large enough to have contained a strongbox, but if it ever had, the box and its contents were long gone.

Charles cursed and flung the candle down. The room pitched into darkness. He thrust Cooper out before him, nearly sending the smaller man sprawling.

Damnation. So close. He'd felt success burning just beneath his skin. If it wasn't there now, it certainly had been. It had to have been.

He lashed out with his foot, sending a book flying across the room. It fell facedown, open, pages bent out at odd angles. Charles stamped on it for good measure.

Leo and his whore weren't going to win that easily. If the money was no longer here, and Leo was still dangling from her apron strings, that could mean only one thing: She had it.

Charles glanced around her well-appointed study. Someone had spent a small fortune on this house, its furnishings, and maintenance. And Mrs. Whedon had quit the field quite abruptly, if his memory served.

Almost as though she'd come in to some kind of windfall.

He picked up the poker and swung it at the wall. Plaster gave way like the chalk cliffs at Dover. Charles swung again, raining dust down onto the books.

Damn her. He swung again, and again.

❦ CHAPTER 15 ❦

Viola clamped her arm to her side, pinning the unruly skirt of her habit up and out of her way, and resolutely walked down the path that led to the stable block. She'd been so sure of her plan to wear breeches, but one look in the mirror had laid that plan to rest.

Leo's buckskins, nobly handed over the night before, had clung to her thighs but sagged about her waist and hips, and the less said about the baggy horror of the seat the better. She was well aware that breeches were always somewhat full in the backside, but clearly they needed to be matched up with the posterior for which they'd been cut and paired with a coat for cover.

As she reached the stable block, she could see Leo running his hands over a gray with a long tail tipped in black. The horse swung its head to look at her, ears swiveling about.

Leo turned. His eyes widened, and his lips quirked with mirth. "No breeches?"

"No, I—"

"Don't think for a moment that I'm going to put on skirts because you changed your mind."

Viola wrinkled her nose at him. "God's honest truth? They didn't fit."

"Vanity won out, did it?"

Viola dropped her skirt and gestured down the length of her oatmeal habit. It strained across her bust, swung about her waist, and had a stain down one side of the enormously long skirt that appeared to be a mix of ruddy earth and grass. "When I tell you this is better, you'll understand the full implication of what I mean when I say the breeches were worse."

He grinned widely. "Beau's a good bit taller than you, but none of that will matter for what we're doing today. Your maid can winkle about with it later if you don't break your neck."

"Your sister won't mind if your mistress steals her habit?"

"I don't think Beau's worn that since she was a hoyden of fifteen. I doubt she'll even notice it's gone, and if she did, no, I don't think she'd care. Come and meet Oleander. She's a sweet-tempered little goer, and I fully expect the two of you to become fast friends."

Viola eyed the mare. Oleander stared back, large brown eyes surveying her with clear contempt. "Do you have something smaller?"

Leo laughed, and the horse blew out a loud and derisive-sounding breath, nostrils fluttering rudely. "The only other horse in the stable trained to carry a lady is Quiz, and since my goal today is something other than cementing your affection for sedan chairs, I'll not put you anywhere near him. Now come here and let me boost you up."

Viola suffered a moment of pure panic as Leo grasped her about the waist and tossed her up into the saddle. She wobbled, and his grip tightened, shoring her up.

"Get your knee around the pommel. Yes, like that. Now other foot in the stirrup." He let go of her waist, hands sliding down her hips and legs, and guided her foot into place. "You want to keep the pommel firmly between your knees and the ball of your foot balanced across the bar of the stirrup."

Leo took the reins from the metal ring they'd been looped through. "Just hold on. Get a feel for the rhythm. No, no. Don't twist about. You'll unbalance yourself and tumble over."

Viola blew a drifting curl out of her eyes and glared at Leo. "Whoever invented the sidesaddle should have been murdered on the spot."

Leo laughed and set her firmly back into position. Blood pounded in her ears, making it impossible to think.

"You can thank Good Queen Bess for having taken a shine to them." His hands pushed up under her skirt, found the naked flesh of her thigh, and checked the placement of her knee over the pommel with ruthless efficiency. Heat flooded through her, bringing a ridiculous surge of longing. The man had bewitched her. They'd made love twice the previous evening and again after breakfast and still she wanted more.

He gave the horse a smart slap on the shoulder, and the mare turned to nuzzle his shoulder. He absently rubbed her head, large capable hands caressing the horse's jaw and ear.

"Don't poker up so. Relax."

"I could happily get down now and never ride again, my lord. In fact, I fear I'm going to slither off at any moment."

Leo shook his head, clearly not taking her words at all seriously. He really couldn't grasp that someone might *not* want to ride. Just like a man, to assume his own passions must be shared by everyone.

"Nonsense, my dear. You've found your seat. Now all you have to do is maintain it. Keep your weight to the left. Lean into the pommel, grip it with your knees, and relax." He made a tsking sound, and the horse ambled forward. Viola clutched at the mane, knees gripping the silly, curved pommel until her thighs shook.

The horse stopped. Her ears went back flat, and her coat twitched in a horribly disconcerting way. "Relax. You're upsetting Oleander."

"*I'm* upsetting *her*?" Indignation bubbled up, choking her.

"Yes, a horse knows what its rider is feeling, and you're telling her that something's wrong. Do you feel the slight hump of her back? Do you see the set of her ears? She doesn't understand why you're so stiff, and she doesn't like it. So relax. I'm not going to let anything happen to you. And neither is Oleander, no matter how much you annoy her."

Viola glared at him again and attempted to do as he bade her. She sat up straight, let go of her death grip on the horse's mane, and took several deep breaths. She felt the mare do likewise, and then the hump left her back and her ears flicked about as though she were awaiting a command.

"See? Now try and keep that position while Oleander begins to walk. We're not going to do anything faster than a walk today. I just want you to catch the rhythm. To learn to feel secure. That's right. It's all right to let your body shift with the horse's. It's preferable in fact."

"I just feel as though I'm liable to tumble over the side at any moment."

"But you won't. Oleander here is too much a lady to tip you off. Even my sister, madcap that she is, has never come off her, much as she's tried. Beau prefers Quiz. Mostly because I think she's trying to break her damn neck. Oleander knows her own limitations. Quiz doesn't think he has any, and neither does Beau."

"*Does* the daughter of a duke have limitations?"

"You should know she does."

"Me?"

"Lady Sarah Lennox's birth didn't preclude scandal and ruin, did it? In fact, I'd be prepared to argue that having so far to fall made it worse. And poor Beau, much as she might argue otherwise, is subject to gravity, just like the rest of us."

Viola bit her lip. She'd never thought about it that way. She herself hadn't had all that far to fall, but yes, many of her friends, in particular the members of The New Female Coterie, had learned the hard way that their birth provided little protection if their relatives abandoned them.

If a woman's family was powerful enough, and if they backed her, she could brazen through almost anything. But how many of her friends had discovered too late that their families were afraid of scandal and wouldn't stand by them?

Her own family had certainly abandoned her when she'd been fool enough to elope. Though at the time she hadn't cared, and perhaps still wouldn't if Stephen hadn't died. It hadn't mattered until then. She'd been too happy to care that her letters had been returned unopened. And she'd assumed she had all the time in the world to bring her parents around.

"I see the secret to making an Amazon of you is to distract you from the fear of falling."

"What—"

His laugh cut her off, and Oleander's step faltered, causing her to slip precariously. Leo caught her before she could fall and he propped her back into place.

"To distract you and not startle you," he added with one of his infectious grins. "Clearly when you're talking, you're too busy to worry about falling. You've made seven circuits of the area with nary a problem, but the second you thought about what you were doing, you nearly tumbled off."

"So I'm to somehow *not* think about what I'm doing?"

"I think what's vital here is that you not think about the consequences of what you're doing. And eventually, all the little actions that keep you in the saddle will become second nature."

Viola raised her brows, doubt pinching them together. What he said was nonsensical.

Leo slipped the reins over the mare's head and held them out to her. "Here, keep your hands busy, too. I'll stay beside you, not to worry. Grasp the reins so." He arranged her fingers on the narrow strips of leather. "Relax your fingers forward when she's moving, and curl them back to stop her. If you keep her softly on the bit, there's no need to saw at her mouth or yank on the reins like a drunken squire."

He stepped back slightly, and Viola eased her grip on the reins. The mare began to walk, and Viola tried to fall back into the rhythm. The mare balked, ears going flat again. Viola dropped the reins and grabbed hold of the horse's mane.

"No, don't try, don't think about it. Pick up the reins again and talk to me."

"About what?"

"Is there nothing you can do without thinking about it? No game you played as a child? Swinging a cricket bat? Hitting a shuttle? Conkers?"

Viola laughed, and the mare sped up into a trot. Viola kept her shoulders squared but allowed her hips to follow the new pattern.

"See there," Leo said with a hint of pride, quickening his pace to keep up with them. "Ease back on the reins, and she'll fall back into a walk." Viola did as he directed, and as promised, Oleander dropped back into a more sedate pace.

"It's like magic."

"No, it's simply a skill, and you just mastered your first lesson. Let's keep at it for a bit longer though. Tell me why the subject of conkers should make you laugh?"

"Conkers were a great passion among my siblings and me. There was an enormous chestnut tree in the village green where we lived when I was small. We used it much as you used your grandmother's folly. It was our Sherwood, our playhouse, and the provider of the largest, toughest conkers in all of Nottinghamshire."

"So, a childhood filled with epic battles?"

Leo couldn't stop himself picturing her as a wild Maid Marian, armed with a mighty chestnut on a string. She laughed, fingers inching up on the reins, seat secure. She'd passed the hardest fence—that of fear—but the light had gone out of her eyes.

"Of one sort or another, yes. Epic battles seem to have been something of a family hobby," Viola said, her mouth tight and hard.

Leo gritted his teeth. He shouldn't have asked. She wasn't one of the bits-o-muslin who'd risen from humble origins, and however pleasant her childhood, some unfortunate event had led to her present circumstances. The fact that he wanted to know the particulars, that he cared at all, was a very bad sign. Caring made the pleasure of their idyll all too real, all too dangerous.

"Isn't that the rule in most families?" Leo said. "Spats among siblings are as natural as those between cats and dogs."

Her chest rose and fell as she struggled to control her breathing. A muscle quivered in her cheek, betraying the suppression of some strong emotion.

"I never fought with my brothers. At least not over anything but whose conker would be king."

Leo nodded, trying to appear as if her answer closed the subject. He'd bet Dyrham itself she was the product of some stalwart Tory bastion of respectability and rigidity.

Had hers been a transgression of epic proportions, or had she been cast out for some small slip that his own family would have glossed over with money and power?

"Lucky brothers. I fought with mine like two dogs

locked in a kennel with only one bone. Still do, in fact, when the occasion calls for it." Leo smiled at her, but she didn't smile back.

Her expression was shuttered, cold. He wanted the light back, badly.

Without a word, she tightened her grip on the reins and tsked, imitating the noise he'd made to set Oleander into motion. The mare's ears perked, and she broke into a trot. Viola maintained her seat with obvious effort, but she kept the pace for a full circle before reining the mare in.

Oleander came to a full stop, and Viola gave Leo a wavering smile. The bleak tightness that gripped his chest loosened its hold. Whatever happened between him and Charles, he was going to make damn sure she wasn't hurt by it. She deserved a better hand than she'd been dealt, that much had become plain.

•

~ CHAPTER 16 ~

A stack of letters lay waiting for Leo on his desk in the library. One from his mother, two from Beau, one from his family solicitor, Mr. Grimble, and one franked by Thane, though it was addressed in Sandison's hand.

Leo cracked the plain wax seal and spread his friend's letter out on the desk. A quick perusal told him everything he needed to know. Charles and his men had overpowered the footman set to guard Viola's house and had pretty much ransacked the place. They'd moved all the large pieces of furniture, opened several walls, and even pulled up some of the floorboards. But they hadn't found anything, or at least they hadn't carted anything off, according to Boaz, who'd come to in time to see them leaving.

Now he really did have to go to town, if for no other reason than to see that Viola's house was restored to order before she herself returned. He read his mother's letter: His brother's wife was pregnant, again; his father and the vicar had fallen out—as with the first bit of news, this was no surprise; and a drunk, Italian prince had come all the way to Scotland to sing under Beau's window, and the duke had nearly set the dogs on him.

His sister's letter was quite predictably filled with the very same news, albeit with a very different tone. Beau thought the Italian prince deserved the dogs, if for no other reason than the fact that his singing was more the croak of a frog than the song of a nightingale. She also thought it disgustingly redundant of their sister-in-law to have fallen pregnant a fourth time after already adding three hearty new Vaughns to the family tree, and she wholeheartedly took their father's side when it came to his disagreement with the vicar (which seemed to have arisen over the propriety of bonfires at midsummer; the duke being for them, the vicar firmly against such pagan goings-on).

Leo laid the letters aside and opened the one from Mr. Grimble. It was a simple piece of business, but it did require his presence and signature, and it would give him all the excuse he needed to make a quick run to London.

He was rereading Beau's letter, and chuckling over her description of her love-struck prince, when Viola wandered into the library. She smiled, glanced at his letter, then turned her back and began to study the volumes that filled the tall cases lining the walls.

Leo let the letter fall to the desktop. Viola paced slowly along the far wall, pulling out first one book and then another, sometimes stopping to glance at a page or two, other times replacing the book unopened.

"Are you looking for anything in particular?"

Viola craned her neck to look at him while she slid her most recent selection back into place. "I was reading Caesar's *Commentarii,* but I forgot to bring it with me. You have quite an eclectic collection here. Everything from *Aristotle's Masterpiece* to *Tom Jones* to the plays of Shakespeare and the poetry of Donne. Did your grandfather build it, or did it come with the house?"

"A little of both, I'm afraid. To tell the truth, it's the family dumping ground for whatever they drag with them on their trips here."

Viola took a few more steps along the bookcase and pulled out a slender volume bound in blue leather. "And who left this?" She crossed the room and handed him the book in question.

Leo glanced at the title and found himself smiling. "That had to be either Sandison or my sister."

Viola raised her brows. "Your sister has read the Earl of Rochester?"

"Beau has read a lot of things a properly brought-up girl oughtn't to have. It comes from having scholars for parents. They shudder at the idea of censoring books. And Sandison is supposedly the illegitimate descendant of the disreputable earl, so it stands to reason he's proud of the man's debauched poetry."

Viola took the book back from him, opened it, and began to read, *"Our dainty fine Dutchesse's have got a Trick, To Doat on a Fool, for the Sake of his Prick, The Fopps were undone, did their Graces but know, The Discretion and vigor of Signior Dildo."* She shushed him when he choked and rapped him on the hand when he finally gave way to outright laughter.

"I prefer his less vulgar works," Leo said. *"Naked she lay, clasped in my longing arms, I filled with love, and she all over charms; Both equally inspired with eager fire, Melting through kindness, flaming in desire."*

"Are you saying you don't find dildos erotic, my lord?"

"Are you saying you do, my dear Mrs. Whedon?"

Viola bit her lips, but the grin still curled up the edges of her mouth. "I can't say, as I've never had to resort to one."

Leo grinned back at her. Viola leaned in, lips meeting his in a feather-light caress.

"See that I don't have to, my lord," she whispered.

"Is that a threat?"

"Well," she smiled down at him, "it's certainly not me begging."

Leo stood and backed her into the desk. "Shall I see if I can make you?"

"Beg for a dildo?"

Leo nipped her earlobe. "If you like, though that's not what I meant." He put her hand over the fall of his breeches and held it there as his cock flared to life. Her hand flexed, cupping his already ridged shaft.

"Is that you begging, my lord?"

Leo chuckled as he lifted her onto the desk and stepped between her thighs. "Not yet, it isn't."

Viola slid her hand along his erection, stroking it through the fabric of his breeches. She squeezed a bit harder as she reached the head, then pushed back down along its length, fingertips dancing over his testicles. Leo pressed himself into her palm.

"Do you really think it's that easy?" Leo pushed her skirts up and out of his way, dragging his nails lightly up the naked flesh of her thigh. The cleft between her thighs was already slick; his fingers were wet as he slid them inside her.

Viola dragged in a quick breath. "Why shouldn't it be?" Her hand continued to stroke him. "And don't say, *'Because I said it isn't.'*" She opened the fall of his breeches, and this time he didn't stop her.

His cock pulsed in her hand, blood rushed through him, leaving him dizzy. He gripped her hips, moving her forward to the edge of the desk. Viola guided him into place, a low purr in the back of her throat.

Leo thrust in, stretching her, filling her. She arched, rocking until her hips met his, until they couldn't get any closer. Leo pushed her back onto the desk, reached across, and gripped its far edge for leverage.

Viola matched his rhythm. She clung to his shoulders, tugging on his coat, wrenching it half off him. Her body was wet and willing and open, inner muscles pulsing.

Her feet cupped his buttocks, pressing him against her as she bucked up off the desk. One hand twisted in his hair, pulling hard, but with a slow, steady pressure that brought pleasure with the pain.

His release engulfed him, washing him over a precipice to where nothing else existed. His world was the heat of her skin against his, the wet embrace of her body, her shuddering gasps.

He lay still for a moment, drifting. He'd come, but his erection would last a few minutes more. Long enough to pitch her over into insensate bliss. He rocked his hips, rubbed against her, bit softly just below her ear. She struggled, pushed, rolled her body beneath his, then finally cried out, the sound dying away to a series of incoherent sobs.

Leo rested atop her, listening to the frantic beat of his own heart. It slowly steadied. Viola stirred beneath him, hands caressing his back, one foot idly tracing along his thigh.

He kissed the hollow of her throat. "And that, my dear, I think even our wicked earl would call a *conflagration*."

❧ CHAPTER 17 ❧

Plaster dust drifted through the air and caught in the beams of light pouring through the windows. Leo rubbed his eyes and surveyed the destruction. It wasn't as bad as he'd thought, but it clearly hadn't been done to unearth the prince's treasure.

Sandison had already had someone in to fix the floors, and the plasterers were hard at work on the walls. It was still all too evident that Charles had taken his temper out on the house, which meant he most certainly hadn't found the money, or anything that might lead him to it.

"I hope Mrs. Whedon's servants are enjoying their holiday. We certainly can't risk them coming home early to find this."

Sandison nodded his pale head. "Would you like to see the priest's hole? It had a few interesting items, but no strongboxes full of gold. We'd already removed the contents before MacDonald's visit."

Leo followed his friend into the drawing room and watched with interest as Sandison ran his hands under the mantel. One of the two bookcases slid back into the wall, revealing a narrow passageway that led to a small, shelf-lined room with a tattered footstool as its only furnishing.

"So what was here?"

Sandison laughed. "A few candle stubs, a crumpled letter, a shagreen case containing a crystal heart, a psalter and rosary, a pair of garters with a Jacobite slogan woven into them, and a child's leather horse. Nothing of import. I've brought it all back. I knew you'd want to see it regardless."

"Lead on, Macduff."

"Lay on," Sandison said with a disbelieving shake of his head as he descended the stairs.

"Lay on?" Leo grinned and poked him with a finger wielded as a sword.

"And damned be him who first cries 'Hold!' "

"No," Leo assured him. "I don't think that's it at all."

"It is, you undereducated cretin," Sandison said as he held open the door to the drawing room. "And highly appropriate to the present circumstances you find yourself in. Everything we found in the priest's hole is there on the table, except for the raggedy footstool, which you've already seen."

Leo studied the letter first: a hastily scrawled note advising the recipient, a Mr. Boutin, to flee the country. The spidery handwriting angled across the page and was signed only with a large, fanciful *C*. He picked up the crystal heart and held it up to the light. Inside, pale hair and gold wire were twisted into the prince's initials.

"A pretty bit of treason, that bauble," Sandison said.

Leo nodded and put it back into its case. "My grand-mother used to tell stories about all the Jacobite ladies in Scotland wearing Stewart Hearts to show their support of the prince's claim to the throne, but I've never seen one."

"It's doubtful we'll ever see another."

"Put it back where you found it," Leo said. "Most of them must have been thrown away or destroyed after the Jacobites lost at Culloden. This one deserves to survive to tell its tale."

The candle guttered in its socket, the flame dying in a pool of wax. Leo moved closer to the remaining one, eyes straining in the bare light of a single candle.

He'd been well and truly engrossed in the first volume of Viola's memoir. She had a lively style. It read more like a novel than a lurid confessional. And the novel in question was more *Tom Jones* than *Fanny Hill*.

Leo flipped back to the beginning and read the opening sentence again: *At the age of nineteen, I became the mistress of the Earl of D—. I shall not tell you the why's or wherefore's of what came before, for they are of no interest to any but myself.* Not a word about what had led to her estrangement from her family. Nothing about how she'd come to be a courtesan. She'd written it as though she truly had sprung from nowhere, fully formed, a god-dess to be worshipped.

The only hint to Viola's origins was a single comment that she'd been introduced to the earl by one of his friends, a man who'd been so enraged by her decision to accept the peer's extramarital offer that he'd ceased speaking to them both.

It was the only bittersweet moment in the entire book. Otherwise it was a parade of decadence and delight. A tale of friendships and rivalries. She'd embraced the life she'd chosen, or that had chosen her. Wholeheartedly, unreservedly, unashamedly.

Such immodesty ought to disgust. Leo searched his emotions, forcing himself to confront every niggling response. No disgust. No derision. Not even mild contempt. There was abundant curiosity, dawning respect, even a smidgen of admiration. Whatever Viola was, whoever Viola was, she was no one's victim.

Viola looked up from her manuscript to catch Nance thrusting something furtively into her pocket. Her maid blushed as Viola raised a brow. What was she up to?

"Nance? Why so mysterious?"

"It's nothing, ma'am. Just hair from your brush."

"But why is it in your pocket?"

The pretty little maid blushed furiously. "It's for the Midsummer-men."

"The what?"

"Midsummer-men, ma'am. You take a pair of orpine cuttings, and you wrap one in your hair and one in your lover's hair—if you can get it—and you tie them together and put them up in the rafters. If they bend toward each other, he loves you. If they bend away, he doesn't. Or that's what the girls in the village told me after church last Sunday."

"And you're making one for me?"

"And his lordship." Her blush grew even more furious.

"Have you made one for yourself?"

Nance nodded and fled through the adjoining door into the bedroom. Viola gave into the mirth bubbling through her. Nance was city-bred, but clearly she was taking to the country. There were several of the footmen who could be in contention, and perhaps even a groom or two. Nance had certainly complained about Leo's footman Sampson enough to indicate a clear inclination.

Viola scratched out the paragraph she'd been working on and bit her lip as she puzzled out what to write next. Usually the words just flowed, but Sir Hugo's chapters were turning out to be slow going. She could find nothing witty to say about him, but neither could she leave him out. She needed the pages, and after the incident at the theatre, people would be expecting something very juicy indeed.

She tossed her quill aside and capped the inkwell. She needed a ride to clear her head. Riding, she'd discovered, provided a wonderful stimulus to her thought process. It was as though the motion of the horse jogged her muse and memories to life.

Viola followed her maid into the bedroom, and Nance assisted her into her habit. Well, into Lady Boudicea's habit. Viola brushed her hands over the oatmeal linen. She was going to have to procure a habit of her own, though Nance had done a splendid job of altering this one to fit her.

Viola topped her curls with Lady Boudicea's straw cocked hat and grabbed her crop. As she descended the stairs, her heart sank into her stomach with a sickening lurch. Her readers would be expecting something about Lord Leonidas. Did he realize that? Was he prepared for it?

⚜ CHAPTER 18 ⚜

When Leo returned to Dyrham, he found Viola confident enough in the saddle to join him on cross-country rides about the estate. She was most comfortable at a trot, but she'd managed a canter on several occasions, and today she should get enough practice in to master that gait, too.

They'd fallen into a schedule of sorts. She wrote all morning, they rode all afternoon, and then they made love all night, sleeping only in fits and starts. She'd woken him from a dead sleep this morning with a hand wrapped around his cock.

She was going to be the death of him, but what a magnificent death it would be.

He reined Meteor in, while Oleander waded across the shallow streambed. Viola let the reins go slack, just as he'd instructed her, then collected them again when they reached dry ground. Pen splashed through behind them and ambled off into the field, snuffling in the tall grass as she went.

Viola glanced over at the folly and then back at him. "Is Kirby Muxloe really as magnificent as you say?"

"Why ask? You can judge for yourself shortly." He urged Meteor forward, and Oleander fell into step beside him as they emerged from the water.

"It's just that I've never seen a castle."

"Liar."

"I'm not lying. Never."

"You've most certainly seen the Tower of London."

"Well yes, but one hardly wants to count that."

Leo chuckled. "And, pray tell, why not?"

Viola shrugged and flicked a large, trailing curl back off her shoulder. "I don't know. It's just so, so . . ."

"Large? Stony? Imposing?"

She laughed, and her dog woofled back, causing her to laugh again. "I don't know. The Tower is just, well, it's the Tower. It's impossible to imagine London without it. And a castle, well, a castle should be a hulking gray ruin, covered in lichen, with the wind whistling through it like a ghost."

"I don't think you'll be disappointed in Kirby Muxloe. Apart from the ghost, it fits your description as though you'd already been there."

They rode across the field and pushed through a gap in the hedge and onto the road. Leo glanced up and down the deserted lane. "Come on then. If we hurry, we can be home in time for dinner."

Viola's laughter drifted back as Oleander broke into a canter, and the two of them shot merrily down the lane. Pen took off in pursuit, a cloud of dust rising from her churning paws. Leo watched them for a moment, something like pride stirring in his chest. With a whoop, he set Meteor after them.

Their pace ate up the miles to the castle. Leo reined in Meteor. Beside him, Oleander slowed as well. "If you look there, just beyond those trees, you'll see the very top of Kirby Muxloe's tower." Viola straightened in the saddle, straining to see. She shook her head, her face a moue of chagrin.

"Not to worry," Leo assured her, "we'll be there momentarily."

As they emerged from the trees, she grinned like a child, a gurgle of delight breaking free. Leo grinned back, well able to remember the first time his grandfather had brought him here.

In the middle of a large moat, the water smooth and dark, stood the earthworks for the base of a grand castle. All that remained were a single tower and the large gatehouse. Viola reined in as they approached the remains of the bridge.

"Is it safe?"

"It's not as old as it looks," Leo responded. "Look below; the supporting timbers are enormous."

He urged Meteor forward, and Oleander followed, their hooves loud as the battering ram of the Roundheads must have been. As they passed through the wide, vaulted entrance, a hare burst across the open, grassy expanse that was all that was left of the castle. Pen gave chase, her excited baying echoing off the stone walls of the gatehouse. The hare disappeared into a hole, and Pen jammed her nose in after it and began to dig.

Leo leapt down and turned to help Viola from her

saddle. She kicked free and slid into his arms, the motion almost without thought now. She tugged away from him, as though she were eager to explore.

"Not so quickly." Leo tightened his grip.

Viola smiled up at him slyly, her arms sliding up his chest until she could clasp her hands at the back of his neck. "Yes, my lord?"

Leo gave her a quick, hard kiss. He held on just long enough to feel her go pliant in his arms. When he broke it off, she was still smiling. "Can we climb the tower?"

"Pick up your skirts, and we'll go exploring." She glanced at their mounts, worry pinching her brow momentarily. "The horses will be fine here. Come on." He held out his hand, and she took it, scooping up her skirts with her free hand.

"Is there a dungeon?"

Leo grinned. "Yes, but it's under the tower, and it's usually flooded. You'll have to look elsewhere for your ghost."

"This will do," Viola said as they reached the entrance. Sunlight poured in through the remnants of a window. The sound of wings filled the air as a small flock of starlings took flight and whizzed about the room.

Viola shuddered. "I don't like starlings. I can't explain it, but I just don't like them. They look at you as though they'd like to peck out your eyes."

She shuddered again, and Leo bit the inside of his cheek to hold back the laugh attempting to work its way out of his chest. What a thing to be afraid of: birds no bigger than your hand. "There are ravens nesting in the top. Shall we forgo the view and make do with the gatehouse?"

"No, they don't bother me the way starlings do. Ravens are honest in their greed. Almost playful. But there's something deceitful about a starling."

Viola let go of Leo's hand and hurried up the dark stairs. The only light came from tiny and very occasional arrow slits. She didn't so much as pause to gaze out of one, the urge to leave the birds behind too strong.

When she reached the ramparts, she pulled off her hat and turned her face up toward the sun. The breeze caught her hair and sent it flying all about her face. She smiled as Leo stooped under the lintel. She knew she was being silly, but she couldn't help it.

Viola spun about to take in the full view. The ruins were amazing, marooned as they were like a private island in the middle of the countryside. If she let her imagination wander, she could almost picture knights upon enormous destriers down in the courtyard and ladies in flowing gowns and bejeweled hats gathered to watch them.

"It makes you feel small, doesn't it?"

"Small?" Leo looked lost.

"Well, maybe not *you*. But it makes *me* feel small. Once upon a time, this was someone's home. That courtyard bustled with life. People worshipped in the chapel. And now it's just this. Empty and tumbling down around us."

"Ah, now you're getting deep and possibly maudlin. None of that. Today is for adventure."

Leo pulled her along the wall. Her skirts slipped from her hand, and she tripped, legs hopelessly tangled. He caught her up and tossed her over his shoulder. Laughing, he ran along the rampart until he reached the entrance to the tower stairs. He ducked under as she squealed, her hat flying out of her hands and rolling away. He charged up the stairs, emerging onto a large, circular battlement with her still balanced on his shoulder.

"There." He set her on her feet. "Dragged through the castle like the spoils of war."

Laughter bubbled up, causing her to gasp for breath. "So you're the marauding knight? You've broken the castle's defenses and are now going to claim the lady of the castle as your own?"

"It's a rather good idea, you must admit."

"Must I?"

"I really think you must. It's surrender or death, my lady."

Viola turned her back to him, putting her hands on the parapet. "But isn't an honorable death what any true lady would choose?"

"Ah, such a loss isn't to be thought of." He crowded her into the battlement, hands pushing her hair aside, mouth exploring her neck. He'd been playing with her a moment before, but now their game had changed. She could feel herself pulled toward him, an invisible wire strung tight and growing tighter still, like a violin being strung to the perfect pitch. Desire swamped her, flooding out all concern for decorum.

"No?" She pressed back, hips circling.

"No, my lady." His arms came around her, hands splayed out over her breasts. Even through her stays, she could feel his palm scrape across her nipples.

His cock was hard against her. She pushed, and he thrust back. His hands slid down to her thighs, and her skirts rose like the curtain at Drury Lane. The leather of his gloves danced along her skin, the distinct edges of the seams trailing along her hip, moving across her belly, then down between her thighs.

She gasped as he touched her. His knees nudged hers apart, and after a moment, his cock pressed for entrance. His circling fingers urged her backward; the thrust of his hips as he pressed inside pushed her into his hand. She fought for breath, her release carrying her away as assuredly as Leo had done only minutes before.

He pressed fully in, then stilled. Leo rested his forehead against the back of her head, his breath hot and unsteady on the nape of her neck. "Any man who wouldn't storm a castle for that isn't a man at all."

Viola tightened herself around him and pushed backward. She didn't want slow and tender. She wanted the conquering knight. His hands gripped her hips, fingers digging in, hips rocking against her. She moaned, wanting more. Needing more. His weight pinned her to the parapet; his cock filled her.

"Again. Come for me one more time." His voice grated over her. His hand slid back around, pushing roughly between her thighs, fingers riding hard against the swollen folds and the sensitive peak hidden between them.

She was gasping, pleasure sliding over into pain and back again, her release teetering just out of reach until it crashed over her and her bones liquefied. Leo made a growling sound that rattled through her, and he pressed infinitesimally deeper as he came.

"Good God, Vi."

She attempted to move, but he held her fast.

A soft tremor rippled through her, and he made a guttural

sound in the back of his throat. "Whatever you do, don't move just yet." She pushed up, feeling the full weight of him. He rubbed his cheek against her neck like a courting cat. "There's nothing better than the throbbing, shuddering afterglow of a woman's release."

"No?" Viola tipped her head, giving him the side of her neck to explore. He was wrong, but the particulars of why and how weren't something that could be explained.

His teeth slid lightly across her skin, and she let the thought go. It wasn't any of her business that Lord Leonidas Vaughn had never been in love.

⤐ CHAPTER 19 ⤐

Light flooded through the mullioned windows of the parlor, bouncing off the Canaletto over the mantel, making the canals of Venice appear to flow across the canvas. Viola stared at it for several minutes, letting her mind wander along streets she'd only ever read about.

She shook off the daydream and returned to the task at hand. With a few precise stitches, she reattached a Dorset thread button to Leo's shirt cuff. It was amazing that they'd found it, lost among the sheets. The earbob she'd lost in the library was still missing.

A sop to the gods or some such. A small price to pay for such pleasure, really.

She could have left the mending to Nance, but her poor maid had enough to do keeping up with the frequent damage to Viola's own wardrobe. Asking her to repair the rents and tears of Leo's clothing as well would be too much.

Besides, Viola rather liked having something to do when Leo was gone for the afternoon. And this task allowed her to play with the memories of just how that particular button had been torn from its cuff, or how a seam had been rent.

She set the repaired shirt aside and reached for the next one in her workbasket. Across the room, Pen stirred in her sleep, feet twitching madly. Viola held the shirt up and turned it over in her hands, hunting for the damage. Ah, yes. This one's seam had given at the shoulder as he'd yanked it off just last night.

She let the linen pool in her lap and fingered the bite mark that lay hidden beneath her fichu. She'd shared her bed with men concerned only with their own pleasure, with men barely even up to claiming that, and with men who'd moved her to orgasm, but she'd not taken any real pleasure in doing so.

She'd never had a lover whose sole goal was her pleasure, or who'd been so genuinely enamored that he'd left marks without even knowing it. There was something about it that left her feeling powerful. Something delightfully wicked. Each mark like a badge of honor.

Still savoring the slight aches of her various well-earned bumps and bruises, Viola put her needle back to work. As she set the final anchor stitch, the door opened and Pen surged to her feet, hackles up.

Mr. Pilcher didn't so much as spare the grumbling dog a glance. "Mr. Sandison has arrived, ma'am. Shall I—"

"Don't bother announcing me, Pilcher." Mr. Sandison burst into the room, pushing past Pilcher with a scapegrace smile. "Mrs. Whedon and I are already acquainted. Good God! What the devil is that?"

Pen's low protest became a full-throated growl. "Pen!"

Viola stood, snapped her fingers, and pointed at the ground. The dog quieted, but moved to place herself between Viola and Sandison.

"Hello, Mr. Sandison. This horrible beast is Penthesilea. And she's being a very bad girl." Pen flopped at Viola's feet, head propped up on her crossed paws. "I'm afraid Lord Leonidas is gone for the afternoon. Have you eaten? Shall I send Pilcher for something from the kitchen?"

"No, no, ma'am. Thank you. I stopped at the Craven Bull not an hour ago." He crossed the room slowly to take the seat farthest from her. "I'm sorry, ma'am, but is that *your* dog?"

Viola nodded, amusement curling her lips into a smile.

"Not quite most ladies' idea of a pet, is she?"

"Pen was something of a volunteer."

His brow wrinkled, one eyebrow rising in question.

"A very enthusiastic volunteer," she continued. "Impossible to deny, you might say."

"Impossible to get out of the carriage, you mean." Leo strode into the room, hair slightly windblown and boots dusty.

Pen leapt up and ran to greet him. Viola's pulse leapt, too. She took a deep, steadying breath. Leo gave Pen a hearty pat, just as he did his horses, and she wriggled with joy, her stub of a tail wagging frantically.

"As I remember it, my lord, you had no problem ordering her out." Viola sat back down and reached for another piece of mending.

"Only to be met with two pairs of pleading eyes. Admit it, Vi, you'd have turned back to London with this beast in tow if I'd not given way." Viola shrugged as Leo

wiped ineffectually at a long smear of slobber Pen had left
upon his breeches. "Don't let that placid expression fool
you, Sandison. Mrs. Whedon is every bit as bad as Beau
when it comes to getting her way."

"No one could be as thoroughly unscrupulous as your
sister when it comes to getting her way. Except, perhaps—"

"My mother." Leo's eyes crinkled with merriment as
he cut off his friend, and they both burst into laughter. Pen
leaned into him, and he dropped one hand to absently
play with her ears. With sudden decision, he pushed her
away. "Come along, Sandison. Come and see my new
colt. He's a thick, heavy-boned Irish beauty. He ought to
be up to even Thane's weight when he's grown."

Mr. Sandison sketched her a slight bow as Leo ushered
him from the room. The door shut on a note of laughter
from them both. Pen whined at the door, then shuffled
across the room to reclaim the sunny spot on the carpet.

"How very domestic."

Leo glared at his friend and refused to be baited.
Sandison knocked the head off an encroaching plant with
his crop and continued toward the stable.

"She's darning your bloody stockings, Mrs. Whedon.
The woman has brought half of London to their knees,
and you've got her doing your mending. You'd think"—he
glanced back over his shoulder to see if his darts were hitting home, and Leo forced his expression to remain as
bland as possible—"a man of your reputation could find
something far more imaginative to keep her busy."

"She seems content enough." Leo thrust his nosy
friend into the cool shade of the stable. He wasn't about to

tell Sandison that she was mending only what she herself had torn asunder, and that without a bit of mending, he'd be wandering about in nothing but his drawers.

Sandison's smile plainly said he didn't believe him in the least. Leo paused to scratch Quiz. The gelding lowered his head and shook it like a dog. Leo dug his fingers into the sensitive spot just beside Quiz's ear.

Sandison picked his way around a pile of droppings. "Too much a gentleman to tell your friends all the glorious details? Lud. It's not as though I can't just read her memoir."

"Ah, but what she chooses to write is her own business, just as what I choose to divulge is mine."

"You always were a tight-lipped bastard, Vaughn."

Leo gave a bark of laughter, and Quiz jerked out of his hands with an affronted snort. "Any further sign of my cousin or the treasure?"

Sandison shrugged one elegant shoulder and flicked a bit of hay from his sleeve. "I saw MacDonald at the Ackroyd route. Got an icy glare and a rude hand gesture from him as he left." Sandison smiled slyly and Leo raised one brow. He knew that look. Sandison meant devilment.

"After all the time I've spent in Mrs. Whedon's house, I do have a very solid idea of her general tastes," Sandison added. He held one hand out to the new colt and clucked his tongue. "Bohea or Pu Erh for tea. Black glycerin soap from Spain for her bath. Her room smells of *Eau de Cologne,* her stockings of lavender...and a copy of Julius Caesar's *Commentarii*—in the original Latin—on her bedside table for a bit of light reading."

"Leave her stockings out of it."

Sandison grinned, then turned his attention back to luring the colt to him. "Noted. What about her shoes? Are they too out of bounds? They do, after all, *touch* her stockings."

"I know this is likely an impossible request, but don't be an ass, Sandison. There was nothing at all? No secret door in the larder? No hidden staircase to an attic room?"

"No, no, and no. I know the trail in the letters leads to number twelve, but perhaps we have only part of the story. Perhaps they took the money with them when they fled. Or maybe it had already gone on to the next stage of its journey before everything fell apart for the prince."

Leo ran a hand over his face. "Perhaps, but I'm not prepared to give up on it just yet. Maybe there's some clue I've missed in the letters."

"Or maybe the letter that would tell us what we need to know is what is missing."

Leo nodded, knowing that his friend's suggestion was all too likely a possibility. "Well, if this turns out to have been nothing but a wild goose chase, I'll simply have to face up to selling Dyrham."

Sandison eyed him sharply. "Is Dyrham really so unsound?"

Leo nodded. "It's a hunting box. A rather grand one, I'll grant you, but it was never meant to be self-supporting. Oh, I could live on here without the prince's treasure, but everything would go to rack and ruin before I was sixty."

"The old duke forget to take the cost into account when he left it to you?"

"I rather imagine that Grandfather didn't give it a second thought. It must have seemed incidental to him. Just one of many small holdings, none of which pulled its own weight."

"But what does that matter when one enjoys them, eh?"

"Exactly. No different than the house in Mayfair, or the one in Bath."

"Except," Sandison said, "that an estate such as this, with a stable full of horses and a full staff, costs a hell of a lot more to maintain."

"That it does."

Sandison whistled softly, and the colt finally stepped up to the door of the box stall. He rubbed his thumb over the animal's wide blaze.

"He's a handsome devil, isn't he?" Leo asked.

"Yes. I imagine Thane will be mad for him."

"As well as my brother, Squire Watt, and a few dozen others. But they'll all be decidedly out. This boy is mine. He's going to be the foundation sire for my stable. It's taken me three years to find just the right blend of blood and bone."

"Going to set yourself up as a gentleman farmer?" Sandison smiled as he stepped away from the stall and brushed off his hands.

"Something like that, yes. If the universe cooperates." Leo paused as the sound of carriage wheels on gravel became distinct. "Ten pounds it's Thane."

"Done. Thane has never beaten Devere anywhere in his life. It's beneath his dignity to rush."

Leo chuckled. Sandison was right about that. The idea of Thane in a heat or a hurry was simply impossible to picture. Even when delivering a speech in the House, he was always calm and precise. But one of these days, the sleepy giant would wake, and Leo was willing to bet his new colt that the result would be more than worth the wait. Today was unlikely to be that day, but Devere wasn't due until tomorrow, so it was even odds as to which of them was in the carriage.

The jingle of the links of a collar reached them and then de Moulines's greyhound came dancing into the stable, quickly followed by Devere and de Moulines himself. The Frenchman whistled, and his dog rushed back to him, a fawning sycophant of the first order.

"You'd best hope Mrs. Whedon's new pet doesn't eat the Dauphin," Sandison called out by way of greeting.

De Moulines gave them both a quizzical look. "Has she adopted a tiger? Or perhaps some poor gypsy's bear?"

"No, just a mongrel mastiff," Leo assured him. "And I'm sure the Dauphin is more than capable of charming away her snarls."

The greyhound, upon hearing his name repeated, slunk forward and thrust his head under Leo's hand. Leo ran his fingers over the silken fur. "That's a good boy. You work the same magic on Pen, and we'll have no worries at all."

❧ CHAPTER 20 ❧

... and though I have often heard him called a brilliant speaker in Parliament, one could have wished to have found him brilliant in other areas. Alas, both his wife and I were doomed to disappointment.

Viola signed the final *t* with a flourish and placed the period with such satisfaction that she nearly punctured the sheet of foolscap. That did very well for Sir Hugo. A niggling bit of disquiet stirred within her. She was very nearly done with her manuscript. She brushed the feather tip of her quill across her chin.

When she was done, there'd be no reason to stay on at Dyrham. She could return to London, to her friends, to her life. She could pick up the strings of gossip, superintend the replanting of her garden...

Viola sighed and caught the feather between her teeth. She would buy a horse when she returned to London. Her afternoon ride was something she was entirely unprepared to give up when she returned to town.

And then there was Leo himself. The very fact that her feelings had become involved at all was something more than worrisome. It was mortifying and untenable.

She was growing too comfortable at Dyrham. It was becoming hard not to think of it as home, as hers. And it had happened with alarming ease. Something about the haphazardly furnished house had simply laid claim to her. Only last evening, she'd caught herself niggling with the idea of a house party, mentally matching up her friends and Lord Leonidas's, planning whom to seat next to whom at dinner…

She dipped her pen into the inkwell, resolute. This was the final section, the final story, and when it was done, so too was her time at Dyrham.

"Deliver him to Dyrham tomorrow. Mr. Pilcher will be expecting you and will have your payment ready." Leo let his hand linger on the chestnut's withers. Fine-boned in the way of Thoroughbreds with a great deal of Arab blood, the gelding had a beautifully sculpted head and a thick, heavy mane. He was the perfect mount for a lady, and he'd suit Viola to a tittle.

The gypsy's nut-brown face crinkled with a smile as he nodded and led the mare away. The man called out something to his fellows in his own tongue, and one of them raced up to take the horse from him.

"Come. Watch the duck racing." De Moulines waved him over. "It is outrageous. Only the English would do something so ridiculous."

Beside him, Devere shook his head, raising his eyes briefly heavenward. "What? Are you trying to tell me the French have no country traditions?"

"Bah." With a flourish, de Moulines took a snuffbox from his pocket and carefully raised a pinch to one nostril. "You can eat French traditions: cheese, wine, pâté. Only the English enjoy being made sport of for their fellows. It is a mystery." He shrugged and slipped the enamel box back into his pocket.

"Oh, do shut up, my fine frog." Sandison poked de Moulines in the ribs with his crop and then gave him a comical *sa-sa,* wielding it as though it were a sword.

The Frenchman made a face, idly brushing a speck of snuff from his coat sleeve. "An appropriate enough weapon for you, Sandison."

The Englishman burst into laughter. "Given your talent with a blade, I'm not likely to attack your person with anything more serious. Now do come along, both of you. There's a filly on the far side I think Vaughn should see. Got a rump that will lift her over a hedge like she has wings."

De Moulines waved them off and wandered away with Devere to watch the duck races. Sandison smiled at Leo and tucked his crop smartly under his arm. "Do you think that showy chestnut is up to Beau's weight?"

"He isn't for my sister."

Sandison raised one brow and stared him down. "So you're buying Mrs. Whedon a horse? Because that delicate creature certainly isn't going to be carrying you."

Leo felt the first hint of embarrassment burning up his neck. He clenched his jaw, teeth grinding against one another till he thought he might crack a molar. Down by the river, a cheer went up as a sopping man emerged, holding a madly flapping duck aloft. A nearby horse tossed its head in protest, and there was a sudden scuffle as its groom was dragged a few feet before regaining control.

"Don't you think she'd rather have something a little more…" Sandison paused, hand circling about dramatically as he hunted for the right word. "Pawnable? Or at least more traditionally lover-like?"

"I think it's none of your bloody business," Leo ground out. Sandison continued to stare at him, a woeful, supercilious expression on his face. Leo flexed his hand, allowing himself the indulgence of at least imagining the satisfaction of sending Sandison sprawling across the grass.

His friend shook his head and heaved a heavyhearted sigh. "What do you think's going to happen when she finds out just why you seduced your way into her life and her bed? Do you even remember that you set this all in motion with a purpose? That you're not really her protector? Good God, man—"

Leo spun about on his heel and strode off in the opposite direction.

"She'll shoot that chestnut, that's what!" Sandison yelled after him.

Leo yanked his hat from his head and swiped his hand over his forehead, rubbing away the itch where the straw had sat too long against the skin. He squinted as the sun slid out from behind a cloud, gilding everything in shimmering heat. If Viola found out what he'd done—why he'd done it—he'd be lucky if she didn't shoot him.

⊱ CHAPTER 21 ⊰

Viola turned the massive brass-and-leather dog collar over in her hands. Leo smiled as she studied it. The brass had been stamped with *Strayed from Dyrham*. He'd been inspired at the horse fair when he'd seen the men selling them. He'd present her with the gelding later.

Her expression went from bland to confused. Her straight brows pinched in, causing a furrow over the bridge of her nose. She looked up at him, blinking rapidly, as though searching for something she couldn't quite grasp.

"In case she goes wandering." Leo took a step toward her. "I thought she'd be safer if—"

"But we—she—I . . ." Her shoulders slumped, her eyes clouded with disquiet. "I don't live at Dyrham."

The floor creaked, and the door banged shut behind him. Leo turned to find his friends had fled. Wise of them. The Dauphin's nails clicked across the floor as he circled back to join Pen on the rug. He whined softly, and the mastiff laid her giant head on his flank.

"I was hoping you'd stay for the summer." Leo plucked

the collar from Viola's unresisting hands and turned to buckle it about Pen's neck. The dog licked his hand, and he ruffled her ears.

"Oh."

Leo swallowed hard and kept his face turned toward the dogs. There was an entire conversation in that simple word. Regret, trepidation, sorrow, fear. He could sense them all swirling around her, much like the starlings at Kirby Muxloe: dark, menacing, and unwelcome. He'd made a mistake, but for the life of him he couldn't fathom what it was.

"I've nearly finished my manuscript, and I was thinking of returning to town next week. Once I've handed it over to Mr. Nesbit, there should be no reason for Sir Hugo to continue his harassment, should there?" She turned her face away, hands fiddling with her skirt, pleating up the fabric.

Leo let every conflicting emotion flood through him, run its course, and then drain away. His hands clenched, the knuckles popping.

"No, no, you're quite right. Returning should be safe enough." Assuming that he could convince his cousin that there really was no treasure. "So if that's your wish," he said, trying to keep his voice even, "my coach awaits your orders. But I'd be happy to deliver your manuscript myself, if you'd trust me with the undertaking."

Viola bit her lip, choking down a sudden desperate sob. It would be so easy to stay. So easy to fall into the illusion that this was her home, that she really was the chatelaine of Dyrham. It was bad enough to want a man as much as she wanted Lord Leonidas, but it was infinitely worse to realize that she wanted a great deal more.

If she could just get back to London, back to her own house, back to a semblance of normalcy, she might survive it. If she stayed here, every day Leo and Dyrham would work their way a little farther under her skin until she couldn't live without them.

And she'd have to, one day. His entreaty for her to stay held enough of an icy splash of reality to steel her. *For the summer.* He'd hoped she would stay until she had to be sent away to make room for his family. He couldn't possibly keep her under the same roof as his beloved, horse-mad sister and brother with the tragically mundane names.

"I find I'm missing London. Lady Ligonier writes that there's to be a grand masquerade at Vauxhall and a balloon ascension in Hyde Park...Besides, we've torn so many of my gowns that I'll soon be as naked as Eve if I don't pay a visit to my modiste."

Her reasons sounded lame even to her own ears, but she could hardly blurt out the truth: that she had to leave before she fell hopelessly in love with him and Dyrham both.

Leo continued to kneel beside the dogs, one hand on each, fingers making swirling patterns in their fur. His coat buckled stiffly across his shoulders, looking as uncomfortable as she felt.

"I've no objection to you naked as Eve in Eden, but I'll admit it might be a tad problematic when there are guests." He stood. Pen gave a protesting whooing bay and pawed at his boot. "I can escort you back on Monday if that's acceptable."

Viola nodded, forcing a smile that felt like the grinning rictus on a puppet's face. The urge to touch him overwhelmed her, and she put out a hand to draw him near. He helped her up, hand engulfing hers, gripping it, hard.

"Don't look so stricken, my dear. You've every right to order your life as you please, and if it's London you want, then so be it, though I admit I prefer life here."

Viola squeezed his hand back and wished his green eye didn't look so defeated. She preferred it here, too. That was the problem.

The steps of the carriage fell with the sound of a death knell, a series of jarring metallic clanks that ended with an ominous clang. She was home.

Sunlight reflected off the pale stone of her house, blinding her momentarily. She missed her footing and stumbled as Lord Leonidas handed her out. Beads of sweat glistened on his brow and lip. He dabbed them away with his handkerchief, then rubbed at his face to clear the fine layer of dust that seemed to coat everything. She could feel it on her own skin like a mask.

At the door he paused, eyes squinting against the light. "I'll leave you now, ma'am."

Viola tightened her grip on his arm, and beneath her hand, the muscle spasmed. She clung harder as her stomach twisted. He was about to give her her *congé*. "Will you be returning tonight?"

The tense lines about his eyes faded a bit. "If I'm welcome, yes."

Viola let her breath out in a rush, a laugh catching the

tail end. "You're not just welcome, my lord." She pressed close, hands spread over his chest, lips finding his for a brief moment. "You're expected. I'll tell Mrs. Draper to have dinner prepared at eight, if that suits you."

Leo nodded, brushed his lips over the back of her hand, then turned and ran lightly down the stairs. Pen whined and nudged her hand with her head until Viola responded and scratched her ear.

Panic subsiding, she stood on her stoop and watched until he, Meteor, and the coach all disappeared around a corner with a final flick of the gelding's long black tail. Pen turned to investigate the entrance hall, and Mrs. Draper practically seethed with disapproval.

"His lordship's man fetched me home this morning, ma'am. I've done the shopping, but if you want anything particular for supper, you'd best tell me now so I can send Mary back out for it." She eyed the dog again and stiffened her spine. "I shall have to send her out anyway, given that no one informed me about your new pet, and I'm certainly not feeding her the prime beef I bought for your table."

"It doesn't matter, Mrs. Draper. I'm sure whatever you intend to serve will be fine. As for Pen, she's happy with scraps."

Mrs. Draper escaped to the kitchen, her mumbled, incoherent protest following her down the corridor. Viola swept up the stairs, wiping her fingers over the dusty railing. She brushed her hands clean on her skirts.

Odd that. There was a layer of fine dust over the entire house: the paneling in the corridor, the rug on the floor, even the knobs to the doors.

Viola fretted and plotted as the hours passed. Finally, she collapsed into a chair before her nerves caused her to worry a hole in the Turkey carpet in her parlor. Her maid was moping below stairs, clearly resentful of having been separated from Leonidas's footman, who'd been left behind at Dyrham. Viola realized with a jolt she'd never asked about Nance's Midsummer-men. Had they portended true love, or had they reared away from one another in aversion? Did she really want to know?

Pen grumbled in her sleep. The dog had long ago eaten her supper and fallen asleep on the chaise she'd promptly claimed as her own. Pen was seemingly content no matter where they were.

Lord Leonidas was late. That simple fact hung over the evening like a shroud. Viola damped down a wave of despair. The ormolu clock on the mantel chimed nine times, and she found herself fighting back tears. She sat listening to her heartbeat, to her dog's soft snores, and the ticking of the clock. Nothing was in time with anything else. Each sound grated, shredding her nerves further.

Mrs. Draper finally shooed her into the dining parlor and forced her to eat. Viola pushed the stewed carp around on her plate. He wasn't coming. The food turned to chalk in her mouth, making it impossible to swallow.

She put the plate on the floor for Pen and refilled her wineglass. She drained it in one long draught. She was going to bed. And she wasn't going to get up for a week. Maybe two.

She was at the top of the stairs when a loud knock arrested her progress. Her hand shook, and she gripped the railing tight. The wine in her stomach swirled with sickening power, and her pulse fluttered with it, battered like a leaf in a storm.

She could hear Mrs. Draper's voice, followed by Lord Leonidas's, then the rapid sound of his boots on the stairs. She twisted about to make it look as though she were descending.

Leo reached the landing and rounded the corner. "I'm so sorry, my dear. I've already made my apologies to Mrs. Draper for ruining her supper. I was unavoidably detained."

Relief turned to anger, quick as a hawk snatching a rabbit from a field. Viola forced herself to smile as the urge to slap him made her fingers flex. A protector being late had never bothered her, had certainly never sent her into a rage. It was his right to keep her at his beck and call.

But Leo was *not* her protector, by his own design. He wasn't paying for the privilege of her indulgence.

He continued up, stopping when his eyes were on level with her own. "I truly am sorry. I meant to send a footman with a note. The women of my family have descended like the monstrous regiment they are. There was no getting away sooner."

One hand snaked out, and his arm slipped around her waist, pulling her down a single step so that she was brought up against the hard wall of his chest. She caught her lower lip between her teeth.

His eyes crinkled with mirth and relief. "See there, you're halfway to forgiving me already." He dipped his head, lips tracing her ear, the heady scent of Bay Rum and clean skin surrounded her. Her fingers curled into his lapels of their own accord.

"Have you eaten?" Her question came out barely louder than a whisper.

He shook his head, hands sliding over her hips.

"Are you hungry?"

"No." He pushed closer, lips finding the pulse point just below her ear.

Her breathing hitched. "Would you like a drink?"

He laughed, the sound bouncing back at them in the narrow stairwell. "Not just now."

He kissed her hard, pressing her into the wall. Her skirts were up, and her thighs were gripping his hips before she quite knew how it had happened. He pushed inside her, arms locked about her, one hand fisting into her hair.

She didn't remember being lifted, couldn't begin to explain when or how he'd freed himself from his breeches. It had all happened at once, as though their melding was some kind of clockwork toy. A naughty version of the chess-playing Turk that had been on display in London just last season.

And she responded as though her body—his body— knew the exact motions necessary to drive her heedlessly, helplessly toward her release. Her hands began to tingle. Her toes curled, the arch of her foot fighting against the unyielding sole of her shoe. And then, poised on the cusp, he came instead, his body pinning her to the wall as he pulsed within her.

Her breath came out with a sob of disappointment. She'd been so damn close. Too close to even think of pretending. Close enough to ache with the loss of it.

"Good Lord, Vi." He rocked gently against her, fabric

working roughly over her clitoris. She tried to catch her breath, but it hitched uncontrollably as he adjusted his position and the angle of their joining. "There's a bed not thirty feet away, and I'm tumbling you on the stairs like a lad having a go at a housemaid." He chuckled, head resting against the wall, breath stirring the curls at the nape of her neck. "I'm not usually so hasty or inept."

Viola smiled into his collar. Relief that he'd arrived, late or not, thrummed through her. Triumph that he wanted her so badly was singing in her blood. She kissed his neck, lips and tongue and teeth sliding over the spot below the ear he always seemed to favor when doing the same to her. He made a happy, rumbling sound deep in his throat, and his cock stirred within her.

"I believe you know how to find the bedroom, my lord. Make it up to me."

∾ CHAPTER 22 ∾

The previous evening's rain had given way to a soft, foggy morning. Trees and eaves dripped; Leo's lashes collected moisture that had to be blinked away. Meteor shook his head, and his bit jangled, the sound seemingly muffled by the enveloping cloud.

Leo posted lazily alongside his sister as they made their way down Rotten Row. He'd returned to his parents' house in the predawn hours to find Beau already dressed in her habit and sipping coffee while she pored over the previous day's *Morning Post*.

Beau, in typical fashion, hadn't so much as batted an eyelash. She'd simply blown into her coffee cup and said, "If you change quickly and come riding with me, Mother need never know you've been out carousing like a tom." Then she'd flipped up the paper in a perfect imitation of their father's technique and soundly ignored him.

After a hurried cup of coffee, he'd allowed her to drag him back out for a morning ride. Leo looked around the deserted park. "No assignation, Beau?"

She threw him a saucy glance. "If there were, I certainly wouldn't have invited *you*. I'd have brought Ezekiel, who knows very well how to keep a secret."

"You would have, if you wanted to make a point with the poor man: Giant brother, beware ye who attempt to trespass."

"I've been in town for less than a week. I've hardly had time to set up a flirt. I'm not *you*. Who is she, by the way?" Her voice took on a quick, eager quality. "Everyone seems to know, but no one will tell me."

Leo shook his head. "Good Lord. You haven't been asking people about me, have you?" Her answering laugh told him clearly that she damn well had been. "Are you determined to brand yourself as the fastest thing Scotland has ever produced?"

Beau made a face at him. "Bah. It's not as though I'm the one keeping a mistress—or a mister—or whatever you'd call a male courtesan. Why don't women keep them anyway? It seems dreadfully unfair. And the only person I asked was Sandison." She sounded highly disgruntled. "All he did was threaten to put me over his knee. Besides, even I know Dally the Tall is the fastest thing Scotland's ever produced, including poor Gunpowder here." She gave her horse a conciliatory pat, as though he were aware he was being disparaged.

"Beau, so help me..."

"So help you what, Brother? You'll tell Mother on me? I'm sure she knows by now. You have a mistress, and I'm a lost cause. Augusta was having vapors over something last night, and unless our brother has gambled away her considerable dowry or taken a mistress of his own—

which I'll admit is doubtful—it must be something to do with you."

Augusta. Wonderful. His brother's wife was devilishly high in the instep and prone to excessive displays of morality.

"You needn't sound as if you wished he had."

Beau made a rude sound by way of retort, and Leo couldn't quite bring himself to disagree. What Arthur saw in Augusta he'd never been able to figure out, but they rubbed along happily enough, as three children in four years surely proved. And they did it mostly in Scotland, which was one of the many reasons he chose to make his home here.

"You can tell me now, or I'll ask Charles when he comes to escort Mother and me to the theatre. And you know Charles will tell me, if only to twit you."

Leo's jaw clenched. Meteor gave a disgruntled crow hop, and Leo forced himself to relax. "You're going to be the death of me, brat."

She grinned, clearly aware that she'd won.

"Promise first that you won't bring this up with Mother."

"I promise. Now tell me, is she very beautiful?"

"Yes, very."

"And are you terribly in love with her?"

The word *"yes"* was on the tip of his tongue. His teeth rattled with the force of holding the word back. Dear God, there was a pretty pickle. "She's a widow, and I like her well enough. That's all you need to know."

"Have I met her?"

"No, and you're not likely to do so."

Beau's smile grew, and her eyes took on a roguish look that he knew all too well. "So she's the kind of woman who's lucky enough not to have to behave herself at Almack's or pretend to enjoy herself at Lady Colpepper's soiree or Mrs. Danhurt's Venetian breakfast."

"Beau!"

"Leo!" she parroted back in the same affronted tone. "I'm two-and-twenty. I've been abducted twice and lived to tell—or not to tell rather—the tale. I'm not a *child*."

"Then do stop acting like one," he retorted, at a loss as to how else to respond. Perhaps they should have left her to Granby that last time...if only she hadn't stabbed him. It was rather poor form to force one's sister to marry a man she'd maimed.

"Fine," Beau spat out. "I suppose I'll ask Charles after all." With one last, defiant glare, she urged her gelding into a canter and quickly pulled away from him. The fog swirled about her mount's legs as though he were preter-natural, a creature of legend leaping forth from the pages of one of the tales their grandmother loved.

Leo trotted after her. Rotten Row ended not too much farther along, and she'd have to return momentarily. If he ran her down, he was likely to get her crop across his cheek for his trouble.

Pride swirled within his chest. It was very hard not to love Beau, even when she was behaving poorly and caus-ing scandals. No, he smiled as she reappeared like the queen she was named for, delivered by the mist. It was *because* she behaved outrageously—as he would himself—that he couldn't help loving her.

．　．　．

Charles handed his hat and gloves to his uncle's butler and stepped past him into the hall. Nothing had changed since he'd first come here as a child of four. The same ugly Chinese vase stood on a table beneath a landscape of the Lochmaben ancestral seat in Scotland, a drafty stone pile, part castle, part Jacobean manor house. In the painting, the trees were smaller than he remembered, but otherwise it was an accurate enough representation.

His aunt greeted him with a forced smile, but his cousin Beau leapt up, stormed across the room to kiss his cheek, and dragged him over to sit beside her on the settee. Lady Glennalmond nodded at him over her tambor frame.

Cold bitch. She always had been. She'd made it perfectly clear over the years that she thought him an interloper. He dragged his gaze away from his eldest cousin's wife, turning his attention to Beau.

"Is the dowager not with you?" he asked.

"I most certainly am, Charles dear." He turned to find his grandmother being escorted in on the arm of his cousin Leonidas. His mouth went dry, and he swallowed thickly. Wasn't Leo supposed to be in the country with his slut?

Charles rose to give his place to the dowager, then followed Leo over to the buffet, where his cousin was pouring himself a drink.

"Hello, Cousin." Leo smiled, clearly pleased with himself.

Charles gave him a tight-lipped nod, visions of pounding his cousin's head in dancing just behind his eyes. "I'm surprised to see you tonight," Charles said. "I would have thought you'd be otherwise occupied. It's amazing how dangerous London's become. *Nothing* seems safe anymore."

One side of Leo's mouth quirked up in an overly confident grin. "I know how to take care of what's mine."

Charles nodded again, the need to make a hit, to wipe that smile from his cousin's face, pulsing through him. "But just what is really yours, Cousin? It can be hard to tell sometimes, can't it?"

Leonidas's brow knit, but the martial light didn't leave his eyes. Game and stupid as always, that was Leo.

"It's all over town that Sir Hugo wants her back. Eventually she's going to need an income again, and you're certainly in no position to provide it. She's above your touch, Leo."

The muscle in Leo's jaw popped as he clenched his teeth. Charles smiled, satisfaction buoying him up. A hit. A very palpable hit.

"Unless," Charles added, unable to stop himself, "Mrs. Whedon has already found what we're seeking, and she's really the one doing the keeping. Perhaps I'll have to ask her the next time our paths cross."

"Shall we go?" Lady Glennalmond announced loudly, breaking in upon their tête-à-tête. "If we tarry much longer, we'll be caught in the general press, and I do so hate being mauled by the crowds."

"And Leo, they will cross. I can guarantee it."

Beau laughed and came to take Charles's arm. "Nonsense, Augusta. You simply like to arrive early so you can spy on everyone else as they arrive. Admit it!"

"Must you be so vulgar?" Lady Glennalmond glared

at them all, clearly wishing she weren't forced to associate with them.

Beau's reply was drowned out by Leo. "It's Beau. Of course she must. If only to infuriate you. May I escort you to the coach, my lady?" He held out his free arm and Lady Glennalmond, very much on her dignity, took it.

"Your sister is-is—" Augusta seemed unable to utter whatever horrible term sprang to mind.

"Is none of your damn business, Augusta," the dowager said with a hint of annoyance. "And so I've told you time and again. Content yourself with having soured Glennalmond past all hope."

Charles found himself grinning. Beau giggled softly and gripped his arm. "You'd think my dear sister-in-law would have learned by now not to attempt to remonstrate with me, at least not in front of Grandmama," Beau whispered. "Oh, and that reminds me. I have a question for you. About Leo. Well, about his mistress, really."

Charles glanced down at her. He was not at all loath to enlighten her if it would cause further problems for her brother. "Certainly, Cousin." He put his hand over hers as they descended the stairs.

"Who is she? No one will tell me."

Charles smiled. Beau was like a loaded gun with a hair trigger, liable to go off at any moment and likely to cause all kinds of damage when she did.

"I don't know that I should tell you, dearest."

She gave him a fake pout. "But you're going to."

"Am I?"

"You know you are, Charlie." She grinned up at him, eyes squeezed nearly shut with glee.

"I suppose I am," he agreed, heaving a dramatic sigh for Beau's benefit. Just how many foxes could he fling into this particular henhouse? "I'm a bit worried about poor Leo. You see, he's become entangled with a very mercenary widow, and I very much fear he's going to be wounded when she throws him over..."

❧ CHAPTER 23 ❧

Red lanterns illuminated the walkways and courtyards. Fire, rather than water, filled the fountains. Smoke drifted over the garden in billowing clouds, adding to the atmosphere. Music filled the space, cutting through the trees and drowning out whatever noises might be coming from the darker walks and bowers that filled the grounds.

Leo found himself searching the crowd yet again. Someone was watching him, or someone was watching Viola. He hadn't been able to pinpoint the source, but the sensation was unmistakable. The creeping sense of dread between his shoulder blades was sharp and distinct.

The guest list was exclusive and particular. The cicisbei of The New Female Coterie filled Vauxhall, along with their chosen prey. The women present were made up of the ranks of the fallen, the more elite prostitutes of Covent Garden, and a few heavily masked women who Leo guessed to be of his own class, just incurably curious or licentious.

"It's quite a theme you've picked, my dear."

Viola twinkled up at him from behind her mask. Kohl rimmed her eyes so that they appeared luminescent. "It seemed appropriate. According to most people, it's hell we're all bound for eventually."

"And with inducements like these"—he waved his hand around at the scantily clad women and general debauchery of the evening—"it's likely tonight will strike a few more names from St. Peter's list." And deservedly so. He didn't think of himself as a prude, but revels such as this had never interested him.

Viola chuckled. "No doubt. Shall we see what we can do about securing our place in the afterlife? Or shall we sneak about and take in the sights?"

Leo felt the slightest bit of shock flood from his chest up to his neck and spread onto his cheeks. "What exactly are you suggesting, my dear?"

Her grin widened, and she shrugged one pale shoulder. "All the world's a stage..." She took him by the hand and, laughing, led him into the darkened lanes that crisscrossed the garden. They slipped past other couples with similar goals. Soft cries filled the night, mingling with calls of nightingales and the crackle of the bonfires.

Viola pushed him off the path. His back hit a tree and she dropped to her knees. His cock swelled in anticipation, his heartbeat surging into it. She deftly opened the fall of his breeches and freed his cock from the layers of linen and silk.

Her lips slid over the engorged head, tongue pressing, sliding, teeth ever so faintly riding along the shaft. Her hand gripped the base, thumb working along the bottom edge in time with her mouth.

Leo leaned back against the tree and tried to remember to breathe. She was indecently, decadently, absurdly good with her mouth. So good he couldn't even bring himself to resent whoever had taught her such skill.

He was fairly certain none of the girls he'd find at Almack's would ever match her, no matter how much tutelage he provided, and lucky him, he'd never have to find out. The beauty of being a younger son was that he'd never have to marry to produce an heir. He would never have to bed a virgin and pray she'd welcome his amorous attentions with something more than resignation to duty.

He rested one shaking hand on Viola's head, wanting to touch her but careful not to destroy her coiffure. A soft titter dragged his attention to the path. A couple stood watching. Excitement pulsed through him. He shut his eyes and concentrated on the sensation of Viola's mouth on his flesh.

He'd been well aware that the risk of being caught added spice to such encounters. He didn't need the further knowledge that actually having an audience had its own cache. Suddenly the appeal of an orgy made perfect sense.

It was too dark to know who they were. Too dark for them to know who he and Viola were, thank all that was holy. The rising edge of his release hit, and he opened his eyes again to discover the couple was gone, off no doubt on their own adventure.

Viola took him a tad deeper into her mouth, and his knees nearly gave out. He came with a groan, wanting to shout. She swallowed and sucked again, the sensation almost too much to bear. She released him, then grinned as he dragged her up off her knees.

"My God, woman."

She traced one finger along his slowly deflating cock. "Am I really your god?"

He laughed. "At the moment, most certainly." He adjusted himself and buttoned up his breeches. She cupped him with one teasing, possessive hand.

"Excellent. Your deity would like a drink."

"And then perhaps a blood sacrifice?"

"Perhaps." Viola took a small metal tin from her pocket and held it out to him. "Ginger drop?"

Leo chuckled and took a small candy from the tin. It was sweet and hot on his tongue, not unlike Viola herself. He pulled her close and kissed her. "Are you sure you wouldn't prefer your own pleasures be attended to first?" He slid one hand down her back to cup her bottom.

Viola kissed him back, tongue delving into his mouth to steal the bit of candy she'd just given him. "Most certain. The more time you have to plan, the more delightful the results are likely to be."

Champagne in hand, Leo raked his gaze over the crowd yet again. A pair of unmistakable green eyes caught his attention. The woman was concealed behind an elaborate devil mask, complete with horns and a pointed beard, and enveloped in a red-and-black shot-silk domino, but the eyes were distinct.

When he discovered who had brought his sister to a courtesan's debacle, there was going to be hell to pay, and not simply because it fit the evening's theme. Damn Beau, she was always causing some kind of dustup.

Her presence shot his plans for the rest of the evening

all to flinders. "Dearest." He handed Viola her glass and bent so as not be overheard. "I've a devil of a problem."

Viola sipped her champagne, tipped her head, and gazed up at him with wide, questioning eyes.

"My sister is here." There was no prevaricating. No point to it. He was going to have to desert her among her friends.

She blanched. "Your sister, but—"

"Yes, Beau. Damn her." Leo grimaced.

Viola's hand locked about his forearm. "Where?"

"In the devil mask and shot-silk domino. Trying to hide in the doorway of the rotunda. I'm terribly sorry, but I have to take her home."

Her grip didn't loosen. "Are you mad?" Viola pushed up her mask, tiny golden horns twisting into her curls. "She'll cause a scene if you storm over there."

"And she'll cause a scandal if I don't."

Viola heaved a sigh, bosom straining against her bodice, making him curse Beau anew. "Don't be ridiculous. Let me go."

Before Leo could protest, she was weaving her way through the crowd, ducking past dancers, eluding would-be partners. He kept his eyes on his sister and tried to pick her escort from the crowd.

Viola pushed past a paunchy priest and shooed away a grinning Lord Harrington, whose only concession to his wife's party was a pair of horns rising from his balding pate.

As she reached the rotunda, it became clear to him that whoever had brought his sister, the bastard was nowhere to be found at that particular moment. She was quite alone. Marooned in the middle of a party she hadn't the slightest excuse to be attending.

"Mrs. Dalrymple!" Viola called out loudly enough for even him to hear. "We thought you in Paris. Is red the new style of toupee there? Very fetching."

His sister stood transfixed. Viola linked arms with her and pulled her out of the rotunda and into the crowd. Beau said something, clearly trying to release herself from Viola's grip.

"Yes, yes. Back from Paris. So very good to see you again." Viola propelled her through the dancers. "No, no, Lord Harrington. I've been looking for Grace all night, and so has Lady Worsley. We're off to find her now."

Beau stiffened as they approached the edge of the crowd and she spotted him waiting. Viola forced her over the last few feet until they were beside him. "Mrs. Dalrymple, may I present Lord Leonidas. He's been eager to make your acquaintance all evening."

Leo bowed, grateful that Viola had set the ruse in motion, and his sister dropped him a stilted curtsy in return. "Shall we stroll, ladies?" He offered them both an arm, and the three of them set off in a wide circle toward the entrance.

"How dare you, Leo." Beau's hushed whisper was laced with anger, possibly with mortification. Good, she ought to be mortified.

"How dare *I*?" He quickened his pace, dragging them both along past the stream of gaudily attired revelers making their way to and from Vauxhall.

Leo handed his sister and Viola into one of the small boats at the end of the Vauxhall stairs and leapt in after them. The waterman pushed off with a jolly shout. Leo crossed his arms and ground his teeth.

"You had no right—"

"Not a word until we get home, *Mrs. Dalrymple.*"

Beau glared at him, then turned her head to stare haughtily across the water. Viola fairly curled into herself beside him, shrinking under the blaze of anger that flickered between him and his unrepentant sister.

At the White Hall Stairs, Leo hailed a hackney, and as soon as they were inside, the shouting began.

"You'd no right! No right at all." Beau ripped off her mask and threw herself back into the corner. Her hair tumbled down, pins scattering unheeded in all directions.

Leo took a deep breath, and then another. "You've been indulged beyond all reason, Beau. But this is too much even for you. Who brought you?"

She glared at him, mouth set in a mulish frown.

"Damn it, Beau. No one who meant you any good would have consented to bring you to a damn courtesan's ball. Who brought you? Palmer? Richardson?" Leo tossed his own mask onto the floor of the cab and raked his hand through his hair. "Maybe Glennalmond was right. Maybe we should have left you to Granby."

Her head snapped up, chin rising as though he'd stuck her. Leo leaned forward. Beau had to understand. Had to be made to understand if her own innate sense of self-preservation was really so utterly lacking. "You're going to reach a place where no one will have you. Where there will be no saving you. Martin and Granby weren't your fault, but this—tonight—this was, darling."

"You don't know anything about it."

"I know whoever brought you wasn't anywhere to be found just now. I know you could be looking at complete ruin right now, at a scandal the likes of which you've never even imagined."

Beau's breath caught on a sob.

"That's enough, my lord." Viola's sudden interjection startled him. "Don't look at me as though you'd like to wring my neck. You're going to make her hysterical, and that will attract exactly the kind of attention you've been attempting to avoid. Once you get her home, you can yell until you shake the slates off the roof, but for now, let her be."

"This doesn't concern you, Mrs. Whedon."

"And I'll be happy enough to be left out of it, *Lord Leonidas*. But at this exact moment, I find myself quite decidedly in the middle of it all, and neither of you is coming off at all well, I'll have you know."

Leo cursed under his breath. Now they were both glaring at him. His evening was rapidly going from bad to worse, and if he couldn't get Beau home without his mother finding out what she'd been up to—or, God forbid, Augusta!—it was likely to get worse yet.

~ CHAPTER 24 ~

Viola ushered her lover's very angry sister into her bedroom and pushed her down into the chair at her dressing table. "Dry your eyes, repair your hair, powder your face, and remove that domino."

Lady Boudicea met her gaze in the slightly tarnished mirror. The poor girl's powder was streaked with tears, the blackening she'd used on her lashes liberally mixed in and running down her cheeks. Viola set a hand on her shoulder, but Leo's sister shook it off.

"He's angry only because he cares," Viola said, "and you should be happy that he does. Not all of us are so lucky."

Pen yawned from the settee Viola had moved into her chamber for her use, and returned to snoring. Viola set out the various things Leo's sister would need to set herself to rights and then left her alone. She'd calm down sooner if left to her own devices. Being badgered or comforted would only prolong things.

Downstairs, she found Lord Leonidas, brandy glass in

hand, staring moodily into the cold grate. He looked up as she came in and tossed back the contents of his glass. He was still stiff with repressed anger, every movement sharp.

"She'll be ready to go in a few minutes."

Leo nodded and wandered across the room to refill his glass. He drained it and filled it again.

Viola sighed. His temper was like a mad dog circling the room. She crossed the floor and took the glass from his hand. She took a sip and wandered back to the chairs that flanked the fireplace.

"Damnation, Vi, she's got to learn. She's got to—" The decanter exploded in the fireplace. Glass and brandy showered across her skirts. "Oh God, Vi. I'm—"

"Drunk and angry and behaving like an ass." She stood up and shook out her skirts. Bits of glass flew out like birds startled from a tree. Her own temper spiraled up, threatening to swamp her better judgment. "Whatever you do, don't come back here until you've mended that temper of yours, my lord. The world may think I'm your mistress, but I'm not being paid to put up with your distempered freaks."

"No, I suppose you're not."

He was staring at her as if he'd never seen her before. A shiver ran down her spine. He looked as though he could quite happily murder her.

The quick patter of feet on the stairs was a welcome interruption. Viola raked her gaze over Leo, shook her head in disgust, and hastened into the hall to find Lady Boudicea standing on the stairs, looking somewhat bewildered but otherwise restored to respectable order.

The girl swallowed, throat working as though raw. "I'm sorry to have put you to so much trouble, ma'am."

"No trouble at all, my dear."

Leo pushed his way into the small hall, and his sister seemed to shrink. She didn't actually flinch, but it was as though Viola could see the girl's spirit crumble away.

Viola put a hand on her arm. "Just remember, not everyone gets a second chance."

"Or a third or a fourth. Which is it now, Beau? How many times have you been snatched from the jaws of scandal?"

Lady Boudicea's chin went up, her expression hardened. She looked very much as her brother had only a few minutes previously. "This would make three," she replied with a hint of defiance.

"Then let's see there's not a fourth, shall we?"

"Sometimes I hate you." Her hands balled into fists, crushing her skirts.

"Sometimes I hate myself."

His sister stepped carefully over the tread they all knew squeaked, skirts carefully held up so she wouldn't risk tripping over them. Leo did likewise, shoes clutched in one hand. They reached her room without waking anyone, and she dragged him inside.

"Leo?" Though she had washed her face, there was still a smudge of kohl along her jaw. He rubbed it away with his thumb, his anger nothing but ash now that she was safely home.

"Go to bed, brat."

Beau bit her lip, eyes dropping to the floor. "I wasn't being so very bad tonight. I swear."

Leo sighed. Beau always had an excuse.

"It was a lark. Nothing more. I wanted to see Mrs. Whedon, and Charles said she'd be there tonight."

Leo's mouth went dry, tongue desiccated to the point of immobility. A strange buzzing filled his ears.

"But when we got there, we got separated in the crowd. And then I couldn't find him..."

The buzzing grew louder, and a sick, panicked feeling swamped him. He'd never imagined Charles would hurt Beau. Him, yes. Viola, yes. But not Beau. It was his fault. His alone. Beau had every right to trust her cousin, every reason to do so. But not anymore. "I'm so sorry, Beau."

Beau's expression changed, the penitent look wiped away by dawning anger. "Are you telling me Charles left me there deliberately? He wouldn't."

"I wouldn't have thought so either, dearest, but he did just that, and I'm afraid he did it because of me."

"No, Leo. Charles wouldn't do that. Not to me. Not because of some stupid fight with you."

The sick feeling in his gut grew stronger. How did you tell someone that a man she'd known her entire life had used her as a pawn in a game that had nothing to do with her?

"Change into your dressing gown and come downstairs. I'll explain everything, or I'll try to do so, at any rate."

Leo slipped down the hall to his own room and ripped off his coat. He was about to break his sister's heart, and all over what appeared to be a nonexistent treasure. He wished to God he'd never found those damn letters, had never shared them with Charles.

When Beau joined him in the drawing room, she was attired in a lawn dressing gown, with her hair neatly braided and her face scrubbed clean. Just as though she'd never left the house that night but had slipped from bed upon hearing him come home.

He poured them both a drink and claimed a seat beside her. Beau blinked at him and sipped at her brandy. Leo raked his hand through his hair and shook it loose from its queue. His scalp tingled almost painfully.

"What do you remember about Grandfather? About his tales of the family and the forty-five?"

Beau cocked her head. "The same things you remember, I'd guess: family and friendship splintered by the war, his guilt over the ruin of Charles's family…"

"The prince's treasure?"

Her eyes widened.

"It's real, Beau. Or at least it was at the time. I found an extended correspondence detailing it at Dyrham."

"First you accuse Charles and now Grandfather? Leo!" She shook her head, hair falling to hide her face.

"No. Good Lord, no. Not Grandfather. Mr. Black, whom he bought Dyrham from, seems to have been deeply involved. And Grandfather's guilt would explain why he bought it—a small, random estate, hundreds of miles from the family seat. He did it so his friend could leave the country before his complicity was found out."

"And the treasure?"

"The letters trace it back to a house in London and no further. We all know it never reached the prince, and though it may have been stolen by whoever had charge of it when Bonnie Prince Charlie fled, Mr. Black's letters indicate otherwise. There's an extended argument about its disposition. Mr. Black arguing for their right to take it; Mr. Connall that they must keep it in trust for the prince, something about leaving it hidden and trusting it to Mr. Thaddeus. Devil knows who that is, for there are no letters from him at all."

"And you think Mr. Connall won?"

"Yes, but only because Mr. Black was forced to flee the country. There's evidence that Mr. Connall did as well. And though I can't prove anything, my gut tells me it's still where Mr. Connall left it."

She raised her brows.

"In number twelve Chapel Street."

"And Mrs. Whedon knows you're looking for it?"

His expression must have told her the answer, though he could have sworn not so much as a muscle twitched or moved.

"Oh, Leo." The look of pity on his sister's face nearly broke him. "She's never going to forgive you."

No, she wasn't, and he was going to have to tell her. It was becoming inevitable. She had to be on her guard, and the excuse of Sir Hugo had been played out.

"And the devil of it is, Beau, I can't find it. And Charles won't believe me."

"I still don't understand. What has this got to do with me?"

"Nothing, except that Charles will do whatever it takes to hobble me, and ruining you would certainly cause me grief. You know Charles's temper. When he works himself up into one of his rages...He wants this, wants it badly, and he's willing to sacrifice whatever it takes to get it. And that includes you."

"It's monstrous. I'd say you were making it up—I *want* to say you're making it up!—but you're not, are you?"

She twisted her empty glass in her fingers. For the second time that evening, her eyes welled up, but this wasn't the angry histrionics of the coach. This was far worse. Something vital had been crushed right out of her.

"I don't think I stand it, Leo."

"Don't you think I understand? Charles always felt more like a brother than Glennalmond, and now…" He let the statement hang in the air. What else was there to say? Their cousin had become a monster.

"So, no treasure, and now your cousin is willing to sacrifice Lady Boudicea on the altar of his ambition?" Sandison, expression somber for once, met Leo's gaze with a look of concern that Leo frankly hadn't been sure his friend was capable of. "You are in a pickle, my friend."

Leo sank lower in his chair, foot propped against the leg of the table. "I'd be willing to let him have the damn treasure at this point, except I don't think it exists."

"Not that MacDonald will ever believe that." Devere leaned forward, propping his chin on his hand, clearly thinking. "Hell, I don't believe it myself, and I've searched that house from cellar to garret."

"We did find an empty safe." Thane's voice rumbled across the table.

"And a secret stair that leads from the main bedchamber up to one of the servant's rooms." Sandison waggled his eyebrows suggestively. "Very handy for some."

"And now you have the additional problem of keeping not only Mrs. Whedon safe from your cousin but your sister and possibly the rest of your family, too." Thane's expression was pinched with irritation.

"Charles isn't fool enough to threaten my mother. At least I don't think he is, and Beau is wise to the game now. But I'd take it as a kindness if you could all keep your eye on her."

Thane nodded, but Devere and Sandison both smiled. "Are you actually giving us permission to dance attendance on your sister?" Devere asked.

Leo narrowed his eyes at them. "Within reason."

"Better the wolves you know…" Sandison added, still grinning.

"Something like that," Leo agreed. "If only it were so easy with Mrs. Whedon."

"Well, it would be if you'd been honest with her from the start." Thane's comment dropped into the circle with the explosive power of a mortar. "You'd have been able to search with impunity. But you were greedy. And foolish. And now it's too late, and if anything happens to her, it's on your head."

The same sickening feeling he'd had when talking to his sister took up residence once more in his gut. Confessing to Viola was going to be a thousand times worse. He'd been hoping his friends might have some other suggestion.

"But if you tell her, she's likely to show you the door."

"And replace you with Throckmorton."

"Or Darnley."

"Or any of the other dozen or so men who're panting to take your place."

Leo blinked as his friends all chimed in like the chorus in a Greek tragedy. "The dozen or so who're what?"

Sandison rolled his eyes in disgust. "She'd retired to write her memoir. Now she's back in the game. There are bets in every book in town as to when she'll throw you over."

"You're not exactly in her normal line, you know," Devere added helpfully. "Not nearly wealthy enough. None of us are. Well"—he paused as he thought about it—"maybe de Moulines. Bastard or no, his father left him quite a tidy fortune."

"Are you joking?"

"Not at all." Sandison knocked back the last of his ale and set his empty glass down hard enough to make it ring. "Even some of her former protectors are keen to reenter the lists. And wouldn't that complicate things?"

❧ CHAPTER 25 ❧

The sequins on Lord Sudbury's waistcoat shimmered as he stood and took her hand. Viola forced a smile. The earl's visit had come on top of several posies from various gentlemen and the mysterious arrival of a pair of gold bangles in the shape of twisting serpents. The gentlemen of the *ton* had clearly decided she was once more on the menu.

Two months ago, she might have jumped at an offer as magnificent as the one he'd just made her. She'd certainly never had such generous terms laid at her feet by any other man. Today she found herself wanting to weep instead.

"I assure you, my lord, should I find myself in the market for a protector, I'll keep your offer very much in mind."

"See that you do, my dear. And mind, I'll best whatever Throckmorton offers you."

"What has Throckmorton offered?" Leo's question startled her into yanking her hand from the earl's. She scrambled to her feet, wiping her hand on her skirt. She had nothing to feel guilty about. Nothing, but her heart was hammering like that of a hare with a hound in fast pursuit.

"My lord, I wasn't expecting you."

"So I see." Leo spoke to her, but his gaze never left the earl.

The earl chuckled to himself and pulled his gloves from his pocket. He slipped them on and wiggled his fingers. "I'll leave you two children to enjoy your spat. I think I'm late meeting my wife at Drury Lane, and explanations can be so tedious. It's best to make them unnecessary, in my experience."

The older man strolled past Lord Leonidas, amusement trailing in his wake. He'd tossed his barb, and it had struck most effectively, judging by the deep furrow between Leo's brows. The sound of the door closing behind him made her jump. Leo flicked his glance over her, eyes as cold as rumor always made them out to be. She'd been beginning to think his reputation in error, but clearly she'd simply never been on the receiving end of one of his snubs. A muscle jumped in his jaw.

She stared him down, holding his gaze as though she could prevent whatever eruption was building inside him by sheer force of will. She'd had nothing to do with the earl's visit, but she'd already heard from Lady Worsley that Mayfair was thick with gossip about her supposed efforts to replace Leo. Judging by his expression, he'd eaten the same scandal broth for luncheon.

And he'd believed it. Her rapid heartbeat stuttered, skipping a beat. She'd thought better of him, or at least she'd trusted him to trust her.

"Shopping for my replacement?" Leo glanced around

the room, taking in the flowers, his eyes finally locking onto the shagreen box on the mantel that contained the bracelets. Such very expensive bracelets, too...

"And if I were, what business would that be of yours, my lord?"

"None at all, I suppose." He wandered slowly across the room, stopping to read cards propped up near the flowers. "Darnley, Throckmorton, and Everesley. And Sudbury on top of them all. Quite a triumph for you."

Viola swallowed hard and turned slowly to face him as he continued his slow approach to the mantel. It felt unsafe to give him her back as he prowled through the room. "Sir Hugo as well. I find I'm suddenly in fashion once again, after having brought you to heel."

He laughed at that, shooting her a look that promised trouble. His blue eye seemed amused, but his green one, ah, his green one was ever the one to watch. He trailed his fingers along the mantel, tapped the shagreen box, then picked it up.

"Very pretty." He studied the bracelets, then clicked the box shut. "Very pretty and very expensive. Throckmorton, I suppose?"

"I haven't the slightest idea." His eyes snapped up, meeting hers. "There was no card," Viola added, twisting the knife.

"Well, someone's feeling generous," Leo drawled, tone as cold as his eyes. "I wonder what for?"

Jealousy swamped him, the tide rising up to choke him. The sting of her hand across his cheek caught him off guard. He grabbed her by the arm and held her fast.

"You're hurting me, my lord."

Viola was panting with fury, but she made no effort to shake off his hold. Her breasts strained against the confinement of her gown. Her tongue darted out to moisten her parted lips. She was as beautiful as ever, and it was killing him.

"Tell me, Mrs. Whedon, am I a fool?" He knew he was. He'd come today with every intention of making a clean breast of things. He'd come with plans to make amends, with every intention of groveling, if need be.

She pulled back. Leo tightened his grip.

"Am I?"

Her eyes narrowed, lashes obscuring the vivid blue. Her nostrils flared. "No more than any other man, my lord."

He let his breath out in a rush and pushed her away from him. If he kept touching her, he was going to either kiss her or throttle her. Viola stumbled and caught herself against the mantel.

"Then how is it that I thought I loved you?"

She went white, then her cheeks flooded with color. "Get out."

"It's not that simple." If only it were. If only he could leave her to Charles with a clean conscience. If only he'd never set this entire disaster into motion in the first place.

She took a long, strangled breath, hands flexing with suppressed rage. A man would have found a violent outlet for such an emotion. Hell, Beau would have reached for a candlestick and beaten him senseless.

"Then make it that simple. My manuscript has been

safely delivered. You've seduced your way into my bed just as you said you would. What's left to do?"

"Vi, I'm—"

"You're what, my lord? You're sorry? You're sorry you caught me playing the whore, or you're sorry I am one? Whichever it is, you're certainly not in love with me." She laughed, even as she blinked back tears. "Give each thing its proper name. If I'm to return to *whore,* then this is lust. You want me. Even now, when it makes you sick to look at me. You want me."

Leo stared at her. Heaven knew he wanted her. That had never been in doubt. From the first moment, when she'd come tumbling down the stairs, to now, his desire had never flagged. And the only thing that made him sick was himself. His damnable temper had taken the bit between its teeth and run away with him again, and this time he couldn't blame Beau, or even Charles.

Viola closed the distance between them, pressed close, breasts against his chest, lips offered for a kiss, hand tracing his cock as it surged to life. "And that makes it all the worse, doesn't it? Wanting something you so obviously shouldn't. So you can fuck me or you can leave, but believe me when I tell you, I know what it is to love, to be loved, and whatever this is"—she brushed her lips over his—"it isn't love."

She dragged him down to sprawl across the carpet, pulled him over her, skirts riding about her waist, thighs gripping his hips. She bit his lip, scraped her teeth along his jaw, fisted her hand in his hair and pulled hard enough to make his eyes water.

Leo kissed her, teeth clashing with hers. He fumbled

with his breeches, freed his cock, and thrust it into her. She made a whimpering sound, but her legs locked around him and she arched beneath him.

She caught his earlobe between her teeth. "You see, simple lust."

He pinned her to the floor, and she clung tighter. She was wrong. There was nothing simple about it, and it complicated everything.

Viola gasped and twisted beneath him. He thrust and rocked and covered her mouth with his own when she tried to speak again. She bucked and throbbed with her release. He spiraled down to oblivion with his own, brought back by her pushing him off her.

Leo blinked in confusion as she stood and shook out her skirts. "Now get out."

She took a step, and he latched onto her skirt with one desperate hand. Threads popped as she was brought up short. He always did make bad worse. It was a talent. A curse. But if he could just stop her from leaving, if she would pause only long enough for him to explain.

Eyes blazing, Viola grabbed the fabric with both hands and yanked it out of his grasp. When he reached for her again, she kicked him and strode out of the room as he shook his stinging hand.

Her voice carried back from the hall, instructing his own footman that he'd be leaving and she wasn't at home, should Leo call again. Leo sat up and cursed aloud. Regret burned through his lungs, ate away at his heart.

He'd made a bloody hash of things, and now she hated him.

What the hell was he going to do?

• • •

The hiss of steel momentarily drowned out all other sound. Leo struck de Moulines in the ribs with enough force to bend the delicate blade into an arch.

"Deux!" The Frenchman took a step back and dropped his foil to a resting position. He brought it back up, the flash of teeth behind his mask distinct. *"Très bon!* Something has lit the fire in your blood today."

Leo nodded and surged forward. His breath was warm within the confines of his mask, and blood pounded in his ears. Their blades kissed and hissed with every parry. In its own way, swordplay was every bit as intimate as sex. Though with blunted tips, it was far less dangerous.

De Moulines took a tactical step back, and Leo lunged forward. The tip of his foil drove hard into the other man's shoulder.

"Trois."

A small flurry of applause went up, and Leo realized with horror that most of the men in Angello's *salle* had stopped to watch their bout. De Moulines swept off his mask. His dark skin shone against the white of his shirt and teeth.

"Again?" The Frenchman's smile widened.

He loved finding someone to test his mettle, but today Leo simply wasn't that man. He shook his head. This had been a bad idea. Winning his first bout against the chevalier should have felt wonderful; instead, his chest ached as though he might cry.

De Moulines clapped him on the shoulder. "Me, I know that look. Come and have a drink, my friend."

Returned to fashionable splendor, de Moulines led him

into The Red Lion. A few of their fellows were dicing in the corner, but otherwise the taproom was nearly empty. Leo called for wine and threw himself down at the table the Frenchman had chosen.

"So," de Moulines said, swirling the wine in his glass, then inhaled before taking a sip. "What has the divine Mrs. Whedon done to turn you into a—what do you English call it?—a fire-drinker?"

"Eater. A fire-eater." Leo drained his glass and poured himself another. "It's what *I've* done."

The Frenchman's mouth curled up at one corner. "Gone and told her the truth, have you? A very bad idea. Me, I tell you so, no?"

Leo shook his head. "My blasted temper. I never got round to telling her the truth . . ."

His friend sipped his wine, offering nothing. Leo took another desperate gulp of his own and told him everything, or at least enough to make the scope of the disaster clear.

"Are you a- a- a—" De Moulines's eyes wandered about the ceiling as he searched for the proper word in English.

"An idiot? A simpleton? A madman? Yes."

"A simpleton. *Oui.* That will do to a nicety." He caught his lips between his teeth. "She doesn't hate you, *mon ami.* Far from it. Sometimes you English are so very, well, *English.*"

"I'm a Scot."

De Moulines waved away his objection. "Bah, your temper, that is Scottish, but this oh-so-droll inability to grasp what the lady is telling you? Very English. *Je vous assure.*"

⚜ CHAPTER 26 ⚜

Viola accepted a glass of sherry from Lady Harrington and sipped it while the excited chatter of her friends washed over her. At her feet, Pen lay panting softly as Lady Grosvenor's pug excitedly groomed the larger dog's ear.

"No word from Lord Leonidas?" Lady Ligonier said softly enough that everyone else continued to listen to Mrs. Newton's tale of her latest conquest.

Viola shook her head. It had been three days since her row with Lord Leonidas, and true to her command, he had not returned. "Not so much as a posy of flowers, though his footmen continue to arrive with clockwork regularity."

Her friend nodded. "He's giving you time to miss him, savvy devil that he is. And it's working, too, from the wan look of you. Do you really want him back?"

Viola felt the tightness in her chest increase, and her eyes welled up. She blinked rapidly to clear them. "Much as I know I should be happy to be shot of him, I don't feel happy about it."

"Then do something about it," Lady Harrington said from across the room. "You girls give me the bellyache sometime. In my day, we weren't too proud or too miss-ish to go after what we wanted."

Lady Ligonier clapped her hand over her mouth, cutting off a giggle like a child caught misbehaving by her governess.

"And take Penelope there with you. The two of you should be more than capable of formulating a plan of attack."

The countess gave them a dismissive wave of her hand and turned her attention back to Lady Grosvenor. Lady Ligonier stood and dragged Viola up from the settee. "Let's go before she decides she wants the details of our plan."

Viola followed her friend out to the hall where they donned their hats and gloves. Pen shuffled out after them, the pug following until Lady Grosvenor called it back.

At the bottom of the steps, Lady Ligonier linked arms with her, and together they set off down the street with Pen and one of Leo's footmen trailing behind them. A coach rolled past them, the team mincing in their traces.

The footman's oath and Pen's growl brought Viola's attention sharply around. The former soldier was struggling with two men in ill-fitting coats. Pen leapt into the fray, her bay startling one of the men into loosening his grip on the footman.

Hands caught her from behind. Lady Ligonier screamed, clinging to Viola. The man tore them apart, sending Penelope crashing to the ground, and dragged Viola into the coach.

The stench of dirt and horse droppings and sweat rolled off the man pinning her to the seat. One hand gripped her wrist till the bones ground against one another; the other hand clamped over her mouth.

Shouts and oaths broke out as the coach rumbled into motion. Her friend's cries for help faded away as the coach rumbled down the street.

"Cooper, Mrs. Whedon isn't going anywhere. You can let go of her now."

The hand left her mouth, and her hands were suddenly free. Viola wiped her lips with the back of her glove, her stomach roiling in protest.

The man with the silky voice wore a coat that fit him to perfection. A sliver of sunlight cut past the curtain and slid across him, flashing off his coat's spangled buttons. And what a coat. Blue leopard-spotted velvet. It was hideous. His easy demeanor seemed entirely out of place with abducting women off the streets and spoke just as eloquently of malice as his coat did of dandyish aspersions.

In the dimness of the coach, Viola could make out that he was not young, certainly in his forties, if not a bit older. She knew with certainty that she'd never seen him before. She pushed back into the squabs, not wanting to touch him or his servant.

Panic seized her lungs and squeezed her heart. There was no air in the coach, just the stench of the stables and the heavy scent of the gentleman's cologne. It was impossible to draw a full breath without choking.

The stranger smiled, and her skin broke out in gooseflesh. "I wouldn't advise it. If you scream, Cooper here has my permission to silence you however he sees fit.

That's right, my dear, sit quietly and behave yourself. You'll live longer."

A commotion in the hall caught Leo's attention. The clear sound of the butler's raised voice preceded the door being thrown open. His sister looked up from the paper and turned her head toward the door.

Lady Ligonier, hat missing, hair wild, with her gown muddied and torn, shoved past the glowering butler. The older man shut the door behind him with a disapproving snap. Leo's pulse jumped. Something was terribly wrong. "My lord, your cousin has—" She glanced at Beau, her words ending abruptly.

"I rather think Lady Boudicea will survive hearing Mrs. Whedon's name spoken in our mother's breakfast parlor."

Lady Ligonier glared at him. "Very well. Your damn cousin has taken Mrs. Whedon, my lord. And I want to know what you're going to do about it."

"Did you actually see him?" Beau asked. The paper had fallen from her hands, one corner drooping into her coffee, the wet stain rapidly wicking across the page.

"His face? No, my lady." Lady Ligonier smoothed her hair back and squared her shoulders. "But the man inside the coach was wearing a blue leopard-spotted coat. It couldn't have been anyone else."

His sister drew a sharp breath. Charles was inordinately proud of that coat. He'd bought it in Paris just before their grandfather died. Just like him to spurn something more nondescript.

"Did you see where they took her?"

Lady Ligonier shook her head. "No, but your footman and Viola's dog gave chase. He said to tell you to wait for him at The Red Lion."

"Thank you, my lady. Beau, can see that a hack is fetched to carry Lady Ligonier home?"

Leo dropped a quick kiss on his sister's brow and raced upstairs to don his coat and boots. He'd have to send footmen racing all over town if he had any hope of rounding up the League.

Leo reached The Red Lion to find Sandison and Thane already awaiting them. Devere and de Moulines arrived on his heels. Other League members, their morning coffee disrupted, pricked up their ears at the obvious signs of action.

His father's footman erupted through the door, his wig clutched in his hand. He was breathing hard, sweat glistening off his dark skin, soaking his wilted collar. One stocking was down around his ankle, and his lip was swollen and bloody.

"Do you know where he's taken Mrs. Whedon, Ezekiel?"

The footman nodded. "Followed them all the way past Denmark Street, my lord. Me and the dog both. Left her there tearing into the front door like a demon possessed."

"How many men did Charles have?"

"I saw only the one, but there could have been more inside."

"Even if he does, we'll have surprise on our side."

"Or so you hope," Devere said, not looking up from the pistol he was busy loading.

∾ CHAPTER 27 ∾

V iola's head rocked back as the gaudily dressed gentleman's lackey backhanded her across the face. She tested her teeth with her tongue, relieved to find they were all still there. Blood pooled in her mouth. She spat onto the already filthy floor of the garret room where they'd taken her.

"Cooper!" The gentleman's tone was full of reproach, but his mouth was fighting an unmistakable smile. Viola shoved her hair back and held the man's gaze. "No need to begin quite so roughly. Help Mrs. Whedon to a chair."

Her hands shook as Cooper half dragged her across the room. A single wooden chair with a broken stretcher sagged beside a grimy window. She fell heavily into the chair, and it creaked alarmingly. *No need to begin quite so roughly,* but clearly every intention of getting there eventually.

"Now, my dear, a few simple answers and you can go home."

The promise rang patently false, but her pulse raced

all the same. The man's eyes weren't merely cold; they were flat. She was a thing when he looked at her, not a person. A thing to be broken and disposed of.

No matter what his questions were or what answers she gave, there was very little chance she'd ever leave this room alive, and they both knew it. The best she could hope for was a delayed sentence while she became Cooper's plaything.

"How much has my cousin told you about the *prince's treasure*?" He twirled his quizzing glass in idle circles, watching the refracted light play across the wall like a child with a cut crystal making rainbows in the nursery.

Viola shook her head, mind racing. The man's brows rose. He tipped his head as he studied her, eyes tracing over her impersonally. "Cooper?"

The servant's open hand across her face knocked her from the chair. "I had hoped you'd be reasonable about this, Mrs. Whedon. I've no desire to see a woman hurt, not even a whore."

Viola climbed shakily to her feet. If she stayed on the floor, Cooper's next blow might be with his foot, and she was fairly certain he'd break a bone if he kicked her. In the distance, a church bell rang and a dog barked furiously.

"I don't know anything about a prince, or a treasure. I don't even know who your cousin is."

The man laughed. "Ah, I've been too precipitate. My apologies. The cousin in question is Leonidas Vaughn, and the treasure was sent by the King of France to support Bonnie Prince Charlie's bid to unseat the Hanoverian usurpers."

"And what does that have to do with me?" Blood trick-led out her nose, tracing a searing path across her lips. She wiped it away with her hand. She stared at the dark stain on the yellow kidskin of her glove and shuddered.

"With you? Why everything, my dear. You have it."

Viola sucked in a breath and wiped her nose again. The gloves were new, but she was very likely going to die today. Her gloves didn't matter. She should be terrified, but there was no room for such an emotion. Anger filled her, welling up inside her until she was choking on it. She flexed her hands. She could rip out the man's eyes, but she'd never make it to the door.

"I might be brought round to believing you don't *know* you have it."

She flattened her hands across her stomach, pressing in against her stays, trying to stanch the urge to vomit. Her stays were suddenly too tight, and they seemed to be getting tighter by the moment.

"Lord Leonidas has never mentioned it to me."

"Would that I could believe you." He nodded, and the lurking Cooper sent her sprawling onto the floor again. The kick that followed threw her hard against the wall. She retched, stomach muscles fighting hard against can-vas and whalebone.

Leo's cousin took a step toward her. Light flashed off the paste buckles on his shoes. He knelt down, knee beside her head, hand forcing her down hard against the floor.

"The evidence is irrefutable." The musk of his cologne washed over her as he leaned in closer. "The money is— or was—hidden somewhere in your house. Leo dragged you off to the hinterlands while his friends searched

your house—oh yes, don't look so surprised, my dear.
I watched them do it!—and then your relationship ends
most abruptly when you return to town. So, we find ourselves with a few possibilities. Either Leo found it and no
longer needs you. Or he told you about it, and you decided
you no longer need him. Or, my favorite option of all, you
already have it. For your sake, I sincerely hope it's one of
the latter."

Viola shook her head. "I broke it off. Didn't know anything about the treasure."

His eyes narrowed. "Unlikely, a woman of your sort
throwing away a duke's son."

"A younger son." She tried to sound as dismissive as
possible. Whatever this man's issues with Leo, jealousy
was right at the forefront. She could almost smell it. It
wafted off him as thickly as the horrible musk he doused
himself in. "Throckmorton has more to offer."

"And that's what it's all about, isn't it? Who has the
most to offer. Right now, I'd say that was me."

He thrust his hand into her hair and held her tight.
Viola stiffened and tried to jerk away. His grip tightened
until she could feel hairs being ripped from her scalp one
by one.

"You really don't know. Damnation!"

He tossed her away from him and stood in one quick
motion, the skirts of his coat flying out over her head like
the wings of a predatory bird. He paced across the room,
worrying at his gloved thumb with his teeth.

"Letter." Viola choked on the word.

"So he did show them to you?" The man's smile of
relief sent another chill through her.

"No." She swallowed, tasting blood. "I could write you one. Tell my servants to give you free rein to search the house yourself."

"I've already searched your house. There's nothing there, which means Leo has it. I wonder what you're worth to him?"

The door shook on its hinges, the frame flexing and bulging. An unholy baying leaked past it, and Viola found herself smiling, though it hurt to do so. She knew that bark. The only thing between her, the door, and Pen were two men who had no idea what was about to befall them.

The dog hit the door again. Leo's cousin took a step backward, drawing a pistol from the pocket of his coat. Viola pushed herself up from the floor, lifted the chair, and swung for his head. It connected with the satisfying sound of wood splintering, and he went sprawling, the gun skittering across the room.

The door gave way with what sounded to Viola like the annunciation of angels—the full-throated growl of one very angry mastiff. Pen launched herself at Cooper, her snarls drowned out by the man's screams as she knocked him to the ground.

Leo's cousin scrambled for the gun, then raced toward her. "You bitch." He caught her by the arm, fingers digging into her.

The open doorway spilled forth a steady stream of men: Leo at the fore, a disheveled and unshaven Sandison at his shoulder, other faces both familiar and unknown all around them. The tide pushed them forward, propelled them inexorably into the room. Her captor's grip tightened momentarily; then he flung her aside.

Pen took a swipe at one of his cousin's henchmen, leaving a bloody bite on his thigh. As she raced to Viola, the League surged in behind Leo, grim determination radiating off them in a palpable wave. Charles met his gaze unflinchingly. No apology, no plea, just a haze of anger and hate leaking out his eyes, hot as the blast from a blacksmith's furnace.

How had they come to this? A year ago, he'd have killed to protect his cousin, and today it was likely he was going to kill him himself. There wasn't any other way out. Charles raised his gun, thumb cocking the hammer in one fluid motion. The deafening report of multiple shots concussed the air, clouding it with smoke. The burning scent of sulfur curled up his nostrils like the stench of the Thames in August.

Leo dropped his pistol, the dull thud as it hit the floor nearly lost in the shuffling clamor of his friends, his cousin's strained moan, and the sound of Pen growling deep in her throat as Devere and Sandison subdued the man she'd bitten.

His cousin lay crumpled on the floor, bent over, barely moving. Charles had given him no choice—would have left him in the same condition, had he been a better shot—but Leo's mouth was filled with the acrid taste of guilt all the same. The choice had been clear: Viola or Charles. But that wasn't to say it had been simple.

How could it be? Love or family. How to choose? How to live with the choice he'd made . . .

The sudden silence that enveloped the room felt almost unnatural, fraught with tension, like the pregnant moment between a lightning strike and the inevitable clap of thunder. A floorboard creaked behind him, and the world whirled back into motion. De Moulines was kneeling beside his cousin, Thane was giving orders in a low rumble, and Viola was sobbing on the floor, arms wrapped around a panting, smiling, blood-drenched dog.

~€ CHAPTER 28 ❧~

Bruises flushed to life as Viola slid into the bath. She hissed and forced more of her battered body into the steaming water. After the grandeur of the bath at Dyrham, a wooden tub in her room seemed almost a punishment.

Nance approached with a sponge, and Viola waved her away. She didn't want anyone touching her, not even her maid. She gripped the cloth-draped rim of the tub, bent forward, and rested her forehead on her arm. Steam washed over her, curling up to caress her face. It permeated her hair until tendrils sagged down around her, the tips slipping into the water.

Her wounds from the last attack had barely healed, and here she was, more battered than she'd ever been in her life. Her brain wouldn't stop making excuses for Leo, inventing scenarios and reasons for his deceptions, playing devil's advocate with a vengeance. But no matter what twisted explanation she reached for, it evaporated before she could fully grasp it, dancing away from her tired brain like a ghostly light on the moors.

He'd used her. That was the only truth. He'd used her, put her in danger, left her unaware and exposed...That horrible truth balanced on a knife's edge with the undeniable fact that she loved him. The two incongruous facts seesawed back and forth, leaving her shaken and sick to the core.

How could she love such a man? And more importantly, how could she stop? Because she had to stop, had to dig the feelings out and crush them under her heel as you would an adder in the garden.

The door opened. The familiar sound of boot heels on the floor made her stiffen, every muscle taut, poised for flight. A hushed interchange, as though beside a deathbed. The swish of fabric as Nance exited. The *snick* of the door closing behind her.

Viola kept her head down. If she looked up, she'd either burst into tears or spring from the bath and claw his eyes out.

The sound of a chair being dragged across the floor was followed by a creak as he disposed himself beside the tub. Even now he intruded, claimed his place, imposed on her peace. He sat quietly, his simple presence filling the room like a heavy-handed concerto pounded out on a perfectly tuned pianoforte.

"You can have the house." Her breath made ripples in the water. "The both of you." He and his damned cousin, who'd been hauled away with a curse for them both on his lips.

He could have the house, if only he'd leave now. Leave now and not touch her. Leave now and not make her struggle with this, not make her face it.

His only reply was the application of the sponge to her

back. Viola pressed her forehead more firmly into her arm and bit her lip. How could she want him, love him, hate him all at the same time? How was it possible not to disintegrate amidst such conflict?

"I don't want the house," he said, each word skittering across her damp skin, distinct and insistent. "And even if Charles lives, giving it to him won't solve anything."

Viola turned her head so she could see him out of her one good eye. Through the curtain of her hair, he looked like a repentant angel: He'd removed his coat at some point since he'd brought her home, along with his cravat. His waistcoat gaped open, all but the last button disengaged. The sponge continued up and down her spine, a steady, reassuring touch in a world that no longer held any such promise.

"But you want the *prince's treasure*."

Leo winced as something that felt oddly like tears balled up behind his sternum. It wasn't a question. Viola turned her face back toward the water, dismissing him. What excuse could he possibly offer? Yes, he still wanted the treasure, but not at this cost. In his selfish heart of hearts, he wanted her and the treasure both. The sad reality was, he wasn't likely to get either, and deservedly so.

Myriad bruises formed a map across her pale skin. Each dark spot marking a betrayal, each scratch and welt marking a path from one lie to another. The whole of it was a brutal reminder that he'd not only failed her, he'd failed himself. Charles, too, if it came right down to it. He sluiced water over each and every mark. When he lifted her hair, she sat up, staring at him blankly.

There was blood on her face, a bruise blooming across one cheek, from the arch of her cheekbone all the way to her jaw, and one eye was swollen nearly shut. He'd seen men survive a bare knuckles boxing match with less to show for it.

At this point, nothing but the truth would do. "Yes, I want the treasure. I need it, in fact. But I'm not certain it exists anymore."

Viola sucked in a breath, like a swimmer emerging from the waves. "So all this has been for nothing? The attacks, the fire, Ned—oh God, Ned." She covered her mouth with her hand, inhaling sharply through her fingers. The water mixed with the dried blood, sending red rivulets down her face and neck. He soaked a towel and handed it to her.

Her face disappeared, hands molding the cloth to her like some ancient, mournful pieta. "All this time, you let me believe it was Sir Hugo behind those men. Sir Hugo and my damn manuscript that got Ned killed. But it was your cousin. And you."

The urge to deny fault burned, but Leo couldn't. He'd set it all in motion. "Yes, I'm as much to blame as Charles, though I took a different tack. I tried to tell Charles his way was too risky, too cruel. I did try to protect you," he added.

"I suppose you did. But as you needed me, I would hardly call your protection altruistic. What happens now? What happens if your family finds out you shot your cousin? Possibly killed him..." Her voice trailed away.

His heartbeat faltered. "They won't find out. Charles won't tell them. Can't tell them. And if he dies, well,

Sandison told the doctor it was a drunken duel. My parents would never understand. Charles is like a son, like a brother…"

"And you love him."

Leo nodded and held out a towel. That was the worst of it. He did—even after seeing what Charles had done to Viola, and the horrors he'd unleashed upon her staff and neighbors. It simply didn't seem real, didn't seem possible, that it had been Charles.

If his family found out, they'd think it was over money. Something petty and rude. He'd never make them understand that the treasure had become the least of it.

Maybe Beau, but not the rest. Not his brother. Certainly not his parents.

Viola rose unsteadily, and he helped her from the tub. Steam rose off her skin as though she were diffusing into the air. The urge to grab her, to establish that she was real and his, surged through him. He crammed it down, ruthlessly.

"I love him, but I chose you."

Her single open eye pinned him in place as neatly as if he were an exotic insect in a display box. "And you're not sure if you can forgive yourself."

"No." Leo shook his head, hair slipping from his queue to hang about his face. "I know I won't be able to forgive myself for even the smallest part of it. Not what I did to Charles; not for what I did to you."

Viola nodded in an entirely noncommittal way and gingerly pulled on her dressing gown. She wrung the water from her hair, a spiraling stream spilling back into the tub.

"I'm not sure I can forgive you either. Damnable, isn't it? Love and hate getting tangled up this way."

Leo held his breath, not entirely sure that she'd said what he thought. Had she been referring to them, or to him and Charles? She didn't wait for a response, retreating to her dressing table where various pots of salve had been left by her maid.

"But do you think it worth finding out?" His question fell into the room, heavy as a stone sinking in water.

Viola studied her face in the mirror, fingering her various cuts and bruises, ignoring him completely. Ignoring things was an art, and she was a master in it. Finally she selected one of the small pots and began anointing her bruises with the salve inside it. When she was done, she turned her head to face him.

"One of the things life has taught me, my lord, is to never discard anything of value. Does it make you wince to be thought of as a thing? To be weighted and accessed as a commodity? Good. Yes, I think it worth finding out, but I make you no promises of forgiveness or understanding. I don't even promise to treat you nicely. Hell, I can't swear I won't stab you in your sleep."

"Hate, love, and the urge to do murder. All the makings of a true Vaughn."

Viola's head snapped around, but she didn't reply. Leo watched quietly as she returned to drying her hair.

It was more than he had any right to expect, though far less than he wanted. She didn't owe him a damn thing, but having sacrificed his cousin—his family—he couldn't help but want more from her, of her. He'd pledged himself to her in that moment, body and soul, and he wanted that in return. Craved it, bone deep.

As for the possibility of being murdered in his sleep, he'd expect no less from any woman in his family if she were treated so abominably. Why should Viola be any different?

CHAPTER 29

Their return to Dyrham was a ludicrous affair that nearly made her wish she'd chosen to remain in town: four easy stages, in the best-sprung coach she'd ever experienced, the seats folded out into a sumptuous bed where she and Pen could curl up and nap the miles away.

Leo handled her as though she were fragile as fine wine, not to be shaken or unduly disturbed. His servants treated her likewise. Only Pen could be trusted to cram her way in, pushing and shoving and demanding attention in her domineering and irresistible way.

The lime avenue alerted her that they'd reached the outskirts of the estate. Pen turned in a restless circle and began to pant. The familiar arch of limbs and leaves stirred an ache of longing behind her sternum. Ridiculous to have become so attached to a house in such a short time.

The coach rolled to a stop, and Pen raised her head, ears pricked, tail churning with excitement. The coach swayed ever so slightly as the footmen jumped down. The door opened, and Pen scrambled out, happy to be home.

Viola's breath caught. Dyrham wasn't home, whether her dog realized that or not. Leo had been right when he'd asserted that London was no place for her to recuperate. Too many chances for someone to see her, for rumors to start, for someone to ask questions. But all the same, she suddenly wished she'd answered differently and had gone instead to stay with Lady Ligonier.

She wanted this to an extent that frightened her. Wanted Leo, too, despite his many betrayals. What might she be willing to give up to have it? To have him? And would it be worth it in the end?

She'd broken so many of her rules with him, for him.

Her poached egg arrived with its usual desultory promptness. A week of sleeping in, wandering about her room, and being kept on nursery rations had her ready to rip the paper from the walls.

The entire household tiptoed around as though she were at death's door. Everything was hushed, well-oiled, fully functional, but deadly dull. The letter announcing that Lord Leonidas's cousin would live had only seemed to makes things worse.

She dumped the egg into the saucer of her teacup and fed it to Pen. The dog swallowed it whole and turned to wipe her face across Viola's dressing gown. Viola stared down at the bits of drool and egg liberally smeared across her knee. At least this one was linen and easily laundered. Silk was going to have to be banished from her wardrobe entirely unless her income from the second installment of her memoir filled her coffers to unknown heights.

Or perhaps she could start a new fashion: watered silk,

à la chien. She rubbed the egg off with a towel from her dressing table. Was there any point in getting dressed today? She turned the idea over in her head.

If she didn't leave this room soon, she was going to go mad. So yes, there was a very good reason to get dressed, even if Leo might not approve. He'd been free to come and go, while she'd been caged like some animal in the Duke of Richmond's menagerie.

A chemise gown worn over her jumps would be decent enough for the close gardens. She wouldn't even venture so far as the folly. She just needed fresh air in her lungs and sunlight on her skin, to look at something other than these four walls and the distant, teasing canopy of trees and the sparkling twist of water.

An hour later, Viola was seated under a bower of laburnum, Pen lying at her feet, watching the butterflies and bees with hawklike interest. It had taken resolution to bully her way past her maid and Leo's butler, but she'd done it.

Off to one side, she could see the duchess's tower. Occasionally, a groom would appear past the corner of the stable block, exercising one of the horses. She saw Oleander, and Quiz, and a flash of blood bay that could only be Meteor. At one point, Nance and Sampson wandered by in the distance.

Nance had been more than eager to return to Dyrham, and it seemed that her feelings were returned in full by Leo's footman. Would Leo mind if Viola stole his footman? She'd need one of her own if she left Leo, and Sampson was the obvious choice.

Nance had rushed to the kitchen upon their return

and rescued the Midsummer-men from the rafters. She'd found both pairs sweetly entwined, and she'd put great stock in them. Viola had wrapped her own in paper and tucked it into a drawer, feeling foolish in the extreme as she did so.

Two dried twigs, tied together and bent in until the flowering heads were united. Nothing but a country superstition, but she couldn't bring herself to toss hers out any more than Nance could.

A bee tumbled slowly from flower to flower, its soft hum providing a lazy contrast to its activity. Viola breathed deeply and concentrated on the feeling of the sun working its way through the layers of her clothing…She woke to Lord Leonidas's chuckle and the sound of Pen's feet churning the gravel walk as she greeted him.

"Not as recovered as you thought, eh?" His long-fingered hand caressed the dog's ear, pulling it softly while Pen leaned into him with all her might.

Viola covered her answering yawn with her hand. "I needed air." Her body hummed in tune with the bees at the sight of him. The sun turned his hair into a dark halo and caught the slight burr of his beard, shadowing his jaw. Shallowness was a sin she'd have to lay claim to, covetousness, too.

"Walls starting to close in on you?"

She nodded. It would all be so much easier if only he weren't so beautiful. It caught one off guard. His green eye was merry again, something it hadn't been even before her abduction. When was the last time she'd seen that particular glint? For the life of her, she simply couldn't remember. Her traitorous heart set her pulse fluttering.

Damn it all, she didn't *want* to want him.

A smile tugged at her mouth, and she gave in, even though the motion pulled at her still-healing lower lip. He was a scoundrel, and he'd nearly got her killed, but that teasing green eye was impossible to resist.

Weak, wanton, and a fool. That's what she'd become. What she'd been reduced to. And she was likely to remain so for as long as the world allowed her. Outside Dyrham, she might come to her senses, but while here, never. Had he known that when he'd swept her out of town? His wicked green eye implied he had.

Leo took Viola's answering smile as an invitation to linger. Since her abduction, she'd been haughty, reticent, angry, dismissive; anything other than welcoming and soft. And he couldn't blame her, though he wanted the lady with the knowing smile back far more than it was safe for a man to want something.

What was it his grandmother always said about provoking the gods? Something about hubris being a man's downfall? He couldn't quite remember, but it amounted to not setting one's heart on something too hard. The swelling around her eye had entirely disappeared, leaving just a purple-black ring. The bruise on her cheek had faded, too, nothing but a sallowness edged in grayish lavender to show where it had been.

Leo tamped down the rising flood of guilt. She didn't want his apologies, and they wouldn't do his cousin a damn bit of good. He'd been given a choice worthy of Solomon, and he'd made it.

He flicked back the skirt of his coat and sat, straddling

the bench where she'd been dozing. She sighed and leaned into him, much as her dog had done moments before. Her head settled on his shoulder, and one hand gripped his waistcoat, fingers curling inside. He could remember his nephews in just such a pose, sleepy and content as he carried them to the nursery.

He wrapped both arms around her and rested his head atop hers. He'd been planning on chasing his invalid back into the house, but this was infinitely preferable. Her hair smelled faintly of citrus, lemons or orange blossom. He buried his nose in her hair, content to wonder, content to wallow in the thrill of simply being allowed to do so.

After several minutes, Viola turned her head slightly and kissed him, lips firm, almost demanding. A tremor ran through her. Leo groaned and kissed her back. It had been forever since he'd touched her, and he'd not been sure he'd ever be allowed to again.

"Come up to the bathhouse." She slid off his lap and tugged him up. A shadow of her coquettish smile slid across her mouth. God, how he wanted that smile back. He'd give just about anything to see it in all its glory.

Fingers twined, they wandered slowly through the garden and up to the path that led from the house to the bathhouse. Once inside, she kissed him again, kept kissing him, lips, tongue, and teeth all brought to bear, even as he fumbled with the series of ties at the back of her chemise gown. The gown fell to the floor in a pool of white linen. She backed away, smiling, eyes never leaving his.

Whatever had happened to her, between them, she was still quite powerfully herself. Still Viola. Wicked charm still infused her eyes. Her naughty dimples appeared for the scantest of moments, flashing like a distant light at sea.

He stepped toward her, and she shook her head, curls swinging about her shoulders as she ripped the ribbon from her hair. For a moment, she was a Greuze painting—a servant girl in dishabille—then quick fingers tugged loose the ties of her jumps, and they, too, were discarded where they fell. Her shift was off in one quick motion, and she went from Greuze to Fragonard.

She tossed her shift at him, a heavy cloud in the steam. Leo snatched it out of the air and brought it to his face, inhaling deeply. If he were as rich as his father, she'd have a new shift every day, and he'd sleep each night with her used one as a pillowcase, resting his head enveloped in her scent. That was reason enough to find the prince's damn treasure.

She'd reached the edge of the pool and was busy removing garters and stockings: sturdy cotton ones, not one whit less enticing than their silk brethren as they rolled down her calf. Desire whipped through him. Battered and bruised, she was still enchanting enough to steal his wits. His pulse pushed down into his groin. His cock throbbed and stiffened.

Viola slipped into the water like an otter escaping a hunt, not bothering with the steps. Leo ripped his own clothes from his body, scattering them as he went, a trail leading back to sanity. She watched him from the far end of the pool, his own personal siren waiting in the mist.

The water verged on too hot, scalding his skin as though he'd walked into the bonfire on Guy Fawkes night. He surfaced beside Viola, rising into her embrace: arms and legs twining about him, hair tangled around them both like a net, mouth meeting his in a kiss hotter than the water would ever be. Her arm slid between them, her hand grasped his engorged cock, and her fingertips teased the folds of his foreskin near the base.

Leo lifted her away from him, pushed her out of the water, and set her on the lip of the pool. Lord knew his cock was more than willing to take the shortest route to fulfillment, but what had been haunting his dreams was her taste. He wanted her panting and sobbing his name as he filled her.

He pushed between her thighs, gripped her hips, and slid her forward until she was perched on the very edge. It was easy to sink down, to thrust his arms under her thighs, encircle her hips, and tilt her up. Viola rocked back, supporting herself with her arms, knees wide, one foot on his shoulder, one trailing down his back.

Sweet flesh on his tongue, Leo opened his mouth wide and sucked hard on her inner thigh. She gasped and squirmed, knees falling just a tad wider. He bit down lightly on the straining tendon that led from thigh to groin, then slid over to delve into her folds, parting her with his tongue. He fastened his mouth over the sensitive peak at the top of her cleft, pressing his chin hard against the opening of her body.

She strained, breath hitching, the foot on his shoulder beginning to tremble. Leo slid his tongue inside her, lapped slowly all the way up her cleft, then renewed his assault on her swollen clitoris.

Her hand smoothed over his head, locked in his hair. Leo smiled to himself, refusing to be dislodged. She was mumbling, brokenly, words interspersed with gasps. "Vaughn...my lord, oh God...Leo! Leo!"

At last. His name on her lips was as sweet as the taste of her on his. Triumph rippled through him as her whole body trembled. He pulled her back into the water, filled her with one hard thrust, and held her there while the last ripples of her release pulsed around him.

Viola clung to him, spine arching, hips circling in a tight little spiral. He trapped her between his body and the wall of the pool. Waves slid over his shoulders, spilled over the lip of the pool, burst between them like a small geyser. His world spiraled down to the joining of their bodies, the pulsing embrace, the surging thrusts, the incoherent gasps and cries.

As he came, he lost his footing, dragging her beneath the water as he fell. Her mouth found his, and her hair swirled out around them. He found the bottom with his feet and stood, arms locked about her.

Heart pounding in his ears, pulsing in his cock, Leo dragged her to the steps and sat down. She propped herself on her knees and slid back just enough that his cock slipped free. His pulse was slowly returning to his chest where it belonged. She kissed his neck, just below his ear, with the slightest hint of teeth. "In another week or two, I think I could safely return to town."

Leo let his breath out through his teeth. *I,* not we. He should have been expecting this; she'd run for the safety and anonymity of London the last time, too. His hands slid up her thighs, gripped her hips lightly, thumbs resting on her hip bones. "Or you could stay here."

She pulled away just enough to look him in the eye,

her hand pressed over his heart, weight bearing down on it. Her perfect brows pinched sharply over her nose.

"Think of it as trying it on for size." His index fingers circled on her naked skin.

Viola shook her head almost imperceptibly. Her lips parted. Then she caught them between her teeth as though she couldn't quite find the words she wanted, or was holding them back. "It's no use trying on something one can't afford." Her head dropped so that her hair swung between them like a curtain. "In fact, it's madness to do so. Leave well enough alone. Though perhaps, being a duke's son, you don't know much about wanting what you can't have, about settling for what you can."

She tensed, as though for flight. Leo tightened his grip, holding her firmly in place. "If I don't know by now, by God, you're teaching me. This isn't enough. Not for me. I don't want a mistress, never have. I don't want a nursery full of bastards. I want a wife, Vi." Her head came up, eyes boring into him. "But you don't want a husband, do you?"

"The son of a duke—"

"A younger son—"

"—to marry his whore?"

"—with a brother and three nephews between him and the title. I can't offer you strawberry leaves—"

"What on earth would I want—" She cut herself off as the meaning dawned on her, eyes widening with indignation. "If you think I'd marry you if you had a title—"

"There's very little chance of one, just to be clear." He relaxed his grip, slid one hand around, fingers brushing her cleft. He spread the other across her lower back. She caught her breath, but didn't move away. "But we could

make Dyrham our own little Strawberry Hill. Fox and
Mrs. Armistead seem happy enough."

"But not married. Can you imagine the scandal if they
did? The great-grandson of Charles II married to a—"

"Stranger things have happened." Leo slid one finger
into her, followed it with a second, and found the still-
swollen peak of her clitoris with his thumb. "Their royal
bastardy being established by the king's penchant for his
own French whore, I see very little for the Foxes and Len-
noxes to cavil at when it comes to Mrs. Armistead."

Her look of outrage gave way to the flush of desire. He
curled his fingers, twisted his hand so that his thumb was
replaced by the heel of his hand.

"Cry *pax* and be done with it, sweetheart. It was a
clumsy proposal—I'm a fool to have said anything at all
just now—and I beg you to forget it."

"It's not the sort of thing one forgets." Viola angled her
hips toward him, holding on to his shoulders for balance.

"Especially if it becomes a recurring theme." Leo
smiled, and her eyes widened, her expression showing a
mercurial flash of outrage before her head dropped back
and her thighs began to tremble.

She might not have said yes, but he'd set the idea running through her brain, as unstoppable as a horse without
bit or bridle. Leo slid a third finger in and leaned forward
to capture a nipple with his teeth. Viola rose up, back
arched, knees gripping his hips, voice intermingling his
name and God's.

"I know a bribe when I see one." Viola eyed Leo with
distrust.

The flashy chestnut gelding he'd presented to her knocked its hoof against the stall door, demanding attention, much as Leo did himself. Arrogant beasts, both of them. Beautiful, too, and likely to be just as temperamental, just as difficult to master.

Their tryst in the bathhouse had opened the floodgates. He was once more in her bed, the penitent at the temple, the lover enshrined, the wooing, would-be husband rampant…and she could sense her defenses crumbling day by day, disappearing with every kiss, every touch, every look.

Leo smiled, refusing to spar with her. For once, his blue eye looked as mischievous as the green one. He'd not a shadow of a doubt how his gift would be received. And he was right. The horse was everything she could have hoped for. Viola turned her back on a still-grinning Leo. The gelding blew out his nose, much as Pen did, and pricked up his ears.

"Yes, that's my pretty boy." She found herself crooning nonsense like a moonling. His nose was impossibly soft against her cupped hands. He lipped her fingers, looking for treats. She heard Leo chuckle as he handed her a lump of sugar. The gelding ate it greedily, lips searching for more.

Viola reached up to scratch behind his ear, and the horse arched his neck and bent lower, pushing back and waggling his head in ecstasy. "You're impossible, my lord."

Leo's answering laugh made her roll her eyes.

"Well," he began with a hint of offense, "the offer of my own noble hand was declined. Laying Dyrham at your feet doesn't seem to have done the trick, not even the bath-house, which you must admit is a strong inducement indeed. I'm simply stacking the deck a tad more in my favor."

Viola rested her forehead against the horse's neck and shut her eyes, letting the scent of horse and hay and dust build a wall around her. Bit by tiny bit, Leo was tying her to Dyrham. And she was letting him. She wanted to be convinced, wanted the warning that screamed in her bones silenced once and for all.

She'd ignored it once, and doing so had led to short-lived and nearly unbearable happiness, followed by unimaginable pain and disillusionment. Opening herself up to such a fate a second time was foolhardy in the extreme.

If she married Lord Leonidas Vaughn, he'd be as trapped as she in the end. Did he have any idea what that meant? If his friends cut him, if his family disowned him, was he prepared for that?

She certainly hadn't been.

CHAPTER 30

Thought this might be of interest. Leo's distinctive scrawl slashed across a slip of foolscap tucked into a magazine. Viola spread open the issue of *The Gentleman's Magazine* that he'd left on the table in the parlor she'd claimed as her own.

Mr. Green's Comments Upon the Further Refinements of Lord Henry's Translation of The Iliad. She dropped the magazine to worry at her thumbnail with her teeth.

The thrill of being truly seen, of being recognized, coursed through her, only to be quickly overborne by the well-ingrained instinct to prevent such insights. Hiding in plain sight had become second nature. Being dragged out into the light of day as herself, as Viola rather than Mrs. Whedon, was somehow almost as frightening as being snatched off the street.

That a man might notice her penchant for sapphires, or her taste in hats, or even keep track of how she took her tea was one thing. It was safely within the bounds of flirtation and seduction. It was expected. Needful even.

That he might delve deep enough to realize that such a topic as this would be of interest set every nerve blazing with alarm. But then none of Leo's gifts or insights fell into the mundane: a mongrel dog, the engraved collar, his penchant for knowing exactly how to tempt her (whether it was into his bed, or merely his home), the horse that must have cost more than most people's yearly income.

She believed that in this moment, in this place, this idyll away from the world, he loved her, but how to trust that it would last? That it was real enough to endure what would come when the scandal sheets were filled with his name and the gossips got their claws into him?

Was love enough if you didn't have trust, too? She could hear her heart clamoring that it was, but her ever-logical brain—crammed to the brim with useless Latin verbiage and sordid Greek plays—refused to agree.

She could get no peace. The Bible had dour things to say about a kingdom divided. How much worse to be a person divided against oneself?

She retrieved the magazine from where it had fallen and ran her fingers over the cover as though she could somehow bring it to life, force it to speak, to give up Leo's secrets.

If he were plain Mr. Vaughn with two thousand a year and a cottage in Cornwall, she could almost have married him without a qualm. But he wasn't, and even if he were, the undercurrents that swirled between them, as dangerous as Scylla and Charybdis, were impossible to dismiss.

Viola threw herself back into her chair and buried herself in *The Gentleman's Magazine*. She was halfway through the article and busy composing a rebuttal in her head when the door to the parlor opened with enough force to rattle the paintings on the wall. Pen hackled, and the woman standing in the doorway, looking very much like Medea triumphant, shushed her with unmistakable authority. Pen cocked her head, her stub of a tail twitching against Viola's skirts.

"Well, I see some of the tale I've been told is true."

Viola scrambled to her feet, magazine falling from her shaking hands. She curtsied and darted a glance at Leo's butler. Pilcher hovered behind the new arrival in a dither that could only be explained by a supreme calamity: welcoming the duchess into a house where her son's mistress was currently resident.

The expression in the woman's blue eyes would have told Viola everything she needed to know, had she been in doubt as to her identity. Everything she'd ever heard about Lord Leonidas's frosty gaze was more than true of his mother. Viola's heart struggled to beat as her blood chilled. She was sinking into an icy pond with no hope of rescue.

"I'm sorry, Your Grace." Her voice came out surprisingly calm. "Your son is away at the moment."

"So I told Her Grace," Pilcher said from the doorway. "It isn't fitting—" His words choked off as the duchess threw him a quelling glance.

She turned back to Viola, resolution in her spine, determination in the set of her shoulders. "I'm well aware Leo is elsewhere today. I came to see you, Mrs. Whedon. But since servants *who should know better by now,*" she said loudly, in a tone that promised dire consequences, "seem to be able to do nothing more than quake and hound me when they *should* be offering me refreshments, I propose you join me in my carriage before I have my say."

She adjusted her hat upon blond curls shot with silver, and spun about, Viola's acquiescence clearly assumed. Viola motioned for Pen to stay and followed the duchess out. The last thing she needed was Pen in a closed coach with Lord Leonidas's mother. Whether the dog loved her or hated her, the duchess's spangled silk wouldn't have survived the encounter.

Viola tasted bile at the back of her throat. There was something truly frightening about the way the duchess carried herself. A threat was implicit in every motion. That she was used to giving orders, and to having them obeyed, was beyond question.

A coachman, two footmen, and a prodigious mountain of baggage sat atop a glossy coach-and-six emblazoned with the ducal crest. Viola followed the duchess into her carriage without gloves or hat, feeling oddly bereft without them, like an unarmed gladiator thrown to the lions. She took the rear-facing seat and spread her skirts about her as though this were no more than a friendly drive in Hyde Park.

No matter what the duchess had to say, Viola refused to cower. But the door shut behind them with a *click* that made her jump. Without a word or motion from the duchess, the carriage rolled into motion. Viola searched for calm, forcing herself to meet the duchess's gaze unflinchingly. She'd faced down angry relatives before, though never under circumstances such as these.

She had done nothing wrong, had nothing to apologize for, nothing to explain. The duchess couldn't even accuse her of being mercenary, as not so much as a ha'penny had changed hands between her and Lord Leonidas. All the same, she could feel an anticipatory quake of nervous energy low in her belly, and it took all her self-control to prevent her foot from shaking and her knee from bobbing.

The duchess pushed the curtains more fully open and continued to simply stare at her in the bright light of day. Viola stared back. Let her look. Let her study every bruise, memorize every mark.

Finally the duchess sighed loudly and said, with something that might have been a smile curling up the edge of her mouth, "My daughter said you had bottom."

Viola's mouth dropped open, and she shut it with a snap. The duchess glanced down as she smoothed out her skirts, shaking them out so they hung perfectly over her knees, as though sitting for a portrait.

"So unlike my boy to become entangled with a courtesan. If I'd heard he'd eloped with one of his friend's wives, I'd have been less surprised...I hear I owe you a deal of thanks for getting Beau out of a scrape. And for that I *do* thank you. Daughters are something of a trial, and I say that having been an enormous trial to my poor papa. Beau is my just deserts, it would seem."

The older woman sucked in one cheek and continued to study her, as though something would announce itself or reveal itself if she just looked hard enough. "I'd like an explanation for the state I find you in from your own mouth, for I'll go to my grave swearing that my Leo couldn't have done that to a woman—any woman, regardless of the provocation—and you don't strike me as the kind to take such treatment lightly."

Viola caught her breath and held it. Her hands crushed the fine linen of her petticoats. She swallowed thickly. Was it possible to tell only part of the story? How much did the duchess know already?

"I can assure Your Grace that it wasn't your son."

The duchess arched a brow. "You should know that London is rife with rumors. One version says my son caught you with another man, murdered you both, and smuggled your corpses out of town—I'm relieved to see that's blatantly untrue. Another says you and he had a row, and after beating you half to death, he then dragged you away and locked you up as though he were a Bluebeard. My personal favorite is that he fought a duel over you and nearly killed a man."

The duchess watched her very carefully. Viola struggled to breathe normally. Did the duchess know about her nephew? And if so, what had she been told? Viola's hands began to shake, and she balled them into fists.

The coach rocked as it made a sharp turn, and the sound of a whip cracking was followed by the unmistakable sensation of speed. Outside, the avenue of limes that marked the entrance to Dyrham was quickly receding.

Leo's mother slid the length of her parasol across the door as though she were barring the gates of a castle. "When I travel, I don't like to waste time."

"Travel? But—"

"Whatever the truth of the matter"—the duchess cut her off, eyes flintier than ever—"am I safe to assume that whoever *did* do that to your pretty face has been dealt with?"

"Yes, Your Grace, but really—"

"Should the duke and I be making plans to save our son from the gallows?"

"I don't know, Your Grace. I don't think so." Panic set her pulse racing. How did you prevent a woman with such knowing eyes from stripping the flesh from your bones until she knew every secret you'd ever had? It felt as though the knowledge of what Leo had done, and why he'd done it, was writ across her face as clearly as the bruises his cousin had put there.

"Very well, keep your secrets. I'd have bet the ducal rubies that no child of mine was fool enough to dawdle here in England if he had reason to flee, but I hadn't thought to add you to the equation."

"And now that you have?"

The duchess smiled, and a shiver traced its way up Viola's spine. This was not a woman to tangle with, and she was very, very angry behind that placid demeanor. "Well, my dear Mrs. Whedon, now that I have, I find I need to know more before I can draw any conclusions."

"Hence my abduction?"

"If you choose to call it that, so be it." The duchess shrugged, eyes continuing to dissect her with unnerving directness. "Let us simply say that I desire to make your acquaintance."

"My acquaintance? Let us lay our cards on the table, Your Grace. You desire that I should remove myself from your son's protection, possibly from England entirely. Correct?"

"Not exactly, my dear. Though it may come to that in the end."

• • •

Pilcher met Leo at the door with a pained look on his craggy face. He seemed to have shrunk beneath his wig, like a snail withdrawing into its shell. A howl erupted from behind the closed doors of the sitting room.

Leo threw his butler a wary look and strode down the corridor. Inside the sitting room, he found Pen guarding a damp copy of *The Gentleman's Magazine*. The note he'd left tucked between its pages had run and blurred under the influence of the dog's drool, and the cover was sadly mangled.

He set the magazine on the table and glanced around the room. Nothing else seemed amiss. He headed back to the hall, Pen at his heels, whining.

"Pilcher, have you seen Mrs. Whedon today?"

"Yes, my lord."

Leo studied his butler, noting his evasive eyes and the hunch of his shoulders. He stood as though he expected a beating. "Was there something you wanted to tell me?"

The man swallowed hard, darting a quick glance upward to meet his eye before ducking his head again. "She said I wasn't to give you the note until dinner, my lord."

The bottom fell out of Leo's world. The checkerboard of the hall floor spun before righting itself. She'd left him. Just like that. Snuck off the first time his back was turned.

Pen circled, her whine rising into an extended grumbling harangue. Leo's pulse settled. Pen was here. Viola would never have left Dyrham without her dog. Never.

He took a deep breath and watched his butler shift uneasily from one foot to the other, hands fretting about his pockets like a pensioner searching for his tobacco pouch.

Leo shackled his temper and held out his hand. Yelling at Pilcher wasn't going to help things. The man looked fagged to death, like he'd been pursued by harpies. After a bit more searching, Pilcher produced a folded piece of foolscap sealed with a large blob of red wax, an all-too-familiar image sunk deeply into it.

Not harpies, Hera. The avenging mother. Leo gave him a sympathetic glance. The poor man. No wonder he looked as though he'd been sucked dry. Her Grace tended to have that effect on people when she was on the march. She'd been wasted as a peeress. If she'd been in charge of Horse Guards, the American colonies would never have been lost.

His gut twisted as he broke the seal. The idea of a confrontation between his mother and Viola was horrifying. Nothing good could come of it, and neither was likely to break or give ground. It would be a *battle royale*.

His mother's command, for he could hardly call what she'd written anything else, was clear and to the point: She'd take Viola to the family seat in Scotland; he was not to show his face for a fortnight. Then, and only then, he would find out what she and Mrs. Whedon had worked out between them.

Oh, there were plenty of pithy comments about his intelligence, his morals, and his duty to his name scrawled across the page as well, with an added soupçon of guilt for involving poor Beau in his sordid doings and leaving her to explain the gossip swirling about them all. There were also several dire threats involved were he to disobey her.

Leo barked out an order for a bag to be packed and a fresh horse saddled, then he returned to his letter. Poor Beau indeed. This must be the first time that their mother had styled her so. Beau would be livid when he showed it to her, if he didn't throttle her instead.

Damn interfering little brat. Why couldn't she have kept her mouth shut? The sound of a carriage brought his head up. His mother had returned. That didn't bode well. He'd be lucky if one of them hadn't drawn blood.

How exactly did one tell one's mother to shove off?

Leo stepped out onto the porch, prepared to retrieve Viola from his mother no matter what the cost. He wanted some magical path to family harmony to appear, but he knew—bone deep and impossible to deny—that Viola was more important than his mother's opinion or consent.

He stopped dead in his tracks as he stared at what appeared to be a rented conveyance. A mismatched team was harnessed to a coach with faded, peeling wheels. The door sprung open, and his sister came tumbling out, looking half wild.

"Leo! Mother, she's—I'm sorry—it's not my fault—I swear to you."

He blinked, his brain refusing to process the scene before him or his sister's disjointed attempts at explanation. Beau latched on to him like a dying sailor finding the last spar of a shipwreck. "Please, Leo. Pay these men. Then come inside and let me explain."

"You have no idea what the past week has been like," Beau began. "Don't you *dare* yell at *me*. It's all over town. You and Mrs. Whedon, various *horrible* rumors about the two of you, about a fight, a duel. Some people are saying you murdered her. Mother's enraged. Augusta—"

"There's no reason to tell me about our brother's wife's reaction. I can well imagine." And he could. Augusta always did make bad worse.

"And to add to it, Charles sent a letter that made Mother angrier than I've ever seen her. I've never actually been afraid of her before; I always thought people were being silly or overly dramatic when they said they feared to cross her. She smashed the Ming vase in the hall and burnt the letter. Then she abandoned me to *Augusta*."

Leo nearly chuckled at the intense sense of outrage and loathing her tone conveyed. Whatever calamity had occurred in the world, nothing could make Beau accept with equanimity being left in the charge of their sister-in-law.

The anger bubbling below his skin began to cool, even as his concern grew. "Do you know what was in Charles's missive?"

Beau shook her head, lower lip caught between her teeth, brow furrowed. "Whatever it was, I don't think it quite served its purpose. She was muttering something about killing him herself before she'd even finished reading it."

The door opened, and Pilcher, somewhat restored in appearance, announced that Leo's horse was saddled and ready. Leo nodded, then laughed at the indignant expression on his sister's face.

"Pilcher, send the horse back to the stable and have them bring the carriage round. Lady Boudicea will be accompanying me."

Beau leapt up, eyes still damp, but smiling. "I promise you won't regret it, Leo."

Leo laughed and shook his head. His mother had kidnapped his mistress, and he was about to go in pursuit with his sister in tow. An evil thought occurred to him. It was no more than Beau deserved. "Don't thank me yet, brat. You've yet to see your traveling companion."

❧ CHAPTER 31 ❧

Two days gone by and still no Leo. Viola sank farther into the seat of his mother's coach and tried to sleep. The duchess pushed late each night, stopping only for a few scant hours to rest, and then they were back on the road, moving steadily north.

What should have been a five- or six-day trip had been shrunk nearly by half. But at every stop, Viola still fully expected to see Leo. Still hoped to see him. Surely a man on horseback could catch a coach, no matter how swiftly it traveled? Surely Leo wasn't going to abandon her to his mother?

She'd been unable to ascertain exactly what the duchess's purpose was in bundling her off to Scotland. She had barely spoken to her once she'd made certain that her son had not been responsible for the beating, and that neither his arrest nor his hanging was imminent.

It was dark outside now, but the nearly full moon provided enough light for Viola to see the duchess fiddling with the buttons on the cuff of her coat. When Leo's mother had instructed her coachman to change the horses and push on at dusk, Viola's heart had sunk a little more.

"Tell me about your family." The question floated out of the dark, almost too soft to hear. It was the first thing the duchess had said to her all day. She'd been brooding silently, staring out the window, or sometimes at Viola, as though searching for the answer to some riddle in her face.

"There's nothing to tell, Your Grace."

"Bah." The older woman leaned forward, her gaze holding Viola's in the dim interior of the coach. "You didn't spring from the ground like a mushroom, and whoever your first protector was, I doubt he found you in a brothel in Covent Garden. A pretty milkmaid you're not."

A smile tugged at Viola's mouth. Her first protector had found her beside his best friend's grave, destitute and heartbroken. And he hadn't really meant to make her his mistress. It had just turned out that way. But she wasn't about to tell Her Grace *that* story.

"I eloped when I was fifteen, and my family cast me off, so I have no family. It's as simple as that."

"And the man?"

"He died."

"Ah, well…" For a moment the duchess seemed very far away, then she let her breath out and smoothed her hair back from her face in a gesture very like her son's when he was anxious. "You know I eloped with Leo's father?"

Viola nodded. Everyone knew that. It had been a grand enough scandal in its day that it was still whispered about whenever the topic of the mad Vaughns came up. One of many examples of outrageous behavior in a family history that stretched back for centuries.

"I rather imagine being an heiress made your decision to do so a bit more forgivable than mine."

"Not at all. It simply means that had he died, I wouldn't have been left with no choices in life and even fewer friends."

Viola laughed, unable not to do so. The duchess had the truth of it, and she wasn't too mealymouthed to admit it. "I was left with one friend."

"And he made you his mistress."

Viola sighed and shook her head. "Not at first. But being already married himself, it was all he could offer in the end: entrée into a world I hadn't even really known existed, a way to avoid the workhouse or something worse, a means to start over."

Leo's mother nodded thoughtfully, one hand twisting the long curl that hung over her shoulder. "A family might be *very* forgiving if the prodigal returned married to the son of a duke."

"Are you offering me a path to forgiveness or a chance to lord my newfound place in the world over them?"

It was the duchess's turn to smile. The first genuine smile Viola had seen. Her lips curled at the corners like those of a little girl. "Whichever you would like, but my real point is that no matter what you say now about having been cast off, they're likely to turn up when they get wind of your new station in life."

"Putting aside the fact that I've no intention of taking up a new station"—Viola ground her teeth as the duchess blinked innocently at her and forged on, refusing to be beguiled or bamboozled—"you want to know if you would be embarrassed by them? More embarrassed than having a grand whore for a daughter-in-law in the first place? Doubtful, Your Grace. Very doubtful. Unless you've an abhorrence for vicars and cadet branches of ancient baronial bloodlines. No? Well, I certainly have."

The duchess nodded noncommittally, and Viola sighed. "My family's presentable," she summed up, "but not *tonnish*. The problem here is that I've no wish to be redeemed."

"Then we do have a problem, Mrs. Whedon. A prime scandal is more than I can ask for from Glennalmond, and I'd not wish it for Beau—so much harder on the girls, unfair as that is—which leaves only poor Leo to kick up a dust in true Vaughn fashion and make his ancestors proud."

"Living with his mistress at Dyrham isn't scandal enough?"

"For you and me, most certainly. For Leonidas?" The duchess shook her head. "I must quote you back to yourself: *doubtful*. He was never a boy to do things by halves. And that's what you're offering him: half a life, a partial commitment, paste in place of a diamond."

Viola's throat tightened and her eyes burned. "I'm offering him what I can."

"No, you're offering him what's safe. And that won't do. Not for Leo. I let Glennalmond settle for a socially grand match with a woman I don't think he gives a fig about, but I'll be damned if either of my other children do so."

"I think you're mad, Your Grace." It was the only conclusion. It wasn't simply a rumor. His entire family was unhinged. "To help your son to such a match. To even countenance, let along promote it…"

The duchess smiled again. "I haven't yet agreed to help my son to anything. I could be wrong, you see. I could be wrong about you, about him. His sister thinks he loves you. I'm not so sure. And I've no idea at all about your finer feelings, and no real right to ask."

"But you're going to."

The duchess shook her head, her expression clearly saying that Viola was a simpleton. "No, I won't believe you whatever you say. How could I?"

"Then why all this?"

"Because there's no other way. His grandfather left him Dyrham for a reason. To anchor him, to offer him something most younger sons lack, a sense of purpose, of belonging."

"And you think he needs a wife."

"I know he needs one. What I don't know is if he needs you to be that wife, or if you're simply an alluring distraction."

"So this is a test. How do you know I've passed?"

The duchess smiled again. "I'll know when my son arrives. I've been expecting him since we set out, and I'm extremely put out that so far he's failed to live up to expectations."

"I've been thinking the same thing, Your Grace. And that was not an admission of love."

The duchess's smile grew, and her eyes crinkled up. "Not on your part, I agree. But do you expect me to believe that you think he'd ride hell-for-leather after you, against my strict orders, simply for lust?"

Viola ground her teeth, trapped in the duchess's laby-
rinthine logic. She hadn't admitted she loved him, but
she'd certainly confirmed for his mother that she believed
he loved her.

"We're never going to catch them."

Leo glanced at his sister over the rim of his mug. He
swallowed and set his ale down on the table. Beau was
ripping a bun into pieces and feeding them to Pen with a
look of angry resignation on her face.

"That was a foregone conclusion as soon as I agreed to
the coach." He tossed the drooling mastiff an entire bun,
then bit into one himself. They were filled with minced
fruit and nuts and still warm from the oven. He chewed
thoughtfully, then swallowed. "Mrs. Whedon's safe enough
with Mother, or from Mother, I should say. It's Charles
I'm worried about."

Beau's head snapped up, her eyes meeting his with a
flash of anger followed by a shimmer of tears. She blinked
them away, and her expression hardened. "If he shows up,
I'll shoot him myself."

"I don't see him being so bold. I think whatever he told
mother, it was designed to put me in her black books and
Mrs. Whedon in her sights. He's expecting Mother to do
his dirty work for him."

"What do you think was in that letter?"

Pen nudged his knee insistently, and Leo tossed her
another bun. "Something along the lines of my attacking
him because he and my mistress had fallen in love. Maybe
he and I fought a duel over my treatment of her. Maybe he
tried to defend her and I attacked him out of hand. What-

ever it was, you can be sure it flirted with the truth just enough to make Mother wonder..."

"With what truth?" Her eyes were wary again, as though she didn't really want to know.

"With the truth that I shot him. And that I did it over Mrs. Whedon. He'd want to be avenged for that before all else."

Beau nodded. "And the rumors of Mrs. Whedon having been badly beaten?"

"Also true."

"But not by you." Revulsion crawled across her face. "Charles can't be fool enough to think that Mother would ever believe such a story."

Leo shook his head. "He was fool enough to believe he could abandon you to whatever fate you met at Vauxhall without repercussions. Do you think if Mother knew about that betrayal he'd still be walking this earth?"

"She does know."

Leo raised one brow. He hadn't thought Beau could surprise him anymore. "And what was her response?"

"That she owed Mrs. Whedon her thanks. I told her when the rumors first started a few weeks ago. I thought it might help calm Mother down. The story about Mrs. Whedon helping me, I mean."

"And did it?"

Beau shook her head ruefully.

Leo grimaced. It wouldn't have. The duchess didn't like loose ends or unpaid debts, and she wasn't a fan of the theory that revenge was a dish best served cold. She was a woman of action. She'd analyze the situation and do what she deemed necessary to bring about a desirable conclusion.

He'd be lucky to ever see Viola again. It would be just like his mother to put her on a ship and send her off to parts unknown with a generous annuity to procure her silence. But his cousin Charles would be damn lucky to survive.

⚡ CHAPTER 32 ⚡

Viola sat down to dinner at Skelton Hall with just the duke and duchess. Lord Glennalmond had ridden out in high dudgeon once he'd grasped that his mother had brought his brother's mistress home with her. If he'd stayed long enough to realize there was a chance she could become his sister-in-law, he might have had apoplexy on the spot.

That she was sitting down to this first meal without Lord Leonidas beside her was nothing short of enraging. He'd not caught up to them by the time they'd reached the Scottish border, nor was he waiting for them at his ancestral home. Worse yet, the duchess had begun to watch her with eyes that held a hint of pity.

It was galling.

Intolerable.

A bath and a change of clothing had done nothing to improve her mood. Lady Boudicea's gowns were tight and loose in all the wrong places, and the skirts were long enough that she was continually tripping over them.

Being obliged to make do with someone else's clothing and cosmetics and, well, everything was more than disconcerting; it verged on enraging.

The duke seemed more amused by his wife's undertaking than anything, cementing Viola's conclusion that the family were not just the eccentrics society made them out to be, but fully mad. He'd heaved a heavy sigh and apologized for his eldest son, then offered his arm and led her into dinner without any further sign of discomposure.

Watched by a veritable horde of footmen, Viola forced herself to eat. Even poached salmon, a favorite dish, was nearly impossible to swallow. She made short work of the lemon ice that ended the meal, however. How bad could things be when there was lemon ice?

When the sweetmeats were gone and the table cleared, the duke nodded to his wife and suggested they all retire to the library. Once there, he poured them all a generous portion of brandy and waved her and his wife to the chairs before the fireplace.

Viola took a moment to shut her eyes and inhale the comforting scents of leather and paper. Lemon ice and a few thousand volumes bound in red Moroccan: paradise.

The duke set his glass down on the mantel and pulled his wig off, rubbing his hand vigorously across his head for a moment before resetting the wig as though donning a hat. "My wife has explained something of the situation you find yourself in, Mrs. Whedon."

Viola gave him her full attention. She could see very little of Lord Leonidas in his mother, or rather she could see very little of the duchess in him. It was more his personality that the duchess had bequeathed to him. His father was a different case entirely—the height, the breadth of shoulder, the finely chiseled profile—they were all present in both father and son. But his father's eyes were kinder. Softer. The mossy green almost turned to brown in the flickering glow of the candles.

The duke set his shoulders against the stone mantel and studied her in return. "If I were to ponder all the details Her Grace imparted, I'd be forced to a conclusion that does my family little credit."

"Then perhaps it's best not to dwell too long upon the topic, Your Grace."

He shook his head a bit sadly, eyes dropping to the rug for a moment. "Perhaps, ma'am, but given a choice between a comfortable lie and an uncomfortable truth, I'd still choose truth. Like my wife, I'd stake my life on the fact that no son of mine would hit a woman, but if I add in the bits of the story our daughter and nephew provided, it becomes glaringly evident that I raised a man who would."

Viola breathed the slightly caustic fumes rising off the brandy deep into her lungs and held her tongue. The duke clearly had a rough grasp of what had happened, but if he wanted more, he'd have to ask his son. She took a sip and let the liquor burn a path to her belly, where it bloomed like courage.

"You see, my dear? Stubborn."

The duke nodded in response to his wife, eyes never leaving Viola. "You needn't bother to tell me I'm right, and please don't bother lying to me or trying to convince me I'm wrong, my dear. I'll have it out of Leonidas when he arrives, every last unsavory detail. And then it will be my duty to see that things are set to rights."

He strode across the room to refill his glass, impatience and irritation coming off him in waves. The duchess followed him with her eyes, a slightly worried frown marring her brow.

"Your Grace?" Viola said.

The duke set the decanter down and turned back to her. He looked tired, eyes shadowed and slightly hollow.

"It's not my place to tell you Lord Leonidas's secrets, but I can assure you that *you* owe me nothing."

The duke's gaze flicked over her, tracing the lingering bruises on her face. "You're wrong there, Mrs. Whedon. Very wrong indeed. Charles may not be my son, but he's my responsibility, and his actions have consequences. They must. As must those of us all."

His tone was sincere, the words almost a vow. Very similar to his son indeed. A family of madmen with a deeply entrenched sense of honor. At least when it came to some things. Seduction and theft were clearly not beyond the pale.

The thought tugged a smile from her. This family made no sense, but they clearly understood where the lines were drawn amongst themselves. But most peers were like that, at least in her limited experience of them.

"Whatever the outcome, you needn't worry about my nephew ever again." The duke returned to close their small circle by the hearth. "As for my son, well, rest assured you'll be provided for whatever the outcome there. If you prefer Paris or Venice or Lake Geneva, you shall have it."

Shock reverberated through her. Whatever she'd been expecting, it hadn't been that. No threat, no bribe, just a promise of security—of freedom and independence—hers for the taking. Her heart's desire only a few short months ago.

"And if I took your offer and your son followed?"

The duke shut his eyes, shaking his head slightly, as though discovering a favorite dog had eaten a shoe. He opened them again with a snap, gaze pinning her to her chair. "Do you mean, what would happen if my son were to refuse to accept your choice, or do you mean, what would happen if you changed your mind?"

"Either."

"Her Grace and I want our children to be happy, within reason of course. If you are our son's choice, so be it. To be frank, I'd have hoped for something else—someone else—for him, but I'll not force him to give you up, to live a lie with some respectable girl, all the while wishing she were you. That kind of stupidity and misery is pointless. But neither will I stand for you stringing him along or for him persecuting you with unwanted attentions, existing on false hope. I'll see this sorted and settled, and once it is, I shall expect everyone to abide by their decision."

Or there will be hell to pay. She could hear the threat as clearly as if the duke had shouted the words into the quiet room.

"And if I were to choose Paris?"

"I'd send you there on the morrow and spare my son the pain and humiliation of a final parting."

"But she's not going to choose Paris, are you, my dear?" The duchess's lips were again curled up into the smile that reminded Viola of a spoiled little girl, convinced she held the world twisted around her little finger.

"No, Your Grace. I hate to inconvenience you all—truly, I do—but I don't believe I am for Paris."

The duke attempted to put a coat of marchpane on it by mumbling, "No inconvenience at all," while the duchess grinned openly.

Viola stared at her, horror mixing with amusement until she was giddy with the dueling sensations. The duchess was enjoying this, was looking forward to the calamity, to the scandal. "Oh yes, my dear, no inconvenience at all. I shall very much enjoy forcing the *ton* to swallow you. And if we're very lucky, a few of them might even choke."

Bedraggled, unwashed, temper rapidly fraying, Leo ushered his sister into their ancestral home. His parents' butler blanched at the sight of him and made a halfhearted attempt to deny him entry.

"My lord, Lady Boudicea is of course welcome, but Her Grace left strict instructions..." His voice dwindled away, as though he were afraid to convey the duchess's orders.

"Barred from the house, am I? Not to worry, Byrne. I'll bide my time in the stables until Her Grace sees fit to bid me come."

The man's face showed clear evidence of his consternation. "I'll have luncheon sent down for your lordship."

"And for one very large dog as well, Byrne. She's currently asleep in the carriage, but when she wakes, I'd be mortified if she ate a stable boy."

Beau laughed and assured the butler that the dog would, under no circumstances, be eating anyone. She gave Leo a repressive glance. "Shall I go up and alert

Mother to your presence, or hide with you among the horses?"

"Go upstairs, brat. It won't harm me to spend a few hours—or days—kicking my heels before Mother deigns to summon me."

"And if it's weeks?" She dimpled as she asked, eyes dancing.

"Then I shall have time to become inured to the scent of manure." Leo bowed to her as though she were a princess and swept back out the grand front door.

If he was lucky, he had a few minutes before his mother became aware of his presence or put her mind to winkling out how unlikely it was for him to await her pleasure in the stables. If he went around the side and took the servants' stairs up, he should be able to make it to the south wing, where guests were housed, before his mother had time to think of it and cut him off. And once he was there, he could simply lie in wait.

Leo raced around the side of the house and slipped up the servants' stairs with a wink for one of the housemaids. The girl watched him with bemused eyes, but she made no attempt to stop him. His mother's orders must not have trickled down so far as the lower servants.

The stairs gave onto a corridor, which led to another flight of stairs concealed behind a bit of paneling. At the top of them, he finally found himself in the guest wing, which seemed eerily quiet. He checked each room in turn, ten of them in all, without finding a single sign of habitation. Everything was covered in Holland cloth and tidily closed up.

That meant his mother had put Viola in the family

wing, which was interesting in and of itself, but also meant the number of rooms she might have been assigned was reduced to two: the Boucher or the Stubbs suite. And there was only one choice there: the Boucher, with his *Triumph of Venus* dominating the room, angry little *putti* glaring out at you while the goddess smiled over her shoulder atop a settee born by dolphins and Triton.

Yes, Her Grace would have found the irony of that room assignment too sweet to forgo. The only question was, had he any chance at all of reaching it undetected?

He wandered back down the servants' stairs and stood studying the house. His own room was easily accessible via the great vines that clad the back side of the house, but not so the Boucher suite. He could storm the main staircase, but the risk of interception and expulsion was greater than merely slipping from his room to the suite beside it...

Decision made, Leo wrenched off his boots and struggled out of his coat. Leaving them at the base of the house, he said a silent prayer that the vines would hold—not a sure thing by any means; he hadn't attempted such since he was a stripling—and began the climb.

Each new footing and handhold sagged as it took his weight. The sensation of the vines being pulled from the stone was distinct and slightly sickening. Near the top, a small wren exploded out of the leaves, and he nearly lost his grip. A wing tip brushed his cheek as he ducked out of its path.

His heart hammered madly. His hands tingled with anticipation, as they did before a fight. He was so close.

The first window was locked, but the second slid up

with only token resistance. Leo heaved himself over the sill and into his room, attempting to be as quiet as possible. The floor protested with every step, and the hinges of his door gave a squeal that seemed destined to wake the dead.

Leo held his breath and counted to ten, but no other door opened along the corridor. Perhaps they were all downstairs and his climb had been for naught. A score of quick steps and he was turning the handle to the Boucher suite; two more and he was inside.

A sleepy "Is it time to dress for dinner already?" greeted him, and he let out a sigh of relief.

"No, my dear. It's time to flee the premises."

"Leo!"

Viola sat bolt upright on the settee she'd been napping on. The book she'd been reading fell to the floor with a muffled *thump*. Leo grinned. That was the first time she'd called him *Leo* without the distraction of lovemaking.

"Come on, Vi. No time to lose. Even now Beau is alerting my mother to our arrival."

She blinked at him and rubbed her eyes. Her hair was tumbled and disordered, and she appeared to be wearing one of his sister's old gowns, pink-sprigged muslin that clashed wildly with her hair. She was lovely, and if he could get her out of the house before his mother caught them, he might just manage to hold on to her. And keeping her had become something of a moral imperative during the past few weeks.

"Come. I've Pen and your trunk outside in a coach."

She shook her head, sending curls bouncing all around her face. Leo's heart sank. He'd been so close to convincing her. So close to bringing her around . . . and his mother had ruined it.

"No, my lord. It's—"

"Back to *my lord,* am I? A moment ago I was *Leo.*"

Viola glared at Leo, sleep vanishing under a surge of annoyance. He was smiling, eyes brimming with mirth. Coatless, hatless, in his stocking feet, he looked like a pirate.

"A moment ago *I* was asleep. And besides, you're late. Days late. And now you have the temerity to—"

He squeezed himself onto the settee beside her, thigh pressed against her, arm slipping behind her, hand gripping her waist. "To rescue you? Most certainly, my love." He dropped his head for a kiss.

"No, my lord." He stopped a hairbreadth away, so close she could have sworn she felt the heat of his lips. "I've been abducted twice in the last month by members of your family. A third time is simply too much to ask."

He rested his forehead against hers, the tips of their noses just touching. His fingers dug into her, and she almost thought she could feel them tremble. "I'm sorry, Vi. I'm so sorry. My mother, my cousin, my whole blasted family. Damnation. I'm not any better than the rest of them."

Viola smiled and kissed him, lips softly molding to his. Now probably wasn't the opportune time to tell him she rather liked his mother. That horrifying disclosure could wait.

He pulled her into his lap and swung around so that he was supine on the settee with her half on top of him. Viola balled up one hand and propped her chin upon it.

"You've a leaf in your hair. Two in fact."

"I came up the ivy."

"Risking life and limb to save me?"

"Quite literally, only to discover that Rapunzel doesn't want to be saved from the tower after all." He let his breath out in a long, slow exhalation. "What have they offered you? An annuity? A new life on the Continent?"

"If I want, yes." She laid her head on his chest, listening to his heartbeat. Outwardly he was calm, resigned, but his rapidly beating heart told a very different story.

"They've also offered—"

"Leonidas Roibert Vaughn!"

Viola pushed herself upright as the duchess burst into the room. Leo swung his legs down and sat up, but didn't rise. His hand fisted in her skirts, holding her on the settee beside him.

"Hello, Mamma."

"Did you read the letter I left you?"

"How else would I have known where to come? Or how urgent the need to follow was? I'd have caught you on the road, save for Beau's presence. Was that your doing also?"

The duchess made a rude sound in the back of her throat, and her gaze met Viola's for a brief moment. Viola choked back the urge to laugh. Had his mother hobbled his pursuit? Such an act did seem to fall within the scope of her genius.

"Mrs. Whedon is still deciding if she wishes to stay or go." She glared at them both, pushing Viola even closer to laughter. "And you were commanded to give her the room to make the decision without undue influence."

Leo stood, towering over his mother. "Mrs. Whedon is

going to be Lady Leonidas before the night is out, so *going,* as you so delicately put it, isn't an option for her."

"I highly doubt that, my boy."

"Eleanor, do stop torturing the children." The duke appeared behind his wife, his wig replaced with a silk banyan cap.

"We've two witnesses now, and no reason to wait."

The duke's expression went from benign amusement to furious in a snap. The tassel on his cap swung jauntily beside his ear, adding an air of the ridiculous to the scene. "You'll be married in the family chapel like a good Christian, or you won't be married at all. Is that clear, Leonidas?"

"You and Mother married over the anvil."

"Your mother wasn't—"

The duke caught himself, cheeks flushed with rage or embarrassment. Viola took pity on him. "Your father wasn't marrying a notorious strumpet, my lord. Best to put as good a face on it as possible, don't you agree? Banns would be in very bad taste, but a priest and a chapel with your family in attendance? I won't be married in any other fashion."

Leo swung about, expression harried and confused, like a man who'd been bitten by his own dog. "Is that a yes?"

"It's not a no. Which is more than you have any right to expect."

"Not a no." Leo grinned at her, suddenly looking very much like his mother as he did so.

"What can I say, my lord?" Viola plucked the leaves from his hair. "Your mother wore me down."

~ CHAPTER 33 ~

The mail coach rocked precariously. Charles winced as the scrawny woman beside him dug her elbow into his bruised ribs as she flailed to retain her seat. The wound Leo's bullet had left was a fiery, throbbing reminder to stick to his purpose. A string of startled oaths erupted from the rooftop passengers, and the same tiresome woman clapped her hands over her ears, pressing the black silk of her bonnet hard against them.

News of his cousin's betrothal had reached him via the dowager, precipitating this uncomfortable and harried trip north. He'd always thought Leo a fool, but this was beyond anything. Bad enough that his cousin had been spoiled and indulged until he believed the universe centered entirely upon him, but now he was set to besmirch his family name by bestowing it upon a whore.

That the duke and duchess would allow such a thing was beyond reason, beyond understanding. At least Lady Glennalmond had fully partaken of his horror. Never before had he felt the slightest bit of sympathy with her, but in this, they were of one mind: The wedding had to be stopped.

She'd paid his passage on the mail, ensuring that he would arrive before the dowager, upon whom the wedding ceremony waited. He'd promised to unite his voice with Glennalmond's in protest. To talk sense into Leonidas. To do whatever it took to see that the wedding didn't happen.

The coach swayed wildly again, another chorus of oaths bursting forth from the roof. Charles smiled at the discomfiture of his fellow passengers. Especially the spindly governess who continually poked and prodded him with every bony joint in her body.

Did Augusta know to what lengths he was willing to go to ensure that Leo didn't have his way this time? He had an inkling that she might. She'd been quite emphatic about preventing the wedding and had laid the entire dilemma at Beau's door, blaming her for running off and alerting her brother before the duchess had time to get Mrs. Whedon safely out of the country.

And she was right. Something had to be done about Beau as well. She was entirely too cocksure for her own good, a terrible hoyden who'd bring nothing but shame to her family. Rather like Leonidas, when one thought about it.

And there was still the matter of the prince's treasure to sort out as well. Charles bent his head to one side, his neck popping audibly as he stretched. Yes, he and his cousin were due for a serious reckoning, and Leo was going to pay in full for all the trouble he'd caused.

• • •

Viola held her breath as the low rumble of a distant argument erupted into full-blown shouting. The modieste brought in from Edinburgh to make her wedding gown was frozen in position, lips pinched closed on her pins, fingers holding the silvery drugget to Viola's corseted torso. The heat of her fingers leaked through the layers of fabric. The gentle pressure threatened to send Viola tumbling over.

The duchess and Lady Boudicea were staring at each other, tension evident in their shoulders and necks. The sound of a door slamming caused everyone to jump. The shouting continued, growing louder, angrier.

"Glennalmond is an ass." Lady Beau's voice broke the silence, and Viola gasped for air. The modieste tsked and set a pin.

"Whether it's true or not, dearest," the duchess said with a wry tone, "it's rude to call your eldest brother an ass. Leave such remarks to Leonidas."

Lady Boudicea rolled her eyes and Viola gave her a weak smile. The brothers had been at each other's throats for days. It was enough to make Viola wish she'd never agreed to postpone the wedding until Leo's grandmother could be fetched from London.

"Lord Glennalmond has a right to his opinion," Viola said.

"No, he doesn't," the duchess said with a hint of asperity. She closed the ladies' magazine she'd been idly perusing and tossed it onto the table beside her. "He has an obligation to accept his father's authority and to support his decision."

"And if His Grace were to decide he'd had enough of

this nonsense and sent me on my way? Would Lord Leonidas also have an obligation to accept his father's authority and decision?" Viola asked.

The duchess made a rude sound, blowing air out her
nose in a little huff. "Yes," she answered plainly. "Though
I doubt very much that he would."

"So they're too similar for their own good?"

"If only they were. No, my dear, they're as dissimilar
as brothers can be, aside from being stubborn, which
comes of being Scottish and entirely too sure of their
place in the world."

"Which comes from being the sons of a duke," Viola
said baldly.

A trill of laughter erupted from the duchess. "Yes, I
rather think you understand perfectly. It's rare that either
of them sets their will against the duke's, however."

Viola caught both lips between her teeth. Yes, she
understood whom she was marrying. Did Lord Leonidas?
If his brother wouldn't bend, wouldn't accept her, could
he live with that estrangement? Could their marriage survive it?

"Stop worrying about Glennalmond," Beau said. "Rosy
pictures of family harmony aside, they've never been
close. Charles was the bigger loss. To all of us."

"Beau!"

"Mamma!" Lady Boudicea parroted back. "I'm sorry,
but it's true. And you know it is. If Leo'd brought home an
heiress, Glennalmond would have said she had a squint. If
he'd brought home a diamond of the first water, Glennalmond would have found fault with her dowry. He's contrary
and prickly and downright impossible most of the time."

"And he's your brother."

"I'm well aware of that fact, and I love him—don't think for a minute I don't—but half the time I'm not sure he loves me. And so, Mrs. Whedon, please don't take his tantrum to heart. When the deed is done and you're Lady Leonidas, he'll come round. I promise."

"I'm not sure I have any right to hope or expect that he will. He's not wrong. I *am* a very poor bargain for his brother in the eyes of the world."

"This isn't about what the world thinks." The duchess fixed them both with a steely eye. "This is about family. Glennalmond will come round, because, however put out he might be at the moment, eventually he'll remember that family comes first."

"Either that or Leo will beat some sense into him," Lady Boudicea said in entirely too cheerful a tone.

∞ CHAPTER 34 ∞

Languid as a cat, Viola stretched beside Leo till her extremities quivered. She made a happy, contented sound and pillowed her head upon his chest, damp skin to damp skin. Leo wrapped one arm around her and twisted one dangling curl around his index finger. Her hair never ceased to amaze him. It was pointless to even resist the urge to touch it, the almost constant need to touch her.

He'd been a bastion of self-denial since his arrival and kept to his own rooms each night. Had kept his hands—and everything else—to himself, doing a fair imitation of a proper affianced gentleman. It had gone smoothly enough until Viola had crept into his room an hour or so ago.

He traced the shell of her ear with a curl-wrapped finger. "My mother says I shouldn't ask about your first marriage or your refusal to invite your parents to bear witness to ours."

"And so you find you can't stop yourself."

He chuckled, and she pulled away slightly, attempting to sit up. He kept his hold on her hair, and she swiveled about to face him.

"Do you mind my asking?"

"No." Her finger circled on his chest, tracing an invisible pattern. "But I'm not certain you'll like—or even understand—the answer."

"To not even write to tell them. It seems—"

"Unnatural?" she asked. "My parents never answered a single letter after I eloped. I'd shamed them, disobeyed them. I put myself outside their circle of responsibility, beyond their ability to love. You look horrified. Don't be. Ours wasn't a warm family to begin with."

"Was he so unworthy, your first husband?"

She laughed, but her eyes were bleak. "I was the unworthy one, not Stephen. He was the son and heir of a baronet, but his parents disapproved, and my father was dependent upon Sir Henry for his living. 'The life of a vicar is a hard one, full of denial and piety. We should all know our place in the world and be grateful for it. Seeking to exalt ourselves is defiance of God's plan for us.'"

The bitter tone of what were undoubtedly family maxims turned his stomach. "And you dared to be ungrateful for what your father thought God's plan?"

"Well, I dared to believe that God helps those who help themselves, and that Stephen loving me might also fall within God's plan."

"Heresy, clearly. For who could possibly love you?" He ran one finger down the side of her face.

She bit his hand hard enough to sting, the smile lurking in the corner of her mouth attempting to work its way up to her eyes. He rubbed at the mark she'd left.

"Defiance was my crime. My sin."

"Hence your defense of Glennalmond." When his

mother had told him, Leo had known some such thing must be at its core.

"I can't stand for there to be discord between the two of you on my account. It's not worth it."

"There you're wrong. *You* are worth it. My brother will come round. See if he doesn't. He'll be at the church, Friday-faced as a wet cat perhaps, but there all the same."

"Under duress."

"No, Father told him to take himself off if he couldn't behave. The only compunction to appear is love. My brother may not like me very much, but that's not what matters."

"Well, then, you're far luckier in your family than I."

Leo nodded again, anger flushing through his veins. Whatever her failings, she'd deserved better from her family, and she deserved better from his brother. Glennalmond couldn't see past the "what" to the "who." Of course, he had much the same problem with his own wife.

"And your husband's family?"

Viola snorted and shook her head. "They blamed me when Stephen died. It was my fault for forcing the estrangement. My fault for taking him away from them. My fault he'd contracted scarlet fever. My fault our child had as well."

He didn't realize she was crying until a sudden smattering of tears traced their way across his skin. "Here now, love." He sat up and wiped his thumbs across her cheeks. She shook her head violently, hair flying, cutting him off. His mother had mentioned the death of her husband, but not that she'd had a child as well.

"They were enraged that I had the temerity to live,

useless and unnecessary as I was," she said, her voice gruff.

"And your own parents?"

"Sent a letter along much to the same effect." She wiped at her eyes and pushed her hair back. "My own vile conduct had landed me where I was, and their death was a judgment upon me. If it hadn't been for my husband's best friend, I'd have ended up in the workhouse."

Leo held his breath, stifling the urge to comment. He might be a scoundrel who'd seduced his way into her bed for money, but he'd never betrayed a friendship as that gentleman had. No, not gentleman. He didn't deserve the title.

"Perhaps I should have done better by him." Her breath shuddered out of her.

"You?" He couldn't keep the indignant note out of his voice.

"Yes, me. I was alone in the world, save for poor William, and I clung to him quite tenaciously. You can't possibly understand what it was like to be a penniless widow at seventeen."

"I'd guess it was terrifying." And unfair. It was probably a good thing she hadn't invited her parents because he wasn't entirely sure he could be civil to them.

"At first, it was just bewildering, but William took care of everything." Her expression softened. Jealousy twisted in his gut like a bad supper. Ridiculous, but there all the same.

"And misery loves company."

"Yes, I rather think it does. And we *were* miserable, the pair of us. We were miserable friends for nearly a year before we became equally miserable lovers for a few short months."

"And then?"

She shrugged. "One day I woke up and just knew that if I didn't find a way out, I'd end up flinging myself into the Thames. I missed Stephen. I missed our child. And though I was past wishing I died with them, I couldn't let them go while William was there to remind me of them. Luckily, a way out promptly presented itself in the form of one Lord Doneraile. William was appalled—that was the first inkling I had that he hadn't thought out what we were doing any further than I had—but he was relieved, I think, in the end. He'd become trapped every bit as much as I."

"So you've no regrets about your career as a courtesan?"

"I might be brought to admit regret for its necessity, but given my options? No. To be perfectly honest, I don't know any successful courtesan who does. Grace Dalrymple? Sophia Baddeley? Elizabeth Armistead? You'd find not an ounce of regret among them. And don't forget, if my parents had taken me back, or I'd chosen the workhouse over my virtue, we'd never have met."

"Which would have been a very great shame indeed." He pulled her up and rolled her beneath him, pinioning her hands over her head.

"I agree, my lord."

Leo kissed her hard. "In a few days' time, I, too, will be able to tease you with your title and call you *my lady,* but for now, I'm of a mind to enjoy the thrill of having Mrs. Whedon in my bed. She's above the touch of a second son like me, you know."

"Yes, so I've been told. But sometimes she, ah…"

Viola gasped as his hand slid between her thighs. "She, ah, makes exceptions."

He slipped two fingers inside her and bent his head to tease her clitoris with his tongue. "Why would she do that?" He blew across her damp flesh, and then fastened his mouth over the sensitive peak.

"Talent. *Oh, God.* The thrill of—*oh, sweet—*"

And then she stopped talking entirely . . . unless repeating his name in all its various combinations counted.

"You get everything, damn you."

Viola forced herself awake, pushed her hair from her eyes and struggled free of the bedding that tangled about her legs like a shroud. She knew that voice. Knew it and had hoped never to hear it again. Had been promised she'd never hear it again by no less a personage than the duke himself.

"Charles, I've told you," Leo said, "there's nothing to *get*. The treasure is not there."

Charles's laugh rattled about the room like a drunk. Viola reached over the side of the bed and fished frantically for her dressing gown. Naked was decidedly not how she wanted to encounter Leo's cousin.

"So you say, but if there's no profit in it, why marry a whore?"

An angry huff was Leo's only response. Viola slid her arms into her dressing gown and closed it as best she could while still seated in bed. The two men were in the far corner of the room. MacDonald stood near the fireplace, rubbing his shoulder. Leo was beside him, his back to the bed, wearing only a pair of linen drawers.

"The only reason for such insanity is that *you* may not

have the treasure, but she does. Why else make a fool of yourself? Why sully the halls of Skelton with such an addition? Do you think I'm stupid, Cousin?"

"No, Charles. I think you're determined to see the worst in the world. The worst in me. The worst in Mrs. Whedon. The worst in Father even. And I think you're so angry you don't even understand that what you see are your own delusions."

"So now I'm mad, am I? And here I thought you were the madman in the family."

"What do you *want*, Charles?"

"What do I want?" Anger and sarcasm dripped off his words, making Viola's skin break out in gooseflesh. "Justice for my family. For the MacDonalds. A new beginning, for them and for me. The usurper's German head on a spike, and our true king on the throne." His voice rose until he was shouting. "What do I want, Cousin? I want what's mine. I want what's right."

"And you think I have it?" Leo spun about as Viola spoke. His cousin shot up from the windowsill, moonlight flashing along the barrel of the small pistol he held in his hand. Viola's stomach clenched. Why had she left Pen sleeping in her room? If she'd brought the dog along, none of this would be happening.

"You must," Charles said, "for I don't, and Leo here wouldn't have any reason to do something so vile as marry a doxy if there wasn't some irresistible inducement to force him to the altar."

"And you think it's the prince's treasure." Viola nodded, mind racing for options. Certainly his shouts must have woken someone by now.

"Yes," Charles spat out.

"Why would I want to share it with your cousin? A younger son, who wants nothing so much as a life in the country surrounded by horses and dogs? Wouldn't I be better off as a wealthy courtesan in some Continental capitol where these things are understood? Or as a wealthy widow with a new name in some Irish hinterland?"

MacDonald made a strangled, inarticulate sound of pure rage. "No! Because you know I'd find you. You know I'd be coming for what's mine. You need my cousin because he's the only thing between you and me."

"So what do you want *here,* tonight?" Viola laced her voice with disdain. "Do you think I brought it with me in a strongbox? Or do you think your cousin is simply going to let you steal me—and it—right out from under his nose?" She advanced on them, keeping MacDonald's attention locked firmly on her. "What's your plan?"

He was gawking at her now, shaking with rage. He cocked the gun and pointed it not at her, but at his cousin. "I think you'll leave with me now, and I think you'll do it because you don't want to watch me shoot Leo. And I will. After all, it would only be fair, seeing as he's already shot me."

Leo cleared his throat, and Viola cursed him under her breath. If she held his cousin's attention, he just might be able to overpower him.

"What if I told you where it was?" Leo said. "What if I took you to it?"

"So you admit you have it. That it's real. That you've been *lying* to me all this time."

Leo nodded, hair swinging about his shoulders. "You

could leave tonight with directions and a letter for the footman who guards Mrs. Whedon's house and the treasure."

"Leave, with no leverage? With no guarantee that you'd not play me false yet again? I think not, Cousin. I think I'll hang on to the one thing I know you value—lord knows why—and let you do the fetching. I'll see you at the Three Swans in Dover a week from tomorrow. If you bring the prince's treasure, I'll tell you where to find Mrs. Whedon."

"So I'm to trust you, where you'd not trust me?" Leo felt each word scrape past his teeth. He flexed his hands and shifted his weight. If only Viola had stayed safely in bed.

"I'm not the one who's been lying here, Cousin." Charles's lips were pursed as he glared at him. He turned his attention to Viola, gesturing with the gun. "Come, Mrs. Whedon. Out we go."

Leo took a step back, as though making room for Charles to walk past him. His hip hit the dressing table and the pitcher rattled unsteadily, the sound of pottery on wood almost like a bell in the silence. And then he was bringing it down on Charles's head, no memory of having picked it up, no time seemingly elapsed between thought and action.

Charles toppled. Water flew in every direction, soaking his cousin's coat and making the floor slick and treacherous.

The gun went off, and Viola screamed. Charles lashed out with his foot, sending Leo crashing down beside him.

A fist connected with Leo's head, making his ears ring. His fist caught his cousin in the mouth, knuckles and teeth meeting with bloody results on both sides.

His cousin cursed and clawed at his face. Leo twisted his head aside to keep his eye from being gouged out. Charles attempted to roll away, catching Leo hard in the stomach with his booted foot.

Leo scrambled after him. He couldn't have Viola. Couldn't be allowed to so much as touch her. Never again. Never. Leo slammed his fist into his cousin's face. Blood poured out Charles's nose, and he went reeling back. His cousin's feet slid out from under him, and his head hit the stone hearth with a sickening crack.

Leo staggered toward him, but was pulled back. He shook the hands off, only to be grabbed again and hauled practically off his feet.

"It's done, boy. It's done." His father released him, and Leo braced himself on the wall. He shook water and blood out of his eyes, air rattling in and out of his lungs like a bellows.

His father knelt beside Charles's prone form. His mother and Beau were swirling about Viola, voices sharp with anger. His brother stood in the doorway, a candle in one hand, something between guilt and horror washing over his face.

Leo's hand shook. "Viola?"

"I'm fine." She sounded as though she were anything but, voice thready and pitched too high.

"She's not fine." His mother's voice cut through the room. "But I don't think we need to fetch a doctor for a mere graze. Just clean the wound and bandage it up."

"But for Charles?" Glennalmond still stood in the doorway, as if what was transpiring were a play on a distant stage, removed from the reality of the audience.

"He's not breathing." The duke stood up, water staining his nightgown where he'd knelt on the wet floor. "Nothing a doctor can do for him either. Glennalmond, see to your brother while your mother tends to Mrs. Whedon. We have very serious arrangements to make in the next few hours, and it's best if we involve as few of the servants as possible."

❧ CHAPTER 35 ❧

Leo held a piece of raw beef to his eye. He'd killed his cousin. Some might say murdered him, though he wasn't going to stand trial for it. His family would see to that. The world outside Skelton Hall would never know what had really happened, though his fellow League members might well guess. Thane had said it was a mistake to let Charles live—and he'd been proven right.

His father and brother had hauled Charles's body into the spare room while his mother did her best to make it appear they'd been caring for an injured man. All to keep Leo's neck from the hangman's noose.

Charles had been put into one of Leo's nightshirts and placed in the bed. The scene had been set: The rags and water and bandages used to treat him and Viola were scattered about, giving a quite convincing impression that every care had been taken to treat Charles's injuries. One of the grooms had been sent to fetch the doctor, who would arrive to find his skills sadly unnecessary.

Beau had been assigned the role of nurse and was

having no trouble whatsoever looking every bit as distressed as one would have expected. Though if one knew her, it was obvious that anger more than grief was fueling her distress.

What a family they were. Glennalmond had even apologized for his behavior and sworn never to breathe a word of the truth to his wife, who they all agreed couldn't be trusted to hold her tongue.

Pen whined and licked Leo's hand, forcing him to stop brooding and turn his attention to her. Viola had locked the dog in with him that morning, then disappeared with his mother to await the doctor. Leo sighed and tossed her the piece of meat. She caught it in midair and promptly sank to the floor to gnaw at it noisily.

While the dog made a mess on the newly cleaned hearth, Leo washed the stink of the meat from his face and hands. Charles had left him with an ugly scratch near his eye, but it didn't seem to be swelling or turning black.

The handle of the door rattled, and Viola slipped into the room. Her gown and artfully arranged fichu hid her bandaged shoulder.

Leo stood. She smiled wanly and hurried across the room to hide her face against his chest. Viola wrapped her arms about his waist, clinging tightly to him, as though she were afraid to let go.

"Take me home." Her voice was muffled by the silk of his banyan. He caught her chin and tipped her head up. Her eyes were shadowed, the skin beneath them almost bruised in appearance. "Promise me, as soon as the funeral is over, you'll take me home."

"Mother will never allow it."

"She suggested it. We can't possibly be married as your cousin is laid in the ground. The vicar would have kittens. He's upset enough as it is. He practically called it a judgment upon us."

A familiar resentment crawled through his veins. "How did Her Grace take it?"

"She growled, called him a mewling old woman, and told him to keep his opinions to himself or find a living elsewhere. He spent the next few minutes sputtering and tripping over his tongue in his eagerness to explain that she'd misunderstood what he meant. The duchess sent him out the door with a flea in his ear, then she swept out to discuss dinner with the housekeeper and I made my escape."

"He can keep his sensibilities and his blessings. I'll get a special license, and we'll be married from Dyrham. The vicar there won't care for anything beyond the fact that we give a good breakfast afterward. A good breakfast and a good hunt, that's about the sum of his worldly desires."

Viola nodded and buried her face in his chest again. He dropped his head so that her curls tickled his nose— sunlight and grass. No matter what else might be awry with the world, Viola smelled of sunshine, grass, and happiness. He pushed his nose a bit deeper into her hair and inhaled again.

"Your mother says they'll be down in October for cub hunting. We can have the wedding then."

"You'll never keep the boys out. You know that? If we have it at Dyrham during hunting season, we'll be overrun with men in dirty boots with dogs at their heels."

She gave a watery laugh, and Pen barked, attempting

to nudge them apart and claim their attention for herself. Leo rubbed the dog's head and kissed Viola on the nape of her neck.

Viola wiggled out of his loose embrace and leaned back so she could stare up at him with damp eyes. She ignored Pen's grumble of protest as the dog was once again cut out.

"Regardless of when or where we marry, I rather expect that hordes of men with dirty boots are an inevitable part of my future. In fact, I'm counting on it. I may even make you write a promise of such into the settlements."

"Settlements?"

"Oh, yes." She met his gaze, a hint of her usual saucy nature in her expression. "I want the money from my memoir tied up for whatever children we might have. Lord knows any daughter of ours is going to need it—"

"And something for the younger sons?"

"That, too."

"Shall there be anything left for us to live on when our horde of children are grown and married?"

"Only if we find the prince's treasure or I continue to make my way as an authoress. I do think that at this point I have quite enough experience to write a horrid novel every bit as good as Mr. Walpole's *The Castle of Otranto*."

"Yes," Leo agreed. "I rather expect you could. Am I in the next volume of your memoir? I assume I must be, but whatever you wrote would have to have been pure fiction."

She smiled tremulously, then caught her lower lip between her teeth. "I could hardly leave you out, but yes, those chapters are almost entirely fictional. The truth, even what little I knew of it at the time, would hardly have been safe to print."

"Shall you write a third volume?"

Viola shook her head. "If people want to read about a whore redeemed, they can read *Moll Flanders*."

Viola pushed a few errant hairs back from her face, fingering them into place as they clung to her damp skin. Summer had arrived in London with a vengeance while they'd been away in Scotland. Those with the means and leisure to flee to the coast had done so. She had both, oddly enough, the unexpectedly lucrative profits from her memoir providing for the former, and her future as Lady Leonidas ensuring the latter.

It was amazing what an engagement to a duke's son and the ensuing scandal did for book sales. Everyone wanted to know just how appalled they should really be, and she had provided them with plenty of exquisitely outrageous exploits to factor into their decision. Though she hadn't included her time with Leo in her book.

Leo had taken to collecting the rude caricatures that filled the print shops and was threatening to decorate the library at Dyrham with them. Just yesterday, his friend Sandison had stopped by to deliver a particularly rude one showing her in bed with Lord Doneraile, with all her subsequent protectors standing in a line outside, awaiting their turn. Leo had been delighted and had pointed out that an illustrated copy of her memoir would make a fortune.

She had a sinking suspicion he hadn't been joking when he'd said it either. Trust a duke's son to find such a scenario amusing, and trust a younger son to see the profit in it.

Before she and Leo packed up and abandoned London for the remainder of the year, she wanted to get the garden's resurrection under way. If she had to come back to a muddy disaster filled with weeds in the spring, she might never want to return to town again.

Between the rain and the horses that'd been stabled there after the fire, there was almost nothing left of what had once been a very pretty garden indeed. The low herbaceous borders were gone—trampled or eaten—as was the small lawn and all the deliciously decadent flowers that had once made the garden her jeweled oasis. One of the two benches had been knocked over and broken, as had two of the three statues that decorated the back wall. Only the one held in place by creeping vines had survived the equine assault.

As she surveyed the space, Leo wandered out of the house, an enormous straw hat in one hand and Pen at his heels. "Put this on before you cook your brain."

Viola grinned and took it from him. "It's not that hot."

"You'll freckle."

"And we can't have that, can we?" She settled the hat on her head, the shade provided by the brim instantly welcome. She'd be damned if she'd admitted it to him though.

"A freckled wife? No, I really don't think we could."

Viola shook her head, amusement bubbling up in her veins. "I rather like the spray you have on the bridge of your nose, but as we know, I have appalling taste."

Leo rubbed his nose, face set into a theatrically tragic mien. "You needn't remind me I'm not as pretty as you. Now just what are you doing out here in the noonday sun?"

"Trying to decide what to do with the garden. I could

simply replant it the way it was, but as Lady Ligonier pointed out when she was here yesterday, it was awfully fusty and old-fashioned."

Leo nodded, pinpoints of light leaking through his hat and scattering across his skin as he moved. "What were you thinking of doing instead?"

Viola tilted her head and squinted at the ruins with one eye, trying to picture what might suit the long and rather narrow space. "I don't know ... maybe something like the wilderness at your parents' house? I love that little walled garden, and I think we might achieve something of the sort here."

"The statues would have to go." He wandered down the steps and tipped one of them over. Pen snuffled along behind him, nosing through the few gallant sprigs that were trying to reassert themselves. The nymph's broken arm and jug lay where the statue had fallen as Leo rolled it over.

"That could only be a further inducement, as far as I'm concerned. I've never liked those dancing nymphs, and I can't even tell what nymph or goddess that one"— she gestured to the one still standing, encased in vines—"is supposed to be. I thought for a long time they were the three graces, but I'm not even sure that's a woman."

Leo picked his way through the detritus and pulled the vines away from the statue. "There's an inscription at the base, but it's all but illegible. If we did a rubbing, it might be easier to decipher." He let the vines fall back into place and dusted off his hands.

Viola shrugged. "If you think it worth the effort. I'd say we have enough mysteries on our hands. Have you found nothing more in the letters?"

Leo shook his head. "You can have a crack at them if you like. I know them by heart, but staring at them for hours on end is beginning to make me question my mental acumen."

Viola grinned up at him. "That's all right, darling. You're pretty enough that I can forgive you for being a touch dim."

"What more can a man ask for than forgiveness of his weaknesses and forgetfulness when it comes to his failings?" He swept off his hat and made her a grand leg.

"Faithfulness?"

He narrowed his eyes at her. "That's more something a man demands."

"Not all men." The corners of her mouth begged to curl up into a smile, but she pressed her lips together to hold it back. Teasing him was too fun, especially when he knew it was all a game: nothing but an avenue to flirtation. "Were you expecting faithfulness? You picked a very poor candidate if you were."

"Baggage."

She smiled and batted her lashes. "You could always make sure I'm too busy to indulge my—what was it they called it in the print you love so much?—my *wanton nature*?"

"You can indulge it all you like…"

"With you." She made a rude little noise to show him what she thought of that solution.

He tried to maintain his composure for a moment longer, but ended up laughing. "Come inside and indulge it now. What could be more wanton than taking me to bed before luncheon?"

"Keeping you there all day?"

"As if you could."

"Is that a bet, my lord?"

"Call it a challenge." His green eye twinkled.

"Ah." Viola sighed and looked him up and down. He was breathtaking, as always. All sharp lines and harsh planes. His full lower lip stretched into a wicked smile.

"You know the difference between a bet and a challenge, of course?" His grin widened.

"A bet has a winner and a loser..." Her hands began to tingle as heat pooled in her belly and her heartbeat redoubled between her thighs.

"But a challenge can be won by all parties concerned."

CHAPTER 36

Leo spread the rubbing of the statue's engraving across the floor and shooed Pen away from it. He'd brought it with him from town, but he was damned if he could make it out. The dog huffed at him and crossed the room to throw herself down at Viola's feet.

Viola absently rubbed the dog with her foot as she paged through the cache of letters. They'd been making a detailed study of them together during the run-up to the wedding, but so far they'd come up with nothing new. She set the last one aside and turned to her notes. "So we know Mr. Black, owner of Dyrham, fled to America with the money your grandfather gave him for the property. He would hardly have needed it if he'd had the prince's treasure."

"And we know Mr. Connall, owner of number twelve at the time, was adamant about leaving it hidden and holding it in trust. We also know he died shortly afterward, and the house was sold to pay his bills. So his widow must not have known about the treasure either."

Viola blew out her breath, setting her fringe dancing. "And then there's Mr. Thaddeus, purported guardian of the money. Do you think he could have taken it?"

"Well, if he did, we'll never find it. But from the tone of the comments about him, I'd wager he wasn't the type to abscond with what was clearly a sacred trust. Did you find anything that sheds any light on where the money might have been hidden?"

She shook her head and tossed her notes down atop the pile of letters. "No, and it's quite irritating, too." She stretched and wandered across the room. She stopped behind him, hands on his back, chin resting on his shoulder as she peered over it. "Any luck with the inscription?"

"Well, I've ascertained that it's in Latin. Not that it was a large strain upon my mental capacity to do so. I think the first word is either *spēs* or *speī,* but the last one is hopelessly degraded."

"What did you say?" She stiffened, raising her head to study the inscription more closely.

"That the first word is *hope.*"

She shook her head, as though trying to clear her thoughts. "No, the other bit: hopelessly. Hopeless. *Spēs, spem, speī, spē.*" She ran off the declensions as though responding to a don. She circled the paper on the floor, then stopped and shook her hands out. "I can almost see it. It's maddening. I know it means something…"

Leo nodded, well acquainted with the sensation of knowing you had the answer but being unable to quite get hold of it. "It will come to you later."

She laughed and nodded. "In the middle of the night."

"Or while riding, or in the bath."

"At whatever moment is most inconvenient. Yes, that's how my mind works as well." Viola shrugged. "No point torturing ourselves over it. Shall we go for one last ride before our friends and family descend upon us?"

"You mean before we throw the foxes among the hens? By all means, let's. Run up and change, and I'll have the horses saddled."

Leo wandered slowly out to the stable block and stood throwing a stick for Pen while Meteor and Oleander were saddled. Viola came running down the path as the girths were being checked, skirts pinned under her elbow.

Leo tossed her up into the saddle, letting his hands linger on her hip and legs as he helped settle her in. "You know, the idea of your friends, my friends, and my family sharing the same roof for even a single night makes me quake with horror and anticipation."

She smiled, eyes filled with glee. "Afraid our wedding breakfast will turn into a bacchanal?"

"The breakfast? No." He swung up onto Meteor and brought the grain-high horse under control. "The night previous..." He let the comment hang as he imagined his friends pursuing hers through the corridors of the house while his parents shut themselves in their room and died of laughter. It was just the sort of thing his mother would appreciate as a very good joke.

"As long as there are no duels, and no one mistakes your sister for one of my friends—which surely isn't possible, as your friends all know your sister, correct?—I think we should be fine."

"We're exceptionally lucky that Augusta is breeding and not feeling up to the trip."

"Aren't we though." Viola tossed him a sly grin over her shoulder. "But I can't help wishing we'd got to see your brother force her into the church."

"You are a monster. Do you know that?"

She shrugged. "I've been called worse, by *you* if memory serves." She winked, and Oleander shot out of the stable yard, shoes ringing on stone like bells.

The scent of orange blossoms filled Viola's head as she stood before the altar. Only the first few pews were filled, Leo's family in the fore, their friends forming a slightly raucous crew behind them.

The spangled net shivered as she took a deep breath. She felt oddly overdressed in the gown the duchess had chosen for her. Like an impostor.

Lord Leonidas kept a firm grip on her hand as they said their vows, as though he knew she might bolt. He held her gaze, his own sincere, both eyes heavy with intention.

Whispers and giggles filtered through the haze that seemed to surround her. Her friends had arrived in force, making up for the fact that she had no family to support her, and they seemed to be enjoying the occasion immensely. There was a burst of laughter when the vicar had recited the part about declaring impediments that only died down when the duke cleared his throat loudly, and with clear implication of dire consequences were his warning to be ignored.

Leo dipped his head slightly, a slight smile hitching up one side of his mouth, and she realized she was supposed to be responding. Her skin burned. The spangled net itched where it touched her skin. She pressed her foot down hard on the coin Lady Beau had slipped into her shoe for luck.

"I, Viola Elizabeth Whedon, take thee, Leonidas Roibert Vaughn, to be my wedded husband, to have and to hold from this day forward, for better for worse, for richer for poorer, in sickness and in health, to love, cherish, and to obey." Leo smirked as she hit *obey,* both eyes teasing her. She raised her brows and finished: "Till death us do part, according to God's holy ordinance; and thereto I give thee my troth."

The vicar nodded approvingly and continued with the ceremony, the words falling from his lips by rote. Another guffaw flickered through the crowd as Leo slipped the ring onto her finger and the words *with my Body I thee worship* passed his lips. And then they were kneeling, and the final prayer was being said over their heads.

She was married. The bubble of panic that had been growing in her chest exploded. A deep breath did nothing to calm her nerves. Her vision wavered, going black for a moment, and she struggled to keep from fainting. If she had the vapors she'd never forgive herself. Leo squeezed her hand and helped her to her feet.

Hope. That's what marriage was about. Hope. *Spēs, spem, speī, spē.* Her heart slowed, and she was finally able to catch her breath.

Viola stopped dead in her tracks, causing Leo to do likewise. He pushed her back into motion, the hand at the small of her back propelling her forward. As they exited the church, his lips brushed her ear. "Is everything all right, Vi?"

Viola nodded, allowing herself a grin of pure delight as her pulse sped for an entirely different reason. She squeezed his arm as their friends cheered them on. Leo handed her into the carriage, smiling, but with a bit of concern hovering about his eyes.

He climbed in after her, his weight causing the pretty little open coach to rock like a skiff pushing off from shore. "Vi?"

"I know where the treasure is."

His brows flew up. "Shall we leave our guests to their own devices and proceed directly to town?"

Viola held her tongue firmly behind her teeth. The secret knowledge burned within her chest like a banked fire. "If I'm right, it's been safely hidden for nearly forty years. It can wait a few more weeks, or until spring. It can wait however long *you* can wait."

"What? Not even a hint? You're my wife. You just swore to love, cherish, and obey."

She smiled and shook her head.

"You're really not going to tell me?"

His look of feigned indignation set her laughing. His mouth quirked up, and he threw himself back on the squabs with an exaggerated sigh.

"You couldn't possibly have intended to hold me to *obey*."

"I suppose not." He leaned close, rubbing his face in her hair, the tip of his nose pressed against the sensitive skin behind her ear. "It's not your strong point, after all, but I'll have cherish and love by all that's holy."

❧ EPILOGUE ❧

London, March 1784

L eo ripped the vines off the statue and studied it closely. It certainly might have once been St. Jude. It was missing an arm, and its features had been worn away by time and rain and lichen, so it was impossible to tell really. It was just a vaguely human-shaped piece of stone, fluted with what might have been the drapery of robes.

"I'd forgotten that the other name for St. Jude was Thaddeus."

"So had I," Viola said from behind him. "But then it came to me in the church."

She was quivering with impatience, like a hound aching to be unleashed. She'd kept her secret all winter long, teasing him with it, clearly reveling in having solved the mystery. But she had dragged him out to the garden the moment they'd arrived in London.

Leo laughed. "In the church? When you had nothing better to be thinking of?"

She wrinkled her nose at him. "No, when the ceremony was over. Marriage is about hope, and it just came to me in a flash. 'Hope' on the inscription. The patron saint of the hopeless is St. Jude, and his other name is Thaddeus. The reason there were no letters from our mysterious Mr. Thaddeus is that he was entirely incapable of writing any."

"Being stone and encased in creeping vines," Leo said.

"Well, here we go. Say a little prayer to St. Jude as I heave him off his pedestal."

Contrary to his words, Leo lifted the statue carefully from its resting place and set it aside. If the treasure was here, St. Jude would become a revered icon in their home, regardless of what the Bible had to say about worshipping false idols. If this Thaddeus had done his job for all these years, he deserved a little pagan worship.

Leo cleared away the remaining vines, and using a spanner from his coach, lifted the platform and sent it sliding off into the dirt. It landed with a crash, crushing plants and gouging brick.

"Well?" Viola pressed close, her hands clutching at his coat. The memory of the first time she'd done so surged through him. He'd known from the moment he'd seen her that he was doomed, but it was turning out to be a far more pleasant fate than he could have ever imagined.

Leo stared down at the large chest that had been concealed inside the stone base. "I think St. Jude just became the patron saint of the Vaughns, at least of the junior branch."

"Lost causes, all of us?" Viola asked with a laugh.

Leo wrapped one arm around her and dragged her forward for a kiss. "Happily lost, but more happily found."

One of the Second Sons
is after an heiress's heart . . .
Her brothers are after *him*.

Please turn this page for
a preview of

RIPE FOR SCANDAL.

I t's not as though this is the first time I've been abducted, you know."

"An old hand at it, are we?"

Lady Boudicea Vaughn bit the inside of her cheek and studied her abductor for a moment. Mr. Nowlin was so cocksure, so confident that he would get away with abducting her and that her family would simply acquiesce to such a marriage—and that she would. It was baffling.

"Yes. Two years ago, it was Mr. Granby. My brothers say perhaps they should have made me marry him. Only by the time they caught up with us, he wasn't willing anymore."

Nowlin grinned at her. Deep dimples appeared on either side of his mouth. It seemed impossible that a man with dimples like those could be so treacherous or that a man so handsome should need to be.

"Scared him off, did you?"

Beau shook her head and batted her eyes. "Stabbed him. With a fork. The tines went all the way into the bone and stuck there. So much howling. So much blood. My brothers caught up with us because we were waiting for the surgeon."

"I guess you'll be eating your meals with a spoon on this trip," he said almost cheerfully.

Beau sighed. He wasn't listening. Having only a spoon wasn't going to stop her. "And before that there was Mr. Martin. I was only seventeen." She shook her head sadly. "He lives abroad now. Only one eye left. Father felt that was punishment enough."

Nowlin frowned, his dimples deserting him momentarily. Beau smiled wider and continued. "It's quite amazing what happens when you press your thumb into a man's eye socket with all your might."

"Well, well. You are a cold bitch, aren't you?"

Beau smiled and tilted her head, looking at him out of her lashes. "I am my mother's daughter. The best outcome here—for you, that is—is that one of the men in my family catch up with us. Left to my own devices, I'm liable to do permanent damage."

"It would cause quite a fuss if you did. Exactly the kind of thing that a woman in your position should be trying to avoid." His words were confident, but the tone was less so.

"And you think blinding a man didn't have that very distinct possibility? But not one whisper of either affair has ever reached the scandalmongers, has it?"

The worried frown returned, marring his handsome face. He rapped on the roof, and the carriage slid to a stop. Beau leaned forward to press her point. "They might— *might*—only have sent you packing back to Ireland. But you had to go and abduct me in public."

Without a word, he jumped down and slammed the door shut behind him, the scraping sound of the lock enraging her further. "They'll have to kill you. You know that?" she yelled after him, giving the door a good kick for emphasis.

Beau crossed her arms and hugged herself. Nowlin might not be ready to let her go yet, but if he failed to see reason, she'd see him cowering and bloody just like the others.

She was ruined already, and they both knew it. What he didn't know was that her father would let her choose ruin and a quiet life abroad, and she wouldn't hesitate to embrace the option. Paris, Vienna, Florence...perhaps even St. Petersburg or Tangiers.

Hours later, the coach suddenly shimmied beneath her, shaking Beau out of a hazy nap. It bounced horribly, then sagged backward as it came to a stop.

A chorus of cursing swirled about her. Beau smiled to herself. There was something wrong with one of the wheels. That would slow them down. And if they had to stop for a repair, Nowlin would have to let her out of the carriage. She straightened her clothing and finger-combed her hair, slipping the pins back into place.

Eventually, the coach resumed its progress, but with a rolling jolt and a scraping sound that spoke all too clearly of increasing damage. After a painfully slow hour, they entered a small village, little more than an inn, a few shops, and a smattering of houses along an otherwise desolate stretch of road.

The minutes stretched. Beau began to fear that Nowlin intended to keep her locked in the coach while the wheel was seen to, but eventually the door opened and he appeared to lead her inside.

"Don't bother telling tales to these kind people," Nowlin announced loudly as he dragged her through the taproom. "I've told them all about your little escapade."

Beau glared at him. Martin had done that, too: poisoned the well so no one would help her. Nowlin pushed her into a private parlor and kicked the door shut behind them.

"Wives who run off and abandon their husbands and bairns don't sit too well with the common folk."

"And I suppose you're the forgiving husband come to fetch me home?"

"And I always will. Don't believe anything different for a moment, my love. Have a seat and eat something." He gestured to the table, where a cold piece of steak and kidney pie sat waiting beside a tankard with a frothy head that promised ale. There were no utensils on the table.

"I see you remembered about the fork."

Nowlin laughed, his misleading dimples peeping out. "No forks, no knives, no candlesticks. I suppose you could hit me with a chair, but if you do, you'll eat the rest of your meals standing at the mantel." He bowed and slipped out of the room.

Beau swallowed down her anger and sat. Her stomach had been growling since dawn. Starving herself wouldn't help her situation one jot. She pulled off her gloves, thrust them into her pocket, and sat.

When she had finished, she pushed the empty plate away and paced the room. A small commode was the room's only other piece of furniture. Beau rifled through it. It held a chamber pot, a few glasses, and an assortment of half-used candles of dubious quality.

She hefted the chamber pot with one hand. It was heavy stoneware. Nothing like the porcelain ones she was used to, with their fanciful flowers or pretty patterns of Oriental splendor. It was...she searched for the proper word: serviceable.

Clubbing Nowlin with it might not get her anywhere, but it certainly couldn't hurt. If she could wound him, it might at least slow them down, or delay them further.

She took up a position a safe distance behind the door and waited. He'd had fair warning, which was more than any woman owed under such circumstances.

The door swung open a few minutes later, and Nowlin, in a fresh change of clothes and newly shaved, stepped through. His cologne preceded him like a dog before its cart, the scent flooding the room.

Fury burst through her. *He* got a change of clothing and a wash, while she was still wearing the same gown he'd abducted her in and hadn't been offered so much as a basin of water to wash her hands in.

She raised the heavy chamber pot as high as the tight sleeves of her jacket would allow and swung hard, putting all her anger and frustration behind it. Nowlin ducked, twisting about to face her, taking only a glancing blow to the head.

With a growl, he caught her wrists and squeezed. The chamber pot slipped from her grasp and hit the floor with the unmistakable sound of pottery breaking.

Beau twisted her wrists, wrenching one free. Nowlin let go of the other and backhanded her across the face, sending her sprawling. Beau hit the wall, tasting blood, pulse hammering through her like a military drum calling the troops to war.

She slid all the way to the floor, keeping the wall at her back. Nowlin stared at her as her hand closed around one of the shards of the pot. The edge was rough, jagged. It would hurt when she slashed it across his handsome face.

"Put it down, my bonny lass, or I swear on St. Patrick's staff, I'll beat you silly."

Beau tightened her grip and got a boot to the stomach for her defiance. She gasped and retched, her vision flickering as pain roiled through her. He'd kicked her hard enough to break the wooden busk of her stays, and now they were gouging into her, making it impossible to draw a free breath.

Nowlin stepped heavily onto her wrist, boot smearing her with mud, and wrenched the pottery shard out of her hand. He jerked her up, fingers digging into the flesh of her arm.

"Would you really rather be dead? That's not the plan, and I'd be hard-pressed to explain it, but you're begging for a beating the likes of which you've clearly never seen. We're leaving now, and you're going to behave yourself on the way to the coach or I truly will make you regret it, lass. Do you understand?"

Beau met his gaze. He didn't even look angry, just grimly determined. The taste of blood in her mouth made her stomach lurch painfully against her broken busk. She turned her head and spat.

"I see that you do understand." His smile returned in full force. "Good."

• • •

The mist had thickened, not quite turning to rain but heavy enough to coat everything with a damp layer of droplets every bit as cold and slippery. Gareth Sandison turned up the collar of his greatcoat and gave Mountebank his head. The gelding picked up the pace, breaking into a trot, as eager as Gareth to reach a warm, dry inn.

A few miles on, clear signs of habitation began. He was nowhere near St. Neots and the Swan and Bell, but whatever village this was would undoubtedly have an inn of some kind. He'd settle for a spot in the taproom at this point.

As Gareth entered the village proper, it wasn't hard to spot the inn. A mail coach was just departing, and a somewhat battered private carriage was drawn up outside, its groom in the process of checking the harness on what looked to be a fresh team. Gareth reined in. Monty shook like a dog beneath him, flinging droplets of water in all directions.

"I know, boy. It's high time we both found ourselves a..." His ability to speak deserted him.

A woman's head of curls broke through the mist, her hair so dark it seemed to bleed right through the gray. Her head was uncharacteristically bowed, but her height was unmistakable. A man ushered her along, hands familiarly at her arm and waist. Not her father. Not either of her brothers. Certainly not one of the handful of men her family might accept as a suitor. Gareth knew them all.

Lady Boudicea Vaughn was eloping.

A red fog filled his head. His vision tunneled out. Monty gave an impatient crow hop, and Gareth forced himself to loosen the reins and relax in the saddle.

The man bundled her into the coach and leapt in after her. The door shut, and the coach rolled into motion. Gareth watched it go. Its wheels sprayed mud in their wake, and it disappeared into the heavy mist in moments.

Monty was cantering after them before Gareth even realized he'd made a decision.

The crack of a gunshot resounded like a clap of thunder. Beau scrambled for the door, only to be dragged back by her hair. The coach skidded to a stop, sliding in the mud with a sickening, sideways lurch. A few shouts, muffled by the rain and the walls of the coach, and then the door was wrenched open and the wide-eyed groom slid hurriedly out of the way.

"Out, everyone out." The command came from some distance away, muffled but loud enough to be heard nonetheless.

Nowlin swore under his breath, let go of her hair, and stepped out. He attempted to keep Beau inside, but she squeezed out past him. This might be her best chance. Her only chance. Highwaymen were, after all, seeking money. And if there was one thing her family had in abundance, it was money.

Rain droplets splattered across her skin, large but infrequent. A man on a large, dappled horse held a gun pointed at them, the barrel nearly the same smoky blue as the mist that swirled around their feet.

His mouth and nose were hidden in his cravat and the turned-up collar of his coat, but she'd know that horse anywhere. Lord knew she'd ridden him often enough before her brother had sold him. She didn't need the corroboration of Sandison's silvery queue and narrowed blue eyes, but she was relieved to see them all the same.

Beau bit her lips and tried to keep from smiling. Nowlin wasn't going to get a chance to follow through with any of his threats. Not today. Not ever. He'd be lucky to continue drawing breath.

"Your purse, sir."

Nowlin glared and tossed his wallet onto the ground at the horse's feet. Monty took a step back, clearly not happy about having things tossed at him in such a fashion.

Sandison's eyes met hers and narrowed, as though he were accessing the situation still. Beau lifted her chin and stared right back. What was he waiting for?

"If the lady would be so kind as to retrieve it for me?"

Beau stepped toward him, but Nowlin blocked her with his arm, doing quite the impression of a man bravely guarding his own. "Get it yourself, roadbird."

"Ah-ah-ah. You were so hasty as to toss it to the ground. And I'm not fool enough to dismount. The lady seems the safest choice."

When Nowlin didn't remove his arm, Sandison trained the gun directly at him. "I suppose I could simply shoot you and then retrieve it myself. In fact, if you persist in this nonsense, I might take pleasure in doing just that."

Nowlin's arm sagged away from her, and Beau stepped around him, trying desperately not to appear too eager. Why didn't Sandison just shoot him? He had a clear shot. Was he choosing this moment in life to become squeamish?

She picked her way through the mud and bent carefully to pick up the wallet, hissing as her stays dug deeper into her flesh. She thrust the wallet into her pocket as

Monty pivoted, swinging his hindquarters about, putting himself between her, Nowlin, and the coach.

Nowlin's shout of protest was lost in the loud report of the pistol and the splintering of wood. Beau grabbed Sandison's arm, fingers gouging into the wet wool of his coat. He swung her up, and Monty sprang away, long legs eating up ground at a thunderous pace.

Gareth wrapped one arm around Lady Boudicea and gave Mountebank his head. The gelding flew through the trees. Small branches snatched at Gareth's hair. One struck his cheek hard enough that he was sure to have a welt.

Beau clutched at his coat, and he tightened his grip. He'd been lucky to get hold of her at all. Retaining her would prove difficult if she fought him. He didn't ever want to explain that he'd had to hurt Leo's sister in any way, for any reason.

"Did you shoot him?" Her question rattled through him, bringing a twinge of conscience in its wake. Lord knew he'd wanted to in the moment, but he understood what might prompt a man to go to such lengths.

If he hadn't been friends with her brother, he might have done the same himself. Now that she was shivering in his arms, the urge to keep her for himself was nearly irresistible. It burned beneath his skin, alive and hot and wicked.

"No, I'll leave that to your brothers. Rescuing you from yourself is effort enough for me."

She moved impatiently in his arms. "Can we stop for a moment?"

Gareth grinned. That was the Beau he knew. Get him to stop: give her swain a chance to catch up, give her a chance to slip away and run back to him. Cunning, conniving, and unstoppable. "Not just yet, brat. I'd like a bit more distance between us and them before I do."

"Agreed, but my busk broke when he kicked me, and it hurts like the devil. Monty's jostling is killing me."

He straightened in the saddle, stiffening his seat, and Monty planted his hooves and skidded to a halt. "He what?"

Gareth swung his leg over Monty's neck and took them both down to the ground in a single motion. This didn't sound like one of her tricks, and the thought of it brought the red haze back to the edge of his vision.

"What do you mean he kicked you?"

Beau swayed unsteadily as she got her feet beneath her. Gareth gripped her shoulders and looked her over. Her hair was a tumbled riot, and there was what looked like a bruise waxing across one cheekbone. She looked exhausted: the hollows beneath her eyes deep and shadowed, the skin almost papery.

"He didn't take it at all kindly when I hit him with a chamber pot." Her fingers popped the hooks that held her jacket closed. "Now help me, please."

Gareth sucked in a breath and did as directed. That might have been the first *please* he'd ever had from her. He tugged off her jacket, stripping the damp silk from her with difficulty. She dragged her trailing hair over one shoulder, and he jerked loose the knot that held her stays laced tightly shut.

"Are you telling me I should have shot him?"

"Yes!"

The venom in that single word took him aback. "My apologies, Bantling. Next time I'll try to do better."

He took a deep breath and whipped the cord free with sharp, deliberate movements, trying not to think about the fact that Lady Boudicea Vaughn was about to stand before him one damp layer from naked. Trying not to compare the reality of it to the daydreams he so often used to while away the time.

Damnation. The reality was so much better...and infinitely worse. The cord swung free of the last hole, and she ripped her stays away from her body, flinging them to the ground as though she despised them as much as she did her abductor.

Her head was bent forward, exposing the nape of her neck, the visible trail of her spine leading down into her shift. He traced it with his finger, stopping only when he reached the tie that held her petticoats in place.

Gareth stared at her back, at the sheer linen clinging damply to her skin, at the ties to her petticoats, laying quiescent beneath his fingertips.

Heaven help him.

THE DISH

Where authors give you the inside scoop!

❤ ❤ ❤ ❤ ❤ ❤ ❤ ❤ ❤ ❤ ❤ ❤ ❤ ❤ ❤ ❤

From the desk of Margaret Mallory

Dear Reader,

I was a late bloomer.

There, I've said it. That single fact defined my adolescence.

When I entered high school at thirteen-going-on-fourteen, I looked like a sixth grader. Was it the braces? The glasses? The flat chest? The short stature? Red hair and freckles did not lend sophistication to this deadly combination. I have a vivid memory of one of my mother's friends looking at me that summer before high school and blurting out, "What a funny-looking kid."

To my *enormous* relief, I entered tenth grade with breasts, contact lenses, and no braces. Boys looked at me differently, girls quit ridiculing me, and adults ceased to speak to me as if I were eleven. And older guys—who had utterly failed to notice my "inner beauty" before—appeared out of nowhere

Although it took my self-esteem years to recover, suffering is never wasted on a writer. With THE GUARDIAN, I wanted to write a story with a heroine who goes through this awkward stage—along with several dangerous adventures—and eventually comes out the other side as a confident, mature woman who feels loved and valued for her beauty inside and out.

Of course, I had to give Sìleas, my ugly-duckling heroine, a hero to die for. Ian MacDonald is the handsome young Highlander she has adored since she could walk.

Sìleas is an awkward, funny-looking thirteen-year-old when Ian rescues her from her latest round of trouble. Ian is not exactly pleased when, as a result of his good deed, he is forced to wed her. Although Sìleas lives in the Scottish Highlands in the year 1513, I know exactly how she felt when she overheard Ian shouting at his father, "Have ye taken a good look at her, da?"

When Ian returns years later, Sìleas is so beautiful she knocks his socks off. Not surprisingly, Ian finds that he is now willing to consummate the marriage. But as Sìleas's self-confidence grows, she knows she deserves a man who loves and respects her.

Our handsome hero has his hands full trying to win his bride while also saving his clan. Eventually, Ian realizes he wants Sìleas's heart as much as he wants her in his bed. I admit that I found it most gratifying to make this handsome Highland warrior suffer until he proves himself worthy of Sìleas. But I had faith in Ian. He always did have a hero's heart.

I hope you enjoy Ian and Sìleas's love story. THE GUARDIAN is the first book in my Return of the Highlanders series about four warriors who return home from fighting in France to find their clan in danger. Each brave warrior must

And then along came Vivina Angelino. From the first book in the Guardian Angelinos series, Vivi was not only vivid and three-dimensional to me, she seemed to liven up every scene. (Make that "take over" every scene.) When I could finally give her free rein as the heroine of FACE OF DANGER, I did what any writer would do. I buckled up and hung on for the ride. There were daily surprises with Vivi, including her back story, which she revealed to me as slowly and carefully as she does to the reader, and the hero.

The interesting thing about Vivi is that she is one of those people—or appears to be on the surface—who knows exactly who she is and doesn't give a flying saucer what other people think. I think we all kind of envy that bone-deep confidence. I know I do! She scoots around Boston on a skateboard (and, yes, this is possible, because this is precisely how my stepson transports himself from home to work in downtown Boston), wears her hair short and spiky, and has a tiny diamond in her nose…not because she's making a statement, but because she likes it. She's a woman, but she's not particularly feminine and she has little regard for fashion, makeup, and the "girlier" things in life. I wanted to know why.

About five years ago, long before I "met" Vivi, I read an article about a woman who looked so much like Demi Moore that she worked as a "celebrity lookalike" at trade shows and special events. Of course, the suspense writer in me instantly asked the "what if" question that is at the heart of every book. What if that lookalike was truly mistaken for the actress by someone with nefarious intentions? What if the lookalike was brave enough to take the job to *intentionally* attract and trap that threatening person?

I held on to that thread of a story, waiting for the right character. I wanted a heroine who is so comfortable in her own skin that assuming someone else's identity would be a little excruciating. Kind of like kicking off sneakers and sliding into stilettos—fun until you try to walk, and near impossible when you have to run for your life. When Vivi Angelino showed up on the scene, I knew I had my girl.

No surprise, Vivi told this story her way. Of course, she chafed at the hair extensions and false eyelashes, but that was only on the surface. Wearing another woman's identity forced this character to understand herself better and to do that, she had to face her past. More importantly, to find the love she so richly deserves, she had to shed the skin she clung to so steadfastly, and discover why she was uncomfortable with the feminine things in life. When she did, well, like everything about Vivi, she surprised me.

She pulled it off though, and now she's FBI Agent Colton Lang's problem. I hope he can control her better than I could.

Enjoy!

Roxanne St. Claire

www.roxannestclaire.com

❤ ❤ ❤ ❤ ❤ ❤ ❤ ❤ ❤ ❤ ❤ ❤ ❤ ❤ ❤ ❤

From the desk of Isobel Carr

Dear Reader,

Do you ever wonder what happens to all the mistresses who are given up by noble heroes so they can have their monogamous happily-ever-after with their virginal brides? Or how all those "spares" get on after they've been made redundant when their elder brother produces an heir? I most certainly do!

In fact, I've always been intrigued by people who take charge, go out on a limb, and make lemonade when the universe keeps handing them lemons. So it comes as little surprise that my series—The League of Second Sons—is about younger sons of the nobility, the untraditional women they fall in love with, and what it takes for two people who aren't going to inherit everything to make a life for themselves.

The League of Second Sons is a secret club for younger sons who've banded together to help one another seize whatever life offers them and make the most of it. These are the men who actually run England. They're elected to the House of Commons, they run their family estates, they're the traditional family sacrifice to the military (the Duke of Wellington and Lord Nelson were both younger sons). They work—in a gentlemanly manner—for what they've got and what they want. They're hungry, in a way that an eldest son, destined for fortune and title, never can be.

Leonidas Vaughn, the hero of the first book, RIPE FOR PLEASURE, is just such a younger son. His father may be a duke, but he's not going to inherit much beyond the small estate his grandfather bequeathed him.

My heroine, Viola Whedon, took a chance on young love that worked out very badly indeed. Since then, she's been level-headed and practical. A rough life in the work-house or a posh life as a mistress was an easy decision, and keeping her heart out of it was never a problem...until now. Brash seduction at the hands of a handsome man who promises to put her desires first sweeps her off her feet and off her guard.

I hope you'll enjoy letting Leo show you what it means to be RIPE FOR PLEASURE.

Isobel Carr

www.isobelcarr.com

♥ ♥ ♥ ♥ ♥ ♥ ♥ ♥ ♥ ♥ ♥ ♥ ♥ ♥ ♥

From the desk of Katie Lane

Dear Reader,

When I was little I used to love watching *The Andy Griffith Show* reruns. I loved everything about Mayberry—from Floyd's barbershop where all the town gossip took place to the tree-lined lake where Andy took his son fishing. I would daydream for hours about living in Mayberry, eating Aunt Bee's home cooking, tagging after Barney to listen to his latest harebrained scheme, or just hanging out with Opie. And even though my life remained in a larger city, these daydreams stuck with me over the years. So much so that I ended up snagging a redheaded, freckled-faced Opie of my own...with one tiny difference.

My Opie came from Texas.

Welcome to Bramble! Mayberry on Texas peyote.

You won't find Andy, Barney, or Aunt Bee in town. But you will find a sheriff who enjoys grand theft auto, a matchmaking mayor, a hairdresser whose "ex's" fill half of Texas, and a bunch of meddling townsfolk. And let's not forget the pretty impostor, the smoking hot cowboy, the feisty actress, and the very naughty bad boy.

So I hope you'll stop by because the folks of Bramble, Texas, are just itchin' to show y'all a knee-slappin' good time. GOING COWBOY CRAZY, my first romance set in Bramble, is out now.

Much Love and Laughter,

Katie Lane

www.katielanebooks.com

Find out more about Forever Romance!

Visit us at
www.hachettebookgroup.com/publishing_forever.aspx

Find us on Facebook
http://www.facebook.com/ForeverRomance

Follow us on Twitter
http://twitter.com/ForeverRomance

NEW AND UPCOMING TITLES

Each month we feature our new titles
and reader favorites.

CONTESTS AND GIVEAWAYS

We give away galleys, autographed copies,
and all kinds of exclusive items.

AUTHOR INFO

You'll find bios, articles, and links to personal websites
for all your favorite authors—and so much more.

GET SOCIAL

Connect with your favorite authors, editors, and
other Forever fans, and share what's important to you.

THE BUZZ

Sign up for our monthly romance newsletter,
and be the first to read all about it.

**If you or someone you know
wants to improve their reading skills,
call the Literacy Help Line.**

WORDS ARE YOUR WHEELS
1-800-228-8813